A Child
My of Own

BOOKS BY VANESSA CARNEVALE

My Life for Yours
Her Tuscan Summer
The Memories of Us

A Child of My Own

VANESSA CARNEVALE

FOREVER

NEW YORK   BOSTON

Copyright © 2021 by Vanessa Carnevale
Reading group guide copyright © 2022 by Vanessa Carnevale and Hachette Book Group, Inc.

Cover design by Alice Moore. Cover image © Trevillion.
Cover copyright © 2022 by Hachette Book Group, Inc.

Forever
Hachette Book Group
1290 Avenue of the Americas, New York, NY 10104
read-forever.com
twitter.com/readforeverpub

First published in 2021 by Bookouture, an imprint of StoryFire Ltd.
First Forever edition: December 2022

Forever is an imprint of Grand Central Publishing. The Forever name and logo are trademarks of Hachette Book Group, Inc.

The publisher is not responsible for websites (or their content) that are not owned by the publisher.

Library of Congress Cataloging-in-Publication Data

Names: Carnevale, Vanessa, author.
Title: A child of my own / Vanessa Carnevale.
Description: First Forever edition. | New York : Forever, 2022. | Summary: "Isla and Ben are devoted parents to their beloved daughter, Reese. She is their little miracle, the child they thought they'd never have until donors made her existence possible. But Isla has never told Reese about her biological parents. She wants to be honest with her daughter, but can she bear to open up old wounds? Then Isla receives a call from Lucy, once her closest friend, and it seems she may need to make a decision sooner than she thought. They haven't spoken in almost ten years, but Lucy has devastating news: she has lost her beloved husband Nate, just after they decided they wanted to become parents after all. Heartbroken for her friend, Isla welcomes Lucy back into her life. But then Lucy comes to Isla with a request that changes everything. If Lucy gets what she wants, Isla's perfect family could be destroyed. But would she deny the woman who helped her become a mother the chance for her own happiness?"—Provided by publisher.
Identifiers: LCCN 2022031712 | ISBN 9781538723876 (trade paperback)
Subjects: LCGFT: Novels.
Classification: LCC PR9619.4.C3677 C48 2022 |
    DDC 823/.92—dc23/eng/20220711
LC record available at https://lccn.loc.gov/2022031712

ISBN: 978-1-5387-2387-6 (trade paperback)

Printed in the United States of America

LSC-C

Printing 1, 2022

For Alli

PROLOGUE

Dear Lucy,

The slopes were calling. Actually, the black run was calling, and I wanted to let you sleep in. I tried to come up with ten compelling reasons as to why we should have a baby over my espresso this morning, but I came up with nothing. Nothing! I don't have specific reasons for wanting this for us, aside from the fact that I feel like I'm ready to become a dad—that I'm ready for us to start a family. Being at home after the accident, I slowed down and it dawned on me that there's space in my life—our life. It's more of a feeling—knowing there's room for more in our life, and the thing that can fill that space is a baby, a child. A little girl with sparkling blue eyes like her mother, who loves to swim in the ocean, or a little guy with wavy nut-brown hair like his dad, who loves to surf on Sundays.

I know we said we'd never do it. But they make really cute kids' surfboards these days, and if we're going to teach a kid to swim, it may as well be in the ocean.

If you're open to the idea after reading this, then we can start arguing about names tomorrow.

In all seriousness, the spare room would look great as a nursery. I guess it comes down to whether you can imagine the way the future might look for us as parents.

Lucy, you and I have so much love to give, and maybe we could extend that love to a baby.

I love you.
Nate

P.S. This is not, and never will be, a deal-breaker for me.
P.P.S. Leo for a boy? Mikayla for a girl? In case you say yes.

CHAPTER ONE

Lucy

Five weeks shy of Christmas, Nate lifts me in his arms to get the last bauble on the tree. We both take a step back to admire it. I had been searching for those snow-filled baubles since June, finally tracking them down in Rüdesheim am Rhein, a small town in Germany. Amazingly, they have traveled nearly ten thousand miles to Australia and arrived intact. Now they catch the light and cast tiny rainbows on the walls, worth every bit of the small fortune they've cost me. It looks like the kind of tree you'd see in an upscale department store. I catch myself smiling at it—or, rather, grinning. I glance over at Nate, who is standing beside me, beaming.

"I have a surprise for you." He pulls a piece of paper from his pocket and hands me a torn-out page from a travel brochure. "How do you feel about a White Christmas this year?"

I smooth the page out and take in the images of snow-capped mountains and a street that looks like a scene out of a vintage snow globe, with a horse and cart to boot. With a gold Sharpie, Nate has scribbled some dates onto the page.

"Chamonix? Leaving *next week*?"

He nods, satisfied with himself.

We've just come out the other side of a three-month renovation of the place we'll call home for the foreseeable future—a two-story Californian bungalow in our dream suburb of Balwyn.

We surpassed our initial budget by twenty-eight percent, and our second budget by thirty-five percent. I was on a first-name basis with the local store managers at Bunnings, Pottery Barn, and Provincial Home Living. There is no doubt in my mind that the Dulux paint guys were expecting an invite to our housewarming barbecue as a thank-you for all their hard work—aka *patience* with me—while I spent several months ferrying sample cans of paint between the store and home until blush-obsessed me landed on *the* color: Elation. Which was not blush at all but a muted pastel blue that Nate said was "just blue."

It wasn't "just blue," I told him. Nothing is ever just something. For instance, our renovation wasn't just a renovation. It was a commitment to the next chapter in our lives. It was a statement. One that said we were in this for the long haul, that neither of us had any desire to be checking out soon. No, this house, *our* house, is going to be the place where we create a life for ourselves that includes all the things we love: strolling on the beach on Saturdays, winery hopping on Sundays—and despite my mother's deepest wish for us, our future does not involve making babies.

"But how can we afford this? We've spent all this money on the house and—"

Nate presses a finger against my lips. "I've been saving up. Plus, we have loads of frequent flyer points."

"Are you sure?"

He tilts his head. *Trust me.* Of course he's sure.

I plant a kiss on his lips. "This is the best Christmas present ever. Aside from the subway tiles in the kitchen." I mean this. The subway tiles are really something. And so is Chamonix in winter.

Nate smiles, his lips pressing against mine. He smells like mint and cardamom—his favorite aftershave that no matter the time of day makes it seem like he's just walked out of the shower. "Nothing is sexier than subway tiles in the kitchen."

He pulls away, but not completely, and for a few moments he stands there, gazing into my eyes like he used to when we first met.

I squint at him. "Is my husband going all romantic on me?"

"Just thinking about how lucky I am—how lucky we are." He reaches for the switch and flicks the tree lights on. It sparks to life, golden flickers starting at the base and working their way up to the peak and back again.

"We were lucky. You were lucky," I say.

"What if it wasn't luck?" comes his reply.

"How else would you describe it?"

"Fate."

"Fate?"

"Yep."

And then, right after that unremarkable "yep," Nate chooses this very moment to tell me he's quit his job. Of course those aren't his exact words. His exact words are, "It's funny how almost losing your life makes you rethink your priorities." Which, coming from Nate, is jaw-droppingly unbelievable since this is a man who risks his life almost every time he goes to work.

Nate's career as a photojournalist means he is often away from home for weeks at a time. Over the years he's experienced a broken leg, a fractured collarbone, an emergency helicopter landing, two cases of frostbite, and a kidnapping in Fallujah that lasted the longest seventy-two hours of my life. He's stayed in a hotel surrounded by rebels, been bitten by a snake, chased by a wild elephant, and while it is all for the sake of capturing humanity, truth, and beauty on film, it isn't exactly the kind of job that falls under the "family-friendly" banner; I've often wondered if it can even be classified as "marriage-friendly." Somehow we've made it work, and I've made as much peace as a loving wife can with the fact that Nate's job often involves a certain level of risk that would make most people uncomfortable. He has traveled to some of the most dangerous places on earth in the fourteen years

I've known him, but nothing prepared me for the call I received six months ago.

Stuart, a guy on Nate's crew, delivered the news over a crackling phone line. I could barely make out his voice. Nate had been involved in a diving accident. His rebreather had failed to keep delivering oxygen. He'd lost consciousness. *Under water*.

And then the phone cut out.

Later, I learned that the crew had managed to resuscitate him, but we all knew what a close call it had been—even if Nate, until this moment, has said little to acknowledge it. He simply came home and said he was taking the rest of the year off. We bought a fixer-upper. A week after we settled on the house, he submitted plans to council for renovations, and a week after they'd been approved, he started knocking down walls.

And now, here he is talking about priorities, and I am pretty certain he isn't referring to the walls needing an undercoat before we splash the "just blue" Elation on them.

"What kind of priorities? Because if you're thinking of knocking out the sunroom wall, I don't think I have it in me."

The sunroom wall has been contentious. Knocking it out would mean a much larger sunroom. Leaving it equates to cozy. We've agreed on cozy.

"Part of me thinks it might finally be time to settle down, to move on to the next phase in our lives," he continues, in a way that is wholly out of character for him. Nate is not of the planning-the-next-stage-of-our-lives variety. No, he is more of the let's-live-life-today-and-work-it-out-tomorrow variety…well, *tomorrow*. Or the next day. Or the day after that.

"The next phase?"

"A baby."

"A what?" Suddenly, those blinking Christmas lights seem more distracting than mesmerizing.

"You know—a little person, grows in there." He points to my midsection.

I laugh it off. Well, more like guffaw. Because, really, what other option do I have? This is borderline ridiculous. And Nate doesn't even break a smile. Sometimes keeping up with him feels like a full-time job. That's the thing about him—he is full of surprises.

"What have you done with my husband?"

"I think I left part of him off the coast of Florida when I flatlined." He helps himself to a candy cane hanging off the tree and starts unwrapping it.

"A baby."

"Large head, button nose. Hopefully eyes like her mother." He pops the candy cane into his mouth and snaps off a piece. He's smiling now.

"Sleepless nights."

"Ball games. Bike rides. Sports matches."

"Babies are expensive," I counter.

"Lucky we have savings."

This is debatable, given the budget blowout and the fact I've already started buying new furniture. Besides, I'm on a career break. Up until recently I worked as a travel presenter for a small TV network. The show I'd been contracted on came to an end, so now, after spending years of my life in hotels and airports, I'm officially out of work and in the process of deciding whether to try my hand at something else.

"You're supposed to be going back to work in February. The Alaska trip. You'll be away for weeks. When would we even...?"

Nate crunches the candy between his teeth. "Quit my job, remember?"

I let out a sigh. No, I can't keep up with him. "What are you planning to do instead?"

"Another fixer-upper."

"Oh," is the only response I manage to summon.

Nate steps forward and presses a finger to my lips. "The baby…
it was just a thought. That's all."

My body floods with relief. "Oh, just a thought," I repeat, only
it comes out in the wrong pitch—like a strangled warble.

"Maybe I'll feel differently tomorrow. This feeling, it might
fizzle out to nothing." He shrugs, like it's no big deal.

The oven timer beeps, shrill and unrelenting.

Nate waggles his eyebrows. "Your sugar cookies are ready."

We don't speak of the *thought* again.

Instead, we spend the next few days trying to come to a
mutual decision about how to best decorate the room across
the hall from the main bedroom, and up until now we haven't
been able to agree on things. Nate isn't the type of guy who
preoccupies himself with how things look so much as with how
things work. He can tell you exactly, and I mean exactly, how
a propulsion system works, or how a toaster is made, or how a
plane can actually stay suspended in the air. Me, on the other
hand? I can't even figure out how to pop the hood of my car. It
isn't exactly like Nate has taken a huge interest in the styling of
our house—he's been quite happy to be the hands-on guy who
fastens the tool belt around his waist and rolls up his sleeves to put
the furniture together, even if he does have an eye for design. We
have similar taste and he usually nods approval whenever I flash
him a peek at my Pinterest board of distressed timber entryway
benches, or natural-fiber rugs I have my eye on. So Nate's recent
noncommittal "mmm" and "yeah, that could look good" responses
to my suggestions for the spare room are plain odd. No matter
how many times I try to get a thumbs-up for the hanging egg
chair and fiddle leaf fig tree, I can't move these items from my
online wish list to my shopping cart.

I do not suspect that Nate's reticence has anything to do with the *thought* he had a few days ago. In my mind, the *thought* has fizzled out, like the way some of Nate's other plans have eventuated into nothing like bath bombs dissolving in a tub, never to be seen again: the time he declared he wanted to learn Japanese, the summer he vowed to give up carbs, the year he said he was going to master the art of French cooking.

"If you're not keen on the hanging chair, why don't we put a day bed in there instead?" I suggest as I trail out to the veranda with a plate of slow-roasted beetroot and potato salad. Nate turns the steaks over and with a quick pump of his fist drizzles lemon juice over them.

He looks at me quizzically.

"The spare room. Peach & Lemon has them on sale right now." I settle the plate in the middle of the table and pour us both a glass of Verdelho, which I brought home from my last work trip to Pico Ruivo.

"Why don't we wait and see?" He looks at me with a thoughtful gaze.

"For what? It's thirty percent off and they never go on sale."

Nate's response comes in the form of an ambiguous shrug that gives nothing away.

I help myself to a cube of cheddar and study him for a beat. "What's going on? Is it because you don't want to put a bed in the spare room? You're going to fulfill your lifelong dream of learning to play the drums and having your own music studio?" Another plan that has dissolved.

"No," he says. "I'm thinking about whether one day we might want to turn it into a nursery."

I gulp in too much air, which I exhale as a hybrid cough-gasp. "A wha—"

Nate waits a second before continuing. "What I'm trying to say is that up until now I thought our plans were solid. Our plan being that we weren't going to have kids. But..."

There it is: *But*.

"Something changed," I say.

"Yeah. Something changed. This year, the house—we're set-tling, Lucy. For the first time in ten years, we've actually got a place where we can anchor ourselves, and when I think about the next ten years, I can't help wondering if there's some space for us to have a..."

"Baby." Nate is actually serious about this. It isn't a flippant thought; he is actually considering converting our spare room into a nursery. This realization feels like someone ordering a burger and fries on my behalf at the McDonald's Drive-Thru instead of asking me what I want. I really don't want a burger and fries. When given the choice, I will always opt for nuggets and a hot apple pie, and Nate knows this. Yes, chicken nuggets are what Lucy Harper can reliably count on as a constant in her life. But not this.

"But I thought we weren't going to... This was never on the radar."

"I know. We don't have to. Like I said, I've just been thinking about it." He bites into a cracker. Fig and pecan. I only ever buy them for him. I prefer the rosemary and olive ones. I am comfortable with the rosemary and olive crackers.

"Sounds like you've been doing some pretty serious thinking," I say.

"It's a pretty big decision."

That is an understatement if I ever did hear one. It is a decision that undoes the decision we've already made. We are not having children—by choice. Not ever. That was the agreement. I've never felt the maternal pull to have children, and besides, I was too busy traveling for my career. Nate was the same—focused on a career he loved, which at times was dangerous. Our lifestyle wouldn't easily accommodate a child. Now things are changing—my career is in limbo and I'm no longer traveling, and Nate won't be either.

Sure, on a practical level there's room for us to make space for a baby, but there's still the issue of whether I can do something I always said I wouldn't.

"But what happens if I don't want this and you do? What then?" Oh, I've read my fair share of women's magazine articles over the years, not to mention watched a ten-part documentary series on this very topic, and I know that a couple's inability to mutually want a baby does not bode well for the longevity of a relationship. Even if they have been married for a decade.

He shrugs. "Then we get a puppy?"

I don't laugh. I've been nagging Nate for a puppy for years. A goldendoodle I'll call Ellie. But even I know that if Nate really wants a baby, a puppy isn't going to satiate that desire any more than a celery stick might satisfy a sugar craving.

Nate leans over and kisses me. "Maybe think about it, and then we can talk some more. When you're ready to, that is."

Silence hangs in the air.

"Lucy?"

"Chicken nuggets," I murmur, mostly to myself.

"I thought we were having grilled steak tonight."

"I'll think about it." Since when does thinking about it have to equate to anything more? I can think about it for five minutes, an hour, a couple of days, or even weeks and then come back to him with my answer. A firm no. Then life can resume as per normal. After all, it's always been a no. A mutually agreed, we-will-not-have-children-ever no. Only Nate's priorities have shifted without me—he's beginning to move in one direction while I, his wife, am lagging behind. If I decide having a baby isn't for me, then Nate will undoubtedly feel the tug, the weight of someone holding him back. I don't want to be this person for Nate. It's not as if I don't like children—I love them. And so does Nate. We are godparents to his brother's son, and as far as I'm concerned, we are pretty darn great at the job. Nate and I have always been on the same page—even when we were faced with the biggest decision of our lives ten years ago. A decision we made in part *because* we never wanted children of our own.

Nate tops up my glass. He flicks his eyes up and holds my gaze. "Left field, huh?"

I have to remind myself to breathe. My insides are like a violin strung too tight.

"I wasn't expecting it either—to feel this way," he admits.

Yet here we are, miles away from where we were—closer to the place we always said we'd never go.

My theory is correct. Nothing is ever just something.

CHAPTER TWO

Isla

Things nobody tells you about becoming a mother: Labor can last for days. Sleep deprivation can last years. Your feet can go up a shoe size, rendering your entire collection of footwear obsolete. Of course these are things you already know at least on some kind of level. (Though I had no idea about the shoes.)

The obvious expectation is that your life will change to revolve around the little person who you're suddenly responsible for. My hairdresser Deb, a random meme I saw on Facebook, and my long-time colleague Monica unanimously agreed that parenting is the most rewarding job in the world while simultaneously being the most difficult. So in some ways, when Reese came along I *was* prepared.

But here's what they didn't tell me: For some parents, the sleep deprivation, the tantrums, the dirty socks left under the coffee table, the spilled bowls of cereal on the kitchen floor, the homework that needs to be kept on top of, form the least worries of all. Nobody gave me advance notice about the emotional toll becoming a mother can have on a person. And I certainly wasn't prepared for the fact that I—Isla Louise Sutherland—would become a mother who worried. About more things than most.

Take, for instance, this morning. About five minutes ago, Mrs. Raynor, Reese's Year Three learning advisor—apparently at this school, the term "teacher" is passé—called me, advising there had been an incident.

"What kind of incident?" I asked, hoping it was a run-of-the-mill knee scrape and a few too many tears. Deep down, I suspected this wasn't the case.

"Why don't you make your way over here and we'll talk about it face to face?" came her reply.

"I'll be there soon," I told her, moments before Natalie and Simon joined me in the light-filled kitchen of one of my most recently listed homes on Botanica Drive. They've brought their checkbook. In fact, Simon even has a pen in his right hand.

"You were right about the sunroom—it'll make a perfect nursery," Natalie declares, rubbing her swollen belly.

Of course I was right about the sunroom. Natalie is merely weeks away from giving birth to her first child, and whenever a pregnant couple books a private inspection before auction, my money is always on the nursery versus the kitchen as the number-one selling point. Certainly the mood board I showed Natalie prior to our meeting has helped. I came prepared, with a business card for the best interior decorator I know, and within moments Simon was nodding away as Natalie "oohed" and "ahhed" her way through the thirty-square stunner with views of the bay.

"Fantastic," I reply. "Did I mention the shoe closet?"

She lets out a gasp—not dissimilar to the kind of sound one makes when they set eyes upon a puppy, or a diamond ring, depending on one's tastes.

"It's perfect," she coos.

"She has quite an extensive collection of shoes," reports Simon, who looks almost pained by this admission.

My gaze momentarily lands on Natalie's swollen feet, squeezed into a pair of Simone Rocha leather sandals, before beaming in their direction. "Shall we get the paperwork started, then?"

They both nod adorably.

I don't have the heart to tell Natalie about what happened to my shoe collection after I gave birth.

A whole thirty-four minutes later, I'm ushered into the vice principal's office to find Reese sitting cross-legged on the floor, playing Fish with a deck of cards. She flicks her eyes up at me briefly before returning her attention to the game.

"Hey, Button," I say, crouching down to her level. "Everything okay?"

She shrugs and gives an almost inaudible response that sounds something like a yes but I can't be sure.

I turn my attention to Mrs. Raynor. "She seems fine to me. What happened this time?" This is the third incident I've been called to in two weeks.

Mrs. Raynor presses her lips together and gestures toward the door that leads to another office. "Reese, I'm going to leave you in charge of Mrs. Hoffman's office for a minute, is that okay? If any of the Year Threes come in for a sticker, they're in her top drawer."

I wait for Reese's response to this. It comes in the form of a curt nod that tells us she gets it.

I enter the cramped meeting room with boxes of Christmas decorations that have obviously been pulled out of storage and are ready to be dusted off for the reception foyer.

Mrs. Raynor closes the door behind us. "Please, take a seat," she says, motioning to an upholstered tweed armchair in a pea-green color.

I obediently sit and cradle my handbag against my chest. Mrs. Raynor swivels closer to me on her chair, the tiny bells on her Christmas earrings jingling as she moves. She looks at me with the eyes of a woman who seems worn out and ready for the school break.

"She's not herself," she says.

"She can get quiet when she's tired," I explain. "Do you think she's coming down with something? Have you checked her temperature?"

Mrs. Raynor shakes her head. "She's removed herself from the company of her usual friendship group except for Bailey. It seems she had another falling-out with Mitchell today and—"

"Mitchell's one of her best friends. They've known each other since kindergarten." This has always been a friendship I've been wary of—not because I don't like Mitchell, but his mother, Liesel, is one of the most infuriating women I know. I've felt this way about her since kindergarten orientation. It might be due to the fact she pulled out a packet of wipes and proceeded to sanitize the plastic chair he was about to sit on after Reese had been sitting on it.

"He made an inappropriate comment. We've spoken to his mother and gave him a red card. We're also going to have to give Reese a red card." Red cards are the equivalent of detentions. Only they result in phone calls to parents who then have to suspend their workdays to come and collect their little offenders.

"What exactly did he say to her?"

"He called her a liar."

This makes no sense. Reese isn't that sensitive. "What was she supposedly lying about?"

Mrs. Raynor hesitates. "Mitchell called her a fake baby. I believe they were talking about . . . conception."

"What?!"

"From what I've been able to gather, it seems Reese told Mitchell and a small group of friends she was made in a Petri dish."

I feel the punch and the subsequent twist in my stomach. "Ugh," I groan.

"I'm sorry, I know this is a sensitive topic—a private matter. I don't want you to feel uncomfortable in any way . . . but I thought you should know because Reese seemed quite upset about it."

"I know what's happened." I rub my temples as I replay some of the moments of last Tuesday night in my mind. At the dinner table over a bowl of spaghetti Bolognese, Reese asked us the million-dollar question: where do babies come from? Ben cleared his throat, ready to lay it all on the table, whereas I jumped in with an abridged version. A very abridged version that went along the lines of, "A Petri dish!"

Our science-obsessed child seemed very impressed by this to-the-point explanation, and by our third or fourth forkfuls of pasta, we'd all moved on, and all was completely forgotten by the time we'd cleared the table.

"We, uh... the other day she asked us about a few things... We didn't go into a whole lot of detail. To be honest, we thought she'd forgotten all about it..."

"Miss Baker found her trying to leave via the side gate."

"Well, I don't blame her." What I really want to say is, "How dare Mitchell make fun of her?" This, the very thing I've wanted to protect Reese from. Couldn't he have picked on something else, like her shoes or her bad taste in music? Anything but this.

Mrs. Raynor gives me a borderline look of disapproval.

"Well, you know what I mean. If someone hurt my feelings like that, I'd want to get away too."

"That was after she punched him in the arm. Hence the red card," adds Mrs. Raynor, almost apologetically.

"She did?" My voice sounds a little too impressed. "I mean, that's terrible." I stand up. "Thanks for keeping me in the loop. You can tell Mitchell's mother that we're sorry but it can't happen again. Because if it does, I can't guarantee she won't punch him in the other arm, and I'm pretty sure that won't feel fake at all." And with that, I toss the incident report into Mrs. Raynor's wastebasket. "Nobody calls my daughter names. She comes to school to learn and be inspired, and it's my job to make sure she knows how to stand up for herself while she's here."

Mrs. Raynor nods quietly. "I'm sorry. We'll make sure to do whatever we can so that it doesn't happen again."

I walk out of Mrs. Raynor's meeting room and into Dierdre Powell. Well, not right into her, but close enough that I can smell her Oscar de la Renta.

Let me be clear, this is not just another Year Three mother. This is Dierdre—president of the PFA, head of the volunteer committee—and if anyone knows anything about the goings-on of the school, it's her. And she just heard my rant.

"Isla, *hello*," she says. "Is everything all right? You seem a little flustered."

"I'm fine. Just organizing a donation for the Christmas trivia night."

She smiles tightly. "I hope you can make it this year. We missed you last year. If you're wanting a table, best get your name down early." That singsong voice of hers has the same effect on me as someone dragging their nails down a chalkboard.

I hate trivia and I do not want a table.

Her gaze drifts to Mrs. Hoffman's office, where Reese is spinning around on a desk chair. "Well, I better get back to the canteen. I need to get the sausage rolls in the oven! Shall I cancel Reese's lunch order?"

"I need to get going too." I muster a smile and tap my watch. "Reese has a dentist appointment. And yes, that would be great, thanks."

I've put out another spot fire. And it's just one more thing they never tell you about becoming a mother.

Peaches, in true Peaches fashion, is yapping at the back door when we get home. Reese drops her school bag in the kitchen and bolts to the door to let her in.

"How about we watch a movie together?" I suggest as I cobble together some ingredients from the fridge to make Reese a fruit smoothie and a sandwich. "You can choose whatever you like."

"I don't want to watch a movie," she says nonchalantly before she disappears around the corner and into her bedroom.

I finish preparing her lunch and go to her room.

"Hey there," I say, leaning against the door frame, plated sandwich in hand. She's threading a friendship bracelet. We learned to make them last week after watching countless YouTube tutorials. Crafts have never been my strong point but she has a knack for things like this. She looks small among the oversized pillows she's leaning against. "You hungry?"

She shakes her head but doesn't look up. "Not really."

"Want to do some baking? We could make a gingerbread house and decorate it?"

"Nah."

"I'll let you do all the frosting. I won't even help. Not one bit."

She shakes her head again.

"You can use food coloring. I won't even complain if you make the frosting green."

"I don't feel like baking."

"Well, how about some painting?"

That question doesn't even elicit eye contact.

"Okay," I say, changing tack. "Uh, are you planning on punching Mitchell again in the near future?"

Reese flicks her eyes up at me.

"Because if you are, we might be in trouble. Sutherlands don't go around punching people, Sport. It's not how we solve problems. We don't let anyone hurt us and we don't hurt other people. Especially with our hands. No hitting. No mean words. Only firm ones."

"I know." She dips her head and stares into her lap, her shoulders slumping slightly forward.

"When you're ready, we can talk about it," I say, softening my tone.

"I just want to be left alone, Mom," she replies, finally making eye contact with me. "I've had a bad day and I need some me time." With that, she turns her attention back to her bracelet while I stand there partly horrified at hearing my nine-going-on-nineteen-year-old daughter utter words that belong to me.

"You can go now," she adds, eyes trained on her beads.

Why didn't anyone tell me there would come a time when my baby would morph into a small-sized adult?

"Okay, I'm going. But I'll be out there if you need me." As I turn my back, her sweet, small voice calls out, "I'm sorry about punching Mitchell, Mom."

I pause. "I know, Sport. I know."

And then, "Mom?"

"Yeah?"

"Mitchell said babies aren't made in science labs, they're made when your parents *kiss*." She screws up her nose the way she does whenever I serve up anything dark green and leafy. "Eadie even said it's true and so did Madison." Madison, who is six months older than Reese and "knows it all," has somehow become the authority on all things this year.

"Did they really?" I say, sounding like I've swallowed a bug. With wings. I'm equal parts stunned and angry. Firstly, Reese only just turned nine! Nine! Secondly, who is Mitchell to rob my daughter of her innocence? Without Ben here to jump in, there is absolutely no way I can tackle this one alone. Reese knows two things. One: she is loved. And two: sometimes doctors help make babies in labs. In a thing called a Petri dish. This is our pathetic way of explaining our daughter's existence to her.

"We'll tell her the bare minimum. We'll drip-feed information until she's old enough to know more," we said flippantly, and without thought of the consequences. Now, here we are, with nobody to blame but ourselves.

"So?" she says, expectantly.

I stand there, blinking at the sandwich, the smell of peanut butter suddenly having a nauseating effect on me.

"It's sort of a special kind of..." I pause, trying to land on a word "...*intimacy* between two people."

"It's *true?*" she exclaims, her eyes wide. "Eww! I'm never kissing *anyone* again." The expression on her face is not dissimilar to the one she made last week when she stepped in dog poop at the park. This is not where I envisaged last week's introduction to how Reese was conceived would take us. In fact, this isn't even close to how I imagined telling her about how babies are made.

"But that's not how every baby is made."

Reese keeps her eyes trained on mine while she waits for me to elaborate. My grip on the plate tightens so I don't lose the sandwich.

"Some babies *are* made in science labs. They're called embryology labs, actually."

"Oh." She goes quiet, like she's thinking about it. "So it is true! To get a baby you have to do an *intimacely* kind of kiss in a science lab?"

I give a small cough and correct her. "Intimate. And it's one or the other. But sometimes you try one way and it doesn't work, so you have to make a choice, and that's when things become a bit more complicated—"

"Elisha's having a birthday party in two weeks. I'm invited."

Elisha. Is she the girl whose parents recently moved to Australia from the UK, or is that Larissa? Either way, this diversion means I can finally relinquish my death grip on the undeserving porcelain plate in my hand. "Oh! Great!" I say, sounding probably a bit too upbeat. "That sounds fantastic."

"It's another roller skating party," she says, rolling her eyes.

"Oh, bummer." I deposit the plate on her desk and step backward.

"Sandwich. Peanut butter. I'll leave it here in case you change your mind."

*

My head is in the refrigerator, relieving it of the wilted head of iceberg and a bag of mushrooms that are half their original size, when I hear the sound of a vehicle pulling into the driveway. A moment later, the doorbell rings. It's Winston, the guy who's been delivering our mail for the past five years.

"You've got mail!" he says in a singsong voice, flashing his toothy grin. He deposits four boxes onto my porch—the result of my recent online Christmas shopping—and then hands me a padded envelope that no doubt contains my latest online book splurge. I've missed my last three book club meetings and am certain Mary-Lou is going to politely ask me to rethink my participation if I miss another.

"How did Sonia go with her interview? That was this week, wasn't it?" Winston has three daughters, the eldest of whom is interviewing for her first job as a flight attendant. I also know his second child, Peyton, plays basketball, and his youngest, Sienna, refuses to eat all vegetables except for red capsicum and cucumber.

"We find out next week."

"Great. Hope it's positive news."

Winston crosses his fingers.

"Hold on a sec. I have those lemons I promised you." I retreat to the kitchen while Peaches takes advantage of Winston's effusive belly rub.

I pass him a bag of lemons from our tree. Winston, following his recent six-week holiday on the Amalfi Coast, is trying his hand at making limoncello.

He lets out a deep belly laugh and peers into the bag.

"I'll have more next week," I say. "As long as you promise not to deliver any bills."

"Speaking of which…" Theatrically, he presents me with a small stack of envelopes. "I was saving the best for last." With that, he chuckles, tips his Nike cap, and jogs back down the driveway.

As I walk down the hallway, I flip through the mail. An electric bill, a copy of *Men's Health*, an invoice for school fees. And then there is an envelope with the unmistakable blue logo that belongs to West Park Fertility Clinic. I tear it open, cast my eyes over it, toss it onto the counter, and groan. Some days, I can almost swear the universe delights in delivering the crappiest kind of news.

CHAPTER THREE

Lucy

It was never a conscious decision. It wasn't even a decision, really. I suppose I've never felt the strong desire that most of my female friends felt when it came to wanting to have children. Unlike them, I didn't catch baby fever and I didn't spend hours fantasizing about what my offspring would look like while creating a lust-worthy Pinterest board to showcase the picture-perfect life I aspired to one day have. Just like I never spent my teen years practicing how to sign Johnny Cataldo's surname in my diary the way Isla did when we were growing up. And believe me, Johnny Cataldo was truly something. I fell in love with him by total accident six months after Isla fell out of love with him when he asked me to the movies to watch *I Know What You Did Last Summer*. By the time the sequel came around, I was convinced that Johnny was the guy I was going to marry. There was nobody, *nobody*, who'd be able to kiss me the way Johnny did. It was all planned out in my mind. After high school, we were going to spend the next few years sailing the Caribbean until we got sick of white sandy beaches and freshly caught seafood. We'd then come home, and he would open up his dream business—a restaurant on the marina—and I would open a travel agency. Of course the plan was destined to fail, but not because I didn't want children. First of all, aside from the fact neither of us could afford a yacht, as a restaurateur it was unlikely he'd be able to join me on what the industry affectionately named "famils"—those wondrous familiarization trips to exotic locations that cost next to nothing. And secondly, by the time we finished high school, Johnny, the high-achiever, was on his way to becoming a dentist. A very fit, tanned, sought-after dentist who would no longer be interested in me or my ambition to travel the world on a yacht.

Life has a funny way of working itself out, because four years after I finished high school, I met Nate. On a yacht. In the Bahamas. I was in my first year on the job as a presenter for a small TV network, working on a new travel series. I was shooting a segment on the best Caribbean islands for destination weddings, and Nate was on assignment trying to map blue holes—underwater caves—which involved swimming through a layer of hydrogen sulfide, among other things, in an effort to understand more about these largely unexplored ecosystems. His crew had a day off and ended up joining ours for lunch when the producer invited them on board.

Nate took a seat next to me and introduced himself.

"I'm Lucy."

"I know," he said casually.

"You know?"

He bit into his club sandwich and started chewing. "Yeah, I've seen your show on TV."

"You have?" I picked a piece of cucumber from the salad on my plate and put it aside.

Nate smiled. "Yeah. I love the show. You're great at what you do."

I watched as Nate proceeded to pull apart what was left of his club sandwich. "I always forget to take out the tomato."

"Yeah, well, I love tomato, but I hate cucumber," I said, opening up my sandwich.

"We should trade," he suggested, and when I looked up, I noticed he was smiling. He was serious. We'd known each other less than ten minutes but here he was, ready to trade his tomato for my cucumber as if we were old friends. That's how it was from the beginning with us. From the start, it felt like I knew him. From the start, it felt like he knew me. From that moment, we knew we would know each other and never, ever let go.

For years, Nate and I practiced the long-distance relationship thing since, until recently, my job meant that I was away from home for forty-two weeks of the year filming episodes. This wasn't as bad as it sounds. Nate's schedule was relatively flexible compared to mine. In between contracts, he'd have time to meet me: Paris, Monte Carlo, Colorado, Bora Bora... Sometimes, if timing worked, and I found myself in the right place, I'd be able to join him.

I haven't thought about Johnny Cataldo in years. So when I bump into him shortly after Nate springs his "thought" on me, I'm floored. All those years of teenage angst to one day see him in the supermarket and feel nothing. *Nothing at all.* There he is, with his thinning salt-and-pepper hair and well-rounded belly, reading the nutrition label on a jar of pickle chips. His front tooth still leans a little to the left. Then again, he pursued general dentistry, not orthodontics, so I suppose it's fair enough. Farther ahead, his graceful wife is pushing a shopping cart, with their youngest strapped to her chest. His twin daughters, with their peachy complexions and curly topknots, gaze up at me and say, "Hello!" as if they belong in a 1950s TV commercial for fabric softener. There's no doubt about it, his children are gorgeous.

"Hello," I reply through a smile.

My hand darts for a jar of pickled artichokes.

"Lucy, is that you?"

I pretend to be absorbed by the artichokes, but it's no use.

"Wow, it's been, how many years?"

I slowly turn to face him. "Too many to count?" I offer. "You live in Melbourne now?"

He nods. "You look great."

"You look … *busy*," I manage, nodding to the girls.

"I watch you—I mean, I sometimes watch. The program on TV—the travel show. You really get around."

"Well, yeah. It kept me busy. We wrapped up the last season recently. I'm fully grounded now."

"So, do you have any …?" He glances around.

"No, it's just me." I raise my hand and waggle my ring finger. "And my husband. Nate. Happily married. Happily just us."

"Oh, good for you." This, of course, is another way of saying what he most likely is thinking: *Why not? By choice? Is there some kind of problem? With your eggs?*

This choice of ours is something my mother, for the most part, fails to accept and something Janet and Terry, Nate's bohemian-like parents, take in their stride.

An awkward beat of silence.

"I thought you were allergic."

"I beg your pardon?"

"Artichokes. Remember that time I kissed you and you broke out … I thought you were allergic to artichokes."

"I was. I am. They're not for me." I slide the jar back on the shelf. "Actually, I thought they were onions."

He points to his left.

"These are onions." He hands me a jar.

"Thank you," I say quietly, stepping aside and back to my cart.

"Funny," he murmurs.

"It wasn't funny," I tell him. "It was the most humiliating day of my life."

And it had been. I mean, it was my *first kiss*. I had to go home and tell my *mother*. And my mother took me to the emergency department and told the doctor, who happened to be Johnny Cataldo's *dad*. They were his artichokes Johnny had eaten for lunch—his prize Jerusalems he'd grown from seed in his very own backyard.

"No, I mean, it's funny. All through high school I thought you were going to be the one with a husband, three kids, and a German shepherd. Like the plan, you know?"

"Actually, that's not how I remember it."

"No?"

"No. The plan involved a yacht…and a restaurant."

Johnny looks confused.

"The Bahamas."

He furrows his brow.

"Sometimes life doesn't always turn out the way we plan it." I hand him back the jar. "I actually don't eat pickled onions. By choice."

Johnny gives me a look that says, *Okay, well, I'll leave you to it, then*, only the words that come out of his mouth are, "Good seeing you, Lucy. Say hi to your mom for me."

That's going to be unlikely. As he turns away, I add, "By the way, I don't have a German shepherd either."

"Give me ten compelling reasons," I say to Nate exactly six days later. We are in Chamonix, in a café bar, La Vue, on our fourth—or is it fifth?—drink. It doesn't really matter because we don't have a family to worry about, or a German shepherd, and we can enjoy six drinks if we choose to! Or seven! Or eight! Well, maybe not eight. Or even seven.

"Oh, geez! We're talking about this again? It was a thought, not a decision." Nate helps himself to a carefully selected cashew from the nut dish.

The truth is I haven't stopped thinking about it. Not since the pickled onion encounter with Johnny Cataldo in the supermarket aisle. Every time I think of the spare room back home, my mind is assaulted by images of pastel bunting and tiny one-piece jumpsuits in terry-toweling, and bottles of baby shampoo reminding me of the fact that until recently, I'd never envisaged myself becoming a mother.

"But there's two of us, and if half of us have a thought, then it means we are on our way to a decision, right?"

Nate looks at me, a little dazed. He's due for a trim and his hair has flopped over his eye, making him appear even more handsome than usual.

"What I mean is—you can't exactly make the decision on your own since there has to be agreement from the other party. Which would be me." I take another sip of my drink. "So it's sort of like you made your half of our decision and you're waiting for me to make mine."

"But I didn't make a decision. I can't make a decision unless *you* have a thought that matches mine."

"A thought," I repeat.

"A thought that is open to discussion about making a decision."

"Right." I pause. "What are we talking about again?"

Nate laughs and tips his head back to drain his glass.

"Having a baby."

"You're having a baby?!" booms a voice from behind me. It's too loud, even for a packed bar filled with people who are listening to the live band playing jazz tunes and not the "Lucy and Nate Life Discussion." It's the waiter, Alec, who seems as excited as my mother would be if she'd heard the news. Not that there is any news. We haven't sorted out our thoughts and decisions. That doesn't stop this Alec guy from bringing his two hands to his cheeks and opening his mouth in pure delight. In that moment I wonder if he belongs on Broadway instead of a Chamonix bar. Yes, I can absolutely envisage him in *West Side Story*.

"Do you dance?" I ask Alec. "Or sing?"

"Do I... what?"

I didn't mean to ask the question out loud. "Oh, nothing, don't mind me."

"She's pregnant," jokes Nate. "It's gone to her head."

I poke Nate in the ribs and he squirms, holding back a laugh as he pulls me into his arms and kisses me on the head.

"Congratulations!" says Alec. He's all perfectly white teeth and I swear I see his left eye sparkle.

"On that note," says Nate, releasing me. He stands up and hands Alec a tip. Then he takes my glass from me and hands it to a stunned Alec, who goes as far as to sniff the glass for offending traces of alcohol.

"Oh, she found out moments after she drank that," explains Nate, waggling his eyebrows.

"Let's get you into bed," says Nate after we tumble out of the bar and into the snow-lined street, past a gaggle of Christmas elves that can't be over the age of twelve. The cold is sobering, the lights so pretty, it almost feels like I'm standing in a snow globe. The sound of French Christmas carols wafts through a partially open apartment window.

"Do you think it's possible to spend your entire life being completely sure about not wanting something, to then do a total backflip and not be making a mistake?" I ask.

Nate stops walking and leans against a lamp post, pulling me close to him. It's started snowing, and his hair is dusted with tiny flakes I brush away with my fingers.

"Yes, I think it's entirely possible."

I feel my eyes start to water. "It's going to ruin us. If we can't agree on this."

"No," he says. "It won't."

"It might," I counter. I place my palm against his chest. "Because it'll leave a hole, right here, if you don't get what you want. I won't be enough."

"You're wrong, Lucy—you will always be enough."

"It happened to Michelle and Evan. She wanted kids. He didn't. They stuck it out for six years and then one morning she woke up, decided it was a deal-breaker, and filed for divorce."

"That's Michelle and Evan. That's not us."

"It could be us. Not today but years from now when I'm no longer fertile and still don't want a baby and you decide you can't get past that."

"So that sums up your thought, then, huh?"

I tilt my head. I'm not sure what he means.

Nate brushes the snowflakes away from my cheek. "You said 'still don't want a baby,' so I'm guessing that's how you feel right now."

I can't detect any dismay in Nate's voice, but his eyes—the way he drops his gaze and blinks—show me he *is* disappointed. At least a little.

"You would make a really great dad," I say. "As for me... I don't think I..." I stop myself. This isn't something I want to get into.

"Yes, you would," he says firmly.

"I don't think I have it in me," I say, hoping we can leave it at that.

"That's what you're worried about, isn't it?"

I'm quick to shake my head, but, of course, I *am* thinking about the fact that maybe there's a reason I don't have the same maternal streak a lot of my friends have.

"This wasn't—isn't—part of the plan."

✳

When I wake up the next morning, Nate's already gone and so are his skis. I find a note on the coffee table.

Dear Lucy,

The slopes were calling. Actually, the black run was calling, and I wanted to let you sleep in. I tried to come up with ten compelling reasons as to why we should have a baby over my espresso this morning, but I came up with nothing. Nothing! I don't have specific reasons for wanting this for us, aside from the fact that I feel like I'm ready to become a dad—that I'm ready for us to start a family.

The breath knocks out of me. He's ready. He wants this. The question is, do I? I finish reading the note and tuck it between the pages of my treasured copy of *The Nightingale* and make my way to La Vue for a coffee. I need a double shot. As I leave, Nate's words are still whirring through my mind. *If you're open to the idea after reading this, then we can start arguing about names tomorrow.* I have always loved the name Leo.

CHAPTER FOUR

Isla

It will go like this: in three to seven days, Ben will go through the stack of paperwork in his study, and he'll find the letter from West Park. He'll skim his eyes over their polite request on thick bond paper for us to finally make up our minds as to what to do with our frozen embryo.

Our last frozen embryo.

Our last frozen embryo that I can't stop thinking about.

In years gone by, Ben and I would quietly consider the options available to us and instead of discussing what needed to be discussed—that is, did we want another baby?—he'd write a check—he's old-school like that—mail it back, and a few days later, we'd be five hundred dollars poorer and our last remaining embryo would stay on ice for another year. All this because up until now it's been easier to keep our potential future-baby chilled than actually have to decide whether we want another child.

Only this letter is different. The ten-year storage limit is almost up and we've finally reached the point where we have no choice but to make a final decision. The Assisted Reproductive Treatment Act states that embryos can't be stored for longer than ten years, so there is going to be no avoiding this discussion.

Ben walks into the kitchen after putting Reese to bed while I'm busy wrestling the cork off a bottle of rosé. He's wearing his favorite top, a grey Lonsdale T-shirt that I bought for him on a trip I took to Singapore with my colleagues for a sales conference earlier this year. The T-shirt was a size too big but now it fits him perfectly—or rather, snugly, especially around the middle.

I wait for him to talk first—*How was your day?* or *Here, let me help you*—but instead he fills a glass of water from the tap, guzzles it, and says, "I think I'll go for a run. Is that okay?"

It makes me think of how much things have changed since we first met. We met by total accident. I'd listed his parents' home for sale, and as I was closing up after the last group left, he came running up the driveway, calling out for me to wait as I went to close the door. It turned out he needed to pick up some sports gear. Only he'd brought Patch, his chocolate goldendoodle, with him, and he happened to trail across the muddy front lawn and straight into the house.

"Sorry! I'm sorry!" he said, following Patch into the house, where he'd leapt onto the cream-colored sofa, which was now stamped with muddy paw prints.

My hand flew to my chest as I watched the sight in front of me unfold.

"It's fine. I'll take care of it," he said, picking Patch up and traipsing through the kitchen to the backyard. He closed the back door and then opened a cupboard under the sink, from where he took out a brand-new cloth and a bottle of cleaning spray.

"Um, excuse me, but I don't think this is appropriate..."

He took a step back. "Oh. Yeah. Sorry. I should have mentioned this before. I'm Ben." He extended a hand to shake mine.

I eyed him suspiciously. "I'm Isla."

"Maeve and Robert's son. I used to live here. I forgot today was the inspection," he said, by way of explanation.

"Oh," I replied, casting my eyes to the family portrait on the wall behind him. There he was—albeit a younger version of him—along with his sister.

Ben looked up at the photo. "Yep. That's me."

I smiled and that's when I felt him look at me—really look at me. And I couldn't explain it, but I liked the way he looked at me.

I started rolling up the cuffs of my shirt. "Your parents are due back home in twenty minutes. Got another cloth?"

Minutes later, we knelt on the living room floor, side by side, shoulders almost touching, scrubbing Patch's paw prints from the sofa, not yet knowing that soon, we'd become inseparable.

"A run?" I gaze at his pristine Nikes—another gift I brought home from overseas. Ben isn't a runner. He's more of a surfer—a channel surfer, that is, who sometimes plays tennis on Saturdays while Reese has her lesson. In fairness, he's what I'd call mildly active—he does occasionally like to surf, is devoted to fishing and jet-skiing, and never complains about bike-riding with Reese on weekends. He just isn't a runner. "In the dark?"

"Plenty of light on the football field."

"Aren't you hungry? There's some leftover casserole on top of the stove."

"I ate at work. But thanks."

Ben's hours are erratic at best. Granted, things have improved in the last year or so since Ben entered into a partnership with Guy, a savvy businessman and long-term loyal friend whose involvement means that Ben now gets to spend every second weekend at home. Evenings are hit-and-miss. Sometimes he's home at six, other nights at nine. Reese and I always set a place for him at the dinner table regardless. Sometimes I wonder if he even notices.

Ben rinses his glass, lets it drain on the rack, and pulls his AirPods from his pocket.

"Don't forget, there's some mail for you in the study."

He nods before plugging his ears with his headphones.

"When you get back we should probably talk about Reese too," I murmur, right as the front door clicks shut behind him.

*

While Ben's on his run, my thoughts turn to the mail. Or specifi-cally, the letter. And Reese. And the fact some kid has the audacity to be calling her a fake baby. Part of me knows it'll blow over soon enough—we are, after all, approaching the end of the school year—but then again, what if this incident becomes a defining moment in Reese's life? The recent school incident makes me wonder whether not telling Reese the full picture was the right thing to do. Then again, she *punched* another child, and this is not the Reese that Ben and I know. Telling her everything might prove to be too much for her to handle.

"Caramel popcorn and rosé? Was your day really that bad?" asks Ben on his return. He pulls his T-shirt off and mops his face with it. Evidently, Ben's run has done wonders for his mood. Here he is again, my involved husband with a side serving of chirpi-ness. I hold the bowl up and offer him some popcorn, which, surprisingly, he declines, patting his stomach. "I don't want to undo the run," he says. He plonks himself on the sofa beside me and checks his Fitbit stats.

"I finally closed a deal for the Di Mauros, but it went downhill after I had to pick Reese up from school."

"Again?"

"Another incident with Mitchell Patchett."

"She threw another sandwich at his face?"

"She punched him."

Ben chuckles. "How's her left hook?" he quips.

I dump the remaining popcorn into the compost bin, the cock-tail of too much sugar and wine settling in the pit of my stomach. "I'm worried about her. It isn't like her to be so . . . aggressive."

Ben opens a bottle of sparkling water and chugs it down. "She's a kid. At least she knows how to stand up for herself. Sounds like this little punk needed to be put in his place."

"He's actually a really great kid—or so I thought until he accused her of lying about how she was conceived. I don't know what's going on with him. And I'd prefer Reese use her words rather than deal with things like this."

"Don't make a big deal about it. It's going to pass."

"It'll pass." I sigh. This is Ben's go-to phrase. Ride the wave, don't pause to worry, and move on. "Of course it will."

"Well, what do you want me to say? They're kids. They don't even know the meaning of what they're saying half the time."

I mustn't look convinced because Ben adds, "I'll talk to Reese about the punching."

"Maybe it's our fault—it's not exactly like we explained it properly to her."

"We could tell her the full story." Ben casually delivers this suggestion in the same tone he uses to suggest Chinese takeout or pizza.

No. Telling her the full story is the very last resort. What Ben is proposing is too much, too hard, too overwhelming. "We can't do that. She's too young."

What I mean to say but don't is, "We can't do that because she might hate us forever."

When I get home late Saturday afternoon after my six open houses, I'm exhausted. I flick my shoes into the dressing room and change out of the eggshell pantsuit I'm wearing, opting for my comfiest pair of shorts and a loose-fitting linen shirt that I knot around the waist. Reese and Ben are in the kitchen making tacos, singing along to tunes from Ben's favorite playlist—a compilation of 1960s classics. Reese knows all the words to "Stand by Me" and is expertly bopping along while she turns a block of cheese into a mountain with each rotation of the cheese grater.

"Oooh, tacos!" I say, pecking her on the cheek.

"And crazy smoothies!" She dismounts the stool she's standing on, and Ben and I watch as she extracts two greyish-tinged milkshakes from the refrigerator. I had a Pepsi in the car on the way home, and what I really would like is a glass of cold Chardonnay, but Reese waits expectantly for us to deliver the verdict.

"Chef Sutherland, you have outdone yourself!" I surreptitiously slosh the too-sweet milkshake down the sink when she turns her back and balances a plate of diced tomato and lettuce to the dining table.

"How much sugar did she put in this?" I say to Ben.

"About a quarter of a cup," he deadpans. "Plus some honey."

"And you let her?"

He smirks and takes two wineglasses down from the overhead cupboards. "Didn't want to spoil the fun. Was also looking forward to seeing the look on your face." Ben picks something green out of his teeth and inspects it. "Is this spinach?"

I laugh and wait for him to fill my glass. "Sounds like the two of you had a good day."

"We had a great day."

As I sip my wine, the unmistakable sound of The Supremes comes over the speaker, and Reese bounces back into the kitchen waving her arms in the air. She starts singing along to "Where Did Our Love Go?" Ben chuckles and reaches for my hand, pulling me toward him before twirling me around. Reese breaks into a fit of laughter, squeezing her body in between us. For two and a half minutes the three of us dance our way to a place of joy, and I can't help wondering if there might be room for one more.

"Did you get a chance to sort through the mail?" I ask after we clear the table. Reese has scooted upstairs to cobble together the supplies she needs for a new school project—one she seems particularly enthusiastic about. Apparently she's interviewing us and I need to find the family photo album, pronto.

"Not yet. Why?" asks Ben.

"West Park."

"That time of year already, huh?"

"Yep," I call out, reaching into the depths of the hallway closet for a photo album. Our one and only photo album of Reese's first three months. The rest of our family photos are confined to USB sticks and an external hard drive I lost the cord to years ago.

I put the album on the table and flip to one of the first photos we ever took of Reese as a newborn.

"She was so tiny," I whisper, holding it up to show Ben.

He smiles fondly at the picture. "And then she turned into a little tornado and wreaked havoc on our lives."

I turn to face him. "We should discuss it."

"The fact our daughter is spirited?"

"Our options." The mere fact I need to point this out slightly irritates me. Then comes the noncommittal *uh-huh* that hangs there, like a promise unfulfilled. It's yet another thing pushed to the bottom of the list—like a bulging linen closet you'll one day get around to tidying.

"I've been thinking—"

"Daddy, do you know how to make a rocket ship?"

Reese chooses that moment to appear in the kitchen carrying a tower of empty cardboard boxes she's collected from the garage.

"I thought you wanted to see baby pictures, Reese."

She grins from above the cardboard boxes and giggles. "I changed my mind."

Ben takes the tower from her and deposits it on the floor. "Do I know how to make a rocket ship? Ha! I am the best maker of rocket ships and I'll do you one better. I can make rocket ships that fly."

"Noooo." Reese cups her mouth with both hands. It's staggering how this child can be so impressed by almost anything that comes out of her father's mouth.

Ben scoops Reese up and hauls her over his shoulder. "It's got everything to do with my special effects supplies."

Reese erupts with giggles. "Show me!"

"About the letter," I say as they exit the room. Reese has to duck her head so it doesn't collide with the light fitting.

"We'll talk tonight," comes Ben's response as he's halfway down the hallway. Yes, this is potentially going to become one more thing Ben and I will sweep to the side. We're getting good at that.

CHAPTER FIVE

Lucy

While Nate's out on his solo ski—a black run on a steep and ungroomed piste on Grands Montets—I try to picture what life might be like for us as parents. On my way to our favorite café bar to meet Nate for lunch, I watch a father zip his son into an oversized snowsuit before hauling him up onto his shoulders while his daughter, probably not much older than eight or nine, trails behind, pulling along a small sled. Can I imagine Nate as a father?

In all honesty, I can. He'd be hands-on and involved—kids love Nate, who is someone full of energy, curious about the world, and unafraid to take risks. Any child would be lucky to have a father like him, just as I'm lucky to have him as a husband. Me, on the other hand—well, I'm not exactly sure where I fit into that picture. Raising kids is a long-term commitment. A permanent commitment. It comes with a huge amount of responsibility, and even if I consider myself to be a reliable and responsible adult, I'm not convinced I wouldn't fail at being a mother—the type of mother my child might want me to be. I can't guarantee my child won't grow up and see me as a failure.

Then there's the other question.

What if I agonize over this choice and finally say yes, only to discover I *can't* get pregnant?

Four years shy of turning forty, I've seen enough of my friends go through fertility treatment and IVF. Haylee, my old next-door neighbor; Phoebe, my old boss, who'd been trying to adopt a child for six years; and, of course, the one I can never forget—Isla. Six failed rounds of IVF and a long road of heartache before the embryo donation that finally gave them a daughter. What makes these women different to me is that all of them wanted children— they knew they wanted to become mothers from the beginning. It was never a matter of "if" for them, more like a matter of "when."

I haven't thought about Isla in months. It's almost Christmas. I wonder how they spend their Christmases. Do they open presents on Christmas Eve or wait until the morning? Is Reese into bicycles or dolls or Lego? What does she look like? Does Isla ever talk to her about me?

I had a best friend once. Her name is Lucy…maybe one day you'll have a chance to meet her.

No. This is highly unlikely. Isla moved on with her life years ago and I'm no longer a part of it. I push the thought away and pull my beanie over my head, stopping to admire a shop window filled with festive decorations when my phone rings.

"Shirley, hello," I say, keeping my tone even.

"It's your mother."

"I know, Mom."

"That's better."

"How can I help—" I stop myself. "How are you?"

"Well, I'm glad you asked. I hope you're not going to rush off and make some excuse about needing to get back to work, because I know for a fact you're on vacation with that boy," she says in the usual way she addresses Nate, and while it might not seem obvious to some, it's because she has a soft spot for him.

"How do you know this?"

"Your brother-in-law."

"You called Liam?" My mother is all kinds of crazy but this is absurd even by Shirley's standards.

"How else was I going to track you down?"

"Mom, you have my mobile number. I don't know why you had to call Liam. How'd you get his number anyway?"

"I had Sheila look him up on that Facebook program."

"You had your assistant stalk him? Geez, Mom!"

"I needed to verify your whereabouts."

"My whereabouts? Well, I can verify that I'm in France."

"On vacation."

"I sure am."

"And you'll be there for Christmas."

"Yes."

"Yes," she repeats. And then she gives a little pause, like she wants to say more but is holding back.

"We'll be home for New Year's," I add, to break the silence.

Again, there's a pause. One that makes me uncomfortable, mostly because Mom always has something to say. Her assistant, Sheila, has taken up ballroom dancing. Her gutters need clearing. She took her new boots out of the box and they have scuff marks on them. She's boycotting coffee pods and investing in macramé shopping bags made by her local women's group. All the normal, above-the-surface-level stuff that allows the two of us to have a relationship. Or should I say, allows me to have a relationship with my mom. The topic of macramé shopping bags leaves no room for tension. Keeping Mom at a distance means I can coast along without having to dredge up all the reasons we can't be as close as she would like. It means I don't have to remind myself of what hurts.

"Mom, are you okay?" I say after a beat. I stop walking and make way for a group of caroling singers to pass by.

"Never been better. I'll speak to you when you get home."

"Merry Christmas, Mom."

*

One of my favorite things about Chamonix is The Nook. Of course it isn't really called The Nook, but Nate and I don't speak much French and it's easier for us to pronounce than Le Petit Moineau, which has something to do with a bird. Not only does it serve the best raclette in all of Chamonix, which we order every single time we set foot in the cozy eatery, but it also has the most sensational views of Mont Blanc. From here, the powdered streets with showy red bows sitting atop the lamp posts look like scenes from a Christmas movie.

"Hey, beautiful," says Nate, right at twelve o'clock, as he presses his lips against mine. His face is dusted with snow and he is still glowing with adrenaline. He blinks, and snowflakes tumble from his eyelashes onto his cheeks.

"Good run?" I can see in his eyes that he's gotten the buzz he's been looking for.

"It's perfect out there. The views—oh my gosh." He presses his fingers against his lips and makes a kissing sound, reminding me of our Italian neighbor back home, Gianluca. "I think we should try Brévent tomorrow. We could take the cable car between the ski areas."

"Okay," I say, my eyes briefly settling on the menu. I look up, and in unison Nate and I say, "The raclette."

"Yum," I say, groaning, thinking about the cheese, the potatoes, the cornichons and associated accompaniments.

We order, making sure not to forget two glasses of Swiss rosé, and for dessert—the pièce de résistance—caramelized pears and baby figs that Nate will pick out and give to me.

"I have some news. Not relating to your letter," I declare after the waiter plonks our dishes in front of us.

Nate presses his fork into the spongy mass that's melted to perfection. "You changed your mind about the wall colors. You're changing to Idaho blue."

"Actually, no. My mom called me."

Nate wipes his mouth, perking to attention. "Do you want to fly out to see her?"

"Gosh, no. She wanted to know what we had planned for Christmas."

"I've got plenty of frequent flyer points. Let's fly her out here." Everything is always so easy for Nate. Black and white. I equally admire and resent him for it.

I give him my best *you cannot be serious* face.

Nate turns his body so he's now looking at me. "Lucy, I'm a guy and even I know that's your mother's code for 'I'm too scared to ask for an invitation.' "

"My mother can't stand snow."

"Come on."

"It's true. I'm telling you—she wouldn't be into it." My mother is of the variety that enjoys sunshine and rolling hills or bodies of water—not snow-capped mountain peaks. Twice a year she runs wellness retreats in Fiji, where she teaches yoga and meditation.

I haven't seen my mother in over a year. It's something Nate and I rarely speak about, if at all. The convenience of having a job that until recently required so much traveling has meant that it's been relatively easy to not be around for birthdays or Christmas or Easter or any family celebration of significance, to keep Mom at arm's length. It's easier that way.

"Do you think she might be lonely?" suggests Nate, who is forever trying to nudge me closer to Mom, despite knowing our history.

"She has Sheila. And Bounce," I reason. Bounce is my mother's fourteen-year-old toy poodle, aptly named for his vivaciousness.

"Didn't he die last year?"

"Who, Bounce?" I screw up my face as I try to remember.

"Yeah, the eight-thousand-dollar vet bill."

"Oh. Yes. He did." I was at LAX waiting to board a flight when she called to give me the news.

"Maybe you should give her another chance," says Nate neutrally.

"I did. I answer her calls, don't I?"

Nate keeps an even gaze on me.

"I even engage in conversation."

Nate doesn't even blink.

"Sometimes *I'm* the one who calls *her*."

"Yeah? When was the last time?" he challenges.

I try to remember. "I was in Cancún, I think?"

Nate counts with his fingers. "That was two months ago!"

"I've been busy. Like I said, she calls me. And when I can, I answer. I listen. We are civil. That's us."

My relationship with my mother is nothing like the relationship Nate has with his parents; the most appropriate way to describe it is that it's easy. They get along easily, they joke around easily, they accept one another easily.

"I think she might be lonely," I admit finally. Ever since my dad passed away, Mom's been single, except for a couple of brief relationships that didn't eventuate into anything serious.

"You think?" replies Nate. "It's just her and Sheila, isn't it? Every Christmas and Easter."

"Yes." Sheila has been her assistant for almost two decades. It works like this: Sheila does the admin and bookwork, and Shirley does most of the talking. Sheila organizes all the retreats—the marketing, the promotion, the transfer buses, the social media—but she also organizes Mom's life, most likely because when she first entered Mom's life, her life needed a lot of organizing.

"Except this Christmas, Sheila isn't in Sorrento or anywhere near the Mornington Peninsula. In fact, she's not even in Australia."

"She's not?"

"No, Lucy, she's in Fiji for the birth of her grandchild."

"I thought she already had the baby."

Nate gives a small raise of his eyebrows. "You don't remember the lengthy voicemail on the landline, do you?"

"Now I feel bad." Admittedly, I don't pay much attention to the messages. Not nearly as much as Nate, who not only plays our voicemails back but takes notes. Notes that I don't bother reading. I feel a flush of shame wash over me. I don't mean to be this way—in fact, I often wonder what things could have been like between me and Mom if she'd been…well…different. If she'd been the mother I needed her to be.

"I'm not saying it to make you feel bad. I know things are complicated with the two of you."

This I can't argue with.

"Maybe I'll go see her once we get back home," I concede. Sorrento is only an hour and a half drive from where Nate and I live in Melbourne. I could easily visit her for a day.

Nate smiles, seemingly satisfied with this idea.

"But you'll have to come with me."

Nate's smile instantly fades.

I waggle a finger at him and his face adorably brightens. "I would be thrilled to accompany you. Your mother loves me."

"She doesn't," I joke. The only reason Mom pretends not to like Nate is because she really, really likes him. And part of her wishes she'd been more involved in my life, which would mean that by default she'd be part of Nate's life too.

"So, what did you think of my letter?" Nate asks.

"I think you have great penmanship."

He guffaws before swallowing his food and looking at me expectantly.

I don't want to give Nate false hope, but at the same time, I don't want to declare a straight-out no. Because if I'm honest, there is a part of me, albeit a small one, that wonders what it might be like to have a child.

"I'm glad it wouldn't be a deal-breaker for you," I say.

"I mean that."

"I don't doubt that you think you mean it."

He scrunches up his face.

"What I mean is, you believe this to be true now—in this moment. But in a few years...I think you might start to think about it differently," I say.

"So, what does that mean? For us? Because you look worried."

"I'm concerned."

"So your mind is made up? No room for a 'maybe yes'?"

"No, actually, there is some room for a yes. I think I need to sit with this some more, that's all."

"I'd never ask you to give up your job if that's a concern."

It isn't, but I'm partly relieved to hear him say this. "Are you saying you'd give up yours?"

"No, but working for myself means I'd be able to be more hands-on in the parenting department."

He makes it sound too easy. Suddenly, a life I couldn't have previously imagined for us flashes before my eyes. A nursery. A basketball ring at the top of the driveway. A rope swing hauled over the limbs of the oak tree in the front yard. Nate mopping up soggy cereal and spilled milk from the kitchen floor while tiny feet press footprints across the floorboards. Lying in bed at night, a tiny body—one that *we* made—sandwiched between us, giggling as we tickle tiny toes.

"Picturing myself as a mother—it feels...I don't know. A bit foreign to me."

"Well, yeah, that makes sense." Nate inches closer to me. "We'd make awesome parents. Especially you."

I squirm. Nate narrows his eyes. "You don't believe me," he says, like it surprises him.

I set my fork down. "I don't think you can count on that from me. It's possible that Shirley did not pass on the best mothering genes."

Nate's jaw squares. "That's what you're scared of? You think you're going to do a Shirley Livingstone on our kid?"

Why is my heart starting to race? I'm suddenly feeling thirsty. I call out to the waiter. "Excuse me, could I have a Coke Zero, please? With ice."

"Lucy," says Nate firmly. "You'd be an incredible mother." He gently guides my face toward his and leans his chin on my shoulder. "Don't let your past rob you of something potentially beautiful in your future. You aren't your mother, Lucy."

I start to notice every family, every baby, every pregnant belly. It's like someone has taken off my glasses and switched them with someone else's. Usually I wander through the world looking for places to shop or eat, or take breathtaking photographs I'll never get around to printing and framing.

We aren't even supposed to be here—in France, drinking mulled wine and cognac-laced hot chocolate—and we definitely aren't supposed to be making decisions that could potentially change the course of our lives forever.

It was simple, really.

Or so I thought.

Within a matter of days, our conversations start to revolve around how our lives could potentially accommodate a family and whether we'd feel comfortable traveling with a baby—yes— or a toddler—yes, again—since this is something neither of us is willing to give up. We map out what we call a "potential five-year plan" and decide to try it on for size. That's to say, we'll spend the next week assuming we *will* be having a baby, with the understanding that if either of us doesn't feel comfortable at any point, we can change our minds and revert to the original plan. Only Nate is still going to pursue a career change. In fact, he's going to start an owner-builder course the moment we get home.

"How much practice do you think we'd need?" I ask, taking my mug from him and setting it down as he inches closer to me.

"Lots," he says as he unclasps my bra.

I slide my arms around his neck and lean back. "If we'd invited my mother and she was here, there's absolutely no way this would be happening right now."

"See, I told you—to every downside there is an upside," he whispers, tossing my bra onto the floor.

We are thinking about becoming parents. Maybe this is our time. Maybe we can do this thing we said we never would.

CHAPTER SIX

Isla

"Don't get your blouse dirty—Grandma and Grandpa will be here any moment," I warn as the KitchenAid spews vanilla cream out of the bowl and onto my dress.

Reese is sitting on a stool at the island counter twisting her tongue. A string of saliva rolls down her chin. She giggles despite herself and proceeds to wipe her face with the cuff of her sleeve before trying again.

"Should have worn an apron," says Reese, noticing my dress, and I marvel at how my daughter, at times, manages to sound exactly like me.

The marks set into the fabric and offer no promise of being removed without the help of stain remover, which wouldn't be a problem except for the fact I chose this particular dress for the occasion. A buttery-yellow cotton wrap dress with flutter sleeves that is more to Mom's taste than my own. When you are the daughter of Elinor Tippett, you learn to make life easier for yourself, and sometimes that involves choosing attire that leaves no opportunity for scrutiny.

"Reese, can you please check the table's set properly? Take the bread basket with you. And the jug of iced tea."

She dutifully slides off the bar stool and not only does she perform these tasks, she even turns on some music and folds the napkins the way I taught her.

"Hey, Button!" calls out Ben, who is almost an hour late. He fist-bumps Reese and pecks me on the cheek before briefly admiring the beef Wellington sitting on the kitchen counter, glazed with egg yolk and ready to slide into the oven. "Sorry I'm late. How far away do you think they are?"

I check the clock. My parents are never late. Ever. Which means we have approximately twenty minutes for Ben to shower, dress, and get wine into the decanter, and for me to change, light the candles, and get the marzipan onto the chilled princess cake. My mother has a thing for fancy desserts, only she's accustomed to someone making them for her—someone who, unlike me, has earned their stripes as a pastry chef.

"Can you roll your tongue, Daddy? Like this. Watch." Reese pokes her tongue out to show him.

Ben mirrors her expression and tries to no avail. "Nope. Can't do it," he returns. "Looks like you discovered a superpower, Button."

"Mom! That means you can do it."

"I've never been able to roll my tongue," I reply.

"Try!"

To appease her, I try, and fail. "Told you. I can't do it."

"But Mrs. Raynor said it's *genetical*. Like if you can roll your tongue, then I can roll my tongue, and if you can't roll your tongue, then Daddy should be able to roll his. 'Cause it's in the family. It's the same thing if I have blue eyes." She cranes her neck to look into Ben's eyes and shakes her head. "Muddy-green," she notes, and records it in her notebook.

"Reese, what are you doing?"

"My school project."

"Which school project is this?"

"I already told you. I'm doing an investigation into what makes us the same and what makes us unique."

"This is why you wanted to see the photo album the other day?"

She gives me a look that says, *Duh.*

Ben is clearly unperturbed by all of this, but suddenly my palms feel clammy.

"I'm pretty sure the tongue-rolling thing is a myth." I'm not lying. I read this in a magazine article once. It said that apparently this genetic trait isn't so clear-cut. All the same, I have to remind myself to take a breath. It's a school project—nothing more.

"Actually, Mrs. Raynor said it's science. This is a real and important investigation. I even wrote down a *hippopothamus.*"

Ben chuckles. "Hy-poth-e-sis."

"Yes," says Reese.

"Maybe Mrs. Raynor should stick to solids, liquids, and gases," I mutter under my breath to Ben, who's already slipping off his tie.

"That's boring, Mom."

"You're nine years old. Since when do they teach kids your age about genetics in school?"

"Pretty sure it's not covering RNA, alleles, and heterozygosity at this level," chimes in Ben.

"I'm left-handed. Daddy, are you?"

"Uh, nope."

She checks her notebook again. "I need to know who in my family can roll their tongue because Mrs. Raynor said—"

"Grandpa Robert. Dad's side. When's this project due?"

"Two weeks. Can I see a photo of Grandpa rolling his tongue?"

"Cab Sav or Shiraz?" asks Ben, who is kneeling by the wine rack and clearly not bothered by Reese's question.

"Anything will do." I finish rolling out the marzipan and notice Reese looking at me expectantly.

"Mom, did you hear me?"

I pause. "The photo?"

She rolls her eyes. "Of Grandpa Robert. For my homework."

"Oh. Remind me tomorrow, okay?"

"Could we go to Officeworks and get a poster?"

"No," I say, more firmly than I mean to.

Ben clears his throat.

"Of course, just not now," I say.

"Obviously! It's nighttime," she replies.

Ben sloshes the contents of a Penfolds 2007 into a decanter and plonks it on the table.

"Time!" I declare, checking the clock.

Ben nods and makes his way down the hallway. I follow him.

"Aargh, I forgot the cob holders."

"Isla, we're entertaining your parents, not the royal family."

For years my parents have been coming to visit once a month, and every month I become overwhelmed with agitation because of it.

Ben slips his shirt off and starts to unbuckle his belt while the shower is running.

I groan as I tear through my wardrobe trying to find something suitable to wear.

"Reese, honey, could you please look for the cob holders? Buffet drawer!"

Ben finishes buttoning his shirt moments before my father's Prius rolls up the driveway.

"They're here!" Reese skips to the front door.

Ben, sensing my agitation, holds me by the shoulders. "Breathe."

That's exactly when I stop breathing.

Reese flings open the door and shows off her best grin. "Grandma! Grandpa!"

Peaches chooses this very moment to bound down the hallway to greet my parents, and as my mother steps through the door, Peaches drops a gift at her feet. One that almost guarantees our evening is ruined before it's begun.

Ben looks at me with wild eyes that mirror my own. "Is that a..."

Dead mouse.

My stomach drops. "Yes," I whisper.

Ben disposes of the mouse without so much as a word, and joins us in the living room. He wastes no time, and without needing any prompting from me, his hands reach for the Billecart-Salmon Rosé in the ice bucket.

"Thank you, Ben. I need something to calm my nerves after the encounter with that filthy rodent." My mother closes her eyes and shudders, which elicits a discreet eye roll from Ben.

"Really, darling, if you're going to have a dog, you must ensure it's properly trained when it comes to these things."

"We're working on it," I reply.

"None of that pink stuff for me," says Dad. He hands Ben a bottle of Dalmore single malt whiskey. "Got any ice?"

"Now?" asks Ben.

Dad throws me a surreptitious wink—one I know all too well. Mom is getting on his nerves again.

"Really, Lewis, it's barely six o'clock."

"I'm perfectly capable of telling the time, Elinor."

Mom ignores him. "Reese, darling, let me take a good look at you. Is this the outfit I bought you at Easter?"

Reese nods and thankfully doesn't out me for insisting she wear it in exchange for half a pack of Hubba Bubba. I probably shouldn't have done this but Reese is not a fan of puffy-sleeved button-up blouses or paperboy-waist daisy pants. "She looks lovely." Mom pauses, turning her attention to me. "Seersucker. That's an interesting choice, darling. I see you cut your hair—those messy beach waves suit you."

I inhale and hold my glass out for Ben to fill. "Low-maintenance. Perfect for summer, actually."

"Well, yes. You do work in real estate. Your work no doubt imposes on family time."

I want to remind her that the work I do is called "making an income" or "providing for my family." Yes, I do work evenings. There's no other choice. This is the industry I work in, and it's an industry that allows me to help keep our family afloat. Besides, I love my job. I am *good* at my job.

This, of course, makes very little difference to my mother. My choice of vocation isn't exactly one she approves of, even if I was responsible for negotiating the sale for the home she now lives in, a far-too-large-for-two sandstone home in Mount Martha with views of the beach that would make anyone throw logic and reason out the window and bid above market. Which is exactly why I didn't let that happen.

"Tell me all about your life, Reese. We'll start with school," says Mom, patting the sofa. "What wonderful things have you been learning about?"

On that note, I retreat to the kitchen, leaving Ben and Dad to discuss all the things they usually do—weather, sport, business, and whiskey, which in recent years has become one of my father's passions. He recently invested in a boutique distillery in South Australia and Ben hasn't heard the end of it.

The pale green marzipan drapes itself beautifully over the domed sponge cake now layered with perfectly set custard. I pipe cream rosettes around the base and finish with a fondant rose on top. By the time I do this, it's time to slide the beef Wellington into the oven and take out the canapés. Smoked salmon and chive vol-au-vents, and a cheese wheel that cost me ninety-five dollars a kilo and smells not too dissimilar to a teenage boy's socks.

When I enter the living room, Reese is sitting on the sofa with a pencil and notebook in hand—one that is unmistakably her science journal, the one covered in a black-and-white photo of Marie Curie we tracked down on the internet. Reese even has photos of Curie on her bedroom wall after we stumbled across a book for young girls about Marie and her life. It also sparked Reese's interest in science, something Ben and I are excited about, even if it does mean embracing all kinds of messy experiments in the kitchen.

My mother glances up at me, her lips pressed tightly together. Her body is turned toward Reese but her back is stiff, her spine as taut as a freshly tuned violin string.

"Darling," she says, her voice even, measured, calm as always. "Reese has a question that I can't possibly answer."

My grip on the platter tightens.

"Button, why don't you put your homework away and try one of these?" I say, inching forward. I practically shove the tray under Reese's nose, and it's a miracle she doesn't dry retch. She hates blue vein cheese.

Mom stares at me, unimpressed.

"It's just a silly school project."

"Is not silly, Mom!" huffs Reese.

"She wants to know who in the family is left-handed, and I can't think of anyone, can you?"

I can. Of course I can.

"Maybe you're special, Button," I say, hoping it can be left at that.

"Of course she's special," chimes in Dad. "Show us what you've got there, Reese." Dad peers over her shoulder and squints at her notebook while she reads from it.

"List five physical and personality traits that make you who you are. So I answered those questions but I want to know other stuff like traits I inher…"

"Inherited," offers Ben.

"…from my parents. That's my science investigation. I'm studying genes and I made a…hypo…" She looks at Ben for encouragement.

"Hypothesis."

"Yes! That's an educated scientific guess about something." She reads aloud from her notebook. "My hypothesis is that my genes come from my mom and dad and grandma and grandpa and we have things in common that are genetic."

Mom pats Reese's knee. "What a lovely little project. I've no doubt you've inherited your manners and good taste from me."

Another discreet eye roll from Ben.

"We also know how to properly set a table, don't we?" she continues.

"Yes!" exclaims Reese.

"And we share the same taste when it comes to cartoons."

Reese giggles and scribbles something in her notebook.

"Mom, please."

Mom raises a hand to quiet me. "You and Grandpa Lewis both love swimming in the ocean. You're as strong a swimmer as he is."

Dad chuckles. "She sure is."

Reese's tongue pokes out of the left corner of her mouth, which moves as she forms the letters to spell "swimming."

Mom turns to me and raises a brow. "Wasn't that hard now, was it?"

After dinner, Ben, Dad and Reese venture back into the living room, and Mom joins me in the kitchen. She slips on a pair of dusty-blue rubber gloves she keeps under my kitchen sink for occasions like these. While I wipe down the stovetop, she submerges her hands into the soapy water and starts rinsing the dishes.

"You'll obviously have to talk to her teacher on Monday."

"Isn't that a bit dramatic? It's a school project, Mom."

"It's a school project today and a potentially larger problem tomorrow. It's something you're going to have to do something about. Ask the teacher to give her an alternative project to work on. This work isn't suitable for her."

"Interfering in my daughter's life like that isn't really my thing."

"Well, is it your thing to let things spiral out of control?"

"It's not out of control. Everything's fine. It's just a silly school project!"

Mom pulls her hands out of the water and leans against the sink.

"Then tell me, darling, why are you trying to clean the stovetop with mayonnaise instead of cleanser?" She lets out an audible sigh. "Talk to the teacher, Isla."

CHAPTER SEVEN

Lucy

"This morning," whispers Nate, planting a kiss on my lips, "you come with me." He zips up his jacket and checks over his avalanche airbag backpack.

"Oh, no." I shake a finger at him. "I love my limbs intact, thank you very much. There is no way I'm doing a black run."

Nate takes full advantage of his puppy-dog eyes, and when his bottom lip protrudes, a part of me almost forgets how much I value my life.

"You do realize that it's more common to suffer a serious injury on this mountain than it is to endure a plane crash?"

He puts his hands on my cheeks and plants a kiss on my forehead. "Actually, there's a one in one-point-four-million chance of dying from a skiing accident, and about one in two hundred thousand from a plane crash, but that's never stopped you from flying. And you know what else? Winter only comes around once a year." He snakes his hand around my waist. "And we love the snow." He kisses my neck. "It's so romantic. Think of the views."

I have to give it to him. We love the snow. The views are unforgettable. It's romantic—we are the couple that can't travel in a cable car without kissing. But I can't pretend I'm not petrified of enduring another knee injury like I did last year. The rehab and physio after my ACL surgery grounded me for well over six weeks. It was nothing short of grueling and not something I wish to repeat.

"How reliable are your sources?" I ask him.

"Depends how highly you regard the back of a cereal box." He grins.

"I'm not ready for it." Not least because it took me all that time to recover from the surgery, something Nate has seemingly forgotten. "Also, I don't remember how to do it."

"It's like having sex, Lucy. It's not something you forget how to do."

"I took *lessons* to learn how to ski. It's an entirely different physical activity."

"What I'm saying is that you're a natural. You can handle the run. There's no way I'd encourage you to do this if I didn't think you could."

Nate's a Level 3 ski instructor and spent most of his twenties teaching people to ski.

I trust him.

So deep down, I know I can do it, mostly because Nate believes I can.

We take the gondola lift from Chamonix to Plan Praz at 2,000 meters, and are the first ones on the 8:50 a.m. cable car to Le Brévent, which affords us views of Mont Blanc massif, the range of glistening peaks, steep valleys, and glaciers that stretch across Italy, France, and Switzerland, and almost makes me forget to breathe.

Along the way, we toss around ideas. Like potential baby names, colors to paint the nursery, what month might be the best one to have a baby, even though we know that Mother Nature doesn't exactly work that way. It doesn't seem so bad, this whole "pretending to want a baby" thing, and if I'm honest, I've started warming to the idea. It might have something to do with how Nate gets a dreamy look in his eyes whenever he talks about being a dad.

"You really want this, don't you?" I say, once we almost reach the summit.

"Only if you do too." Nate's lips brush my ear. "We nearly forgot."

"About?"

"Our thing." He guides my face toward his, the goggles around his neck click-clacking awkwardly against mine.

"Will we still be able to do this kind of thing?"

"Pretty sure I'll still be able to kiss you, yes."

"Seriously. We like to travel a lot."

"We discussed this. So will our kids." Nate leans back into his seat and gazes out the window. "We'll teach them to ski here."

Nate makes it sound so easy. It makes me wonder if I'm over-thinking things. Would we even be able to afford trips to Europe after having a baby? If I was to consult my friend Kelly about this question, I am almost certain the answer would be a resounding no. Her first Christmas with her twins caused the maxing-out of a credit card, and let's not forget the lengths she went to for their first birthday. I advised her that there are things like boxed cake mixes, but she insisted on the three-tier, fondant-draped designer torte, knowing full well it would cost her the equivalent of two on-sale return flights to Fiji.

Admittedly, the idea of a trip back here with mini snowboards and cute little helmets and tiny snow boots and mittens elicits a fuzzy kind of feeling in me. Chamonix is where Nate proposed. We were both working in Europe and spent our first anniversary as a couple here. The weekend involved lots of near misses and tumbling over each other in the snow, but by the end I'd gotten the hang of it and never looked back. Whenever I found myself on location in places like Japan or New Zealand or Europe in winter, Nate and I would always try to steal a sneaky weekend to hit the slopes. Nate is by a long mile a better skier than me. During his teens he volunteered for the ski patrol and worked as an instructor. He's done dozens of black diamond ski runs and lives for the day I'll be able to join him on one. That, however, is never going to happen. This is how things are with Nate and me. I see something as too hard, too big, too scary, and he boils it down to fear and lack of confidence and encourages me to do it anyway. Maybe that's partly why I love him. Being around Nate makes me a more adventurous person. I learned to ski. I overcame my fear of spiders and driving at night. And monkeys. Yes. Monkeys. I trotted through a monkey forest in Bali with a monkey on my shoulder, and I have Nate to thank for it and photographic evidence to prove it.

Monkeys aside, Nate is the voice of reason, the solid rock, the guy that helps me truly see the world while living in it.

We dismount from the cable car and stop to take in the panoramic view. Nate digs his skis into the snow and stares out into the white vastness. We are up here early, the snow untouched since we are the only ones around. For a moment, I forget about my knee, my apprehension, and the fact I'm coming closer than I ever have before to committing to having a *baby*.

"How about we try the ridge at the top?" he suggests.

The ridge. Nate's favorite off-piste area to ski. Why? Because of the steep chutes above the piste. Steep chutes that are susceptible to avalanches. Steep chutes that, to me, are terrifying mostly because of the fact that one awkward fall could send me off a cliff.

I've skied that area before—but only once, two years ago, on a dare after I lost a game of Monopoly—and it wasn't easy, even if I did have a lingering tinge of an adrenaline spike that was quite enjoyable. Not that I ever admitted that to Nate. Since then, I've lifted my game at Monopoly and made it my mission to buy property as aggressively as possible and as early as possible. So far, the strategy has worked. But here we are. This isn't a dare.

It's purely Nate being Nate, wanting to experience the thrill of off-piste skiing, something that in all likelihood we'll have to give up, at least to some degree, if one day in the not-too-distant future we are to become parents.

And that's why I say yes.

Nate takes the lead as we follow the Bozon run until we take a sharp right turn. He stops in front of an avalanche rope warning that asks us to check whether we are equipped. The warning appears so much bigger than I remember. As a matter of course, Nate is wearing his avalanche airbag—he's not that arrogant about safety equipment—but mine, the bright blue bag that would aid my survival if I happened to get caught in a slide by landing me at the surface of an enormous pile of snow, is back at the chalet.

"I don't have my backpack," I say.

Nate's already slipping his pack off his shoulders. "Wear mine," he says.

"But what if—"

"It's fine. I've got my transceiver," he says, patting his jacket pocket.

"You know this means that tomorrow I get to drag you to the day spa."

"We traveled nearly ten thousand miles for snow and you want to waste a day in a spa?"

He lifts the pack and slings it over my arms. I turn around to face him, and he smiles as he clips my helmet buckle closed before pressing a kiss on my lips.

"Not an entire day. Three hours, actually. We can explore the Christmas market after that," I say chirpily. I poke him with my ski pole. "I'm kidding. But only about the day spa. After we ski, we explore the market. And join in with the Christmas carols."

"Only if we pass by the pub first."

"Deal."

"You know, it's not too late to invite your mom," he says, five minutes into the hike.

"What? Here?"

Nate stops walking. "Yeah, why not?"

"She would never come."

"She would probably jump at the chance, actually. To be with you."

"Maybe next Christmas," I reply. I sink my ski pole into the snow and continue walking. "Why do you keep bringing her up?" I ask, huffing as we push uphill. This hike is harder than I remember and the couloirs to my right are unsettling me.

"I'm not. I've just been thinking about family, that's all."

"Too much thinking," I reply, eyes trained on the horizon.

Nate doesn't reply, instead maneuvering our conversation toward something a bit safer. Lunch. The man is always thinking about food. When we get to Col du Brévent, he pulls out a chocolate bar and offers me a bite as we admire the alpine bliss. From here we can see the Bozon piste below, as well as Chamonix village.

"It's something, isn't it?"

I nod, taking in the scene. He puts his arm around my waist and pulls me closer to him.

"You ready?" he says eventually.

I tighten my grip around my ski poles and adjust my goggles before giving him a quick nod. "Me first. So I don't chicken out."

Nate grins. "I'll give you a head start."

He was right about me being ready to ski again. As soon as I set off, I feel myself come alive. All the fears I have about skiing off-piste recede. At a certain point, I realize that Nate still hasn't caught up to me. I come to a stop and wait, taking the opportunity to readjust my knee brace. When I look up again, that's when I see it—like a flash out of the corner of my eye. A body. A man's body. It's hurtling down the slope in the kind of way no human body should. My breath hitches in my chest as I register the snow kicking up behind him—his body tumbling, over and over and over through the snow, bouncing almost as he somersaults down the hill, the movements so fast and unnatural that I can do nothing but watch. I want to call out for Nate—he'd know how to call for help. But my voice, it's out of reach—like my vocal cords have forgotten to work. That's when I notice the man's jacket. It's cobalt-blue and it matches mine. I bought it on sale last year from my local ski gear shop. It was the last one on the rack. I'd told myself there was absolutely no way I was going to leave it behind.

I once read that when you are faced with an emergency, you don't process what is actually happening until much later. Suddenly, I'm on my knees beside him, ripping the goggles away from my face so I can see him better.

"You're okay. You're fine. You're going to be fine," I repeat, over and over, my hands hovering above his body, unsure of where or how to touch him. His leg is outstretched at an angle that makes my stomach churn, and his helmet... his helmet is damaged, clearly defeated by the rock that broke his fall.

"Nate! Nate... open your eyes."

"Answer me! *Nate*, answer me if you can hear me!"

Too afraid to move him, I call out into the vastness of our surroundings for help, my voice echoing into the emptiness.

There's barely any color in his face, and I can't tell whether he's breathing. I tear my gloves off and with trembling hands place my fingers against his neck below his ears. When I can't feel anything, I move my fingers into a slightly different position. There. A pulse. It's weak, but there.

I call out again. Nothing.

Transceiver.

He has a transceiver.

A transceiver I have no idea how to actually use. I pull it out of his pocket anyway, and when my trembling fingers have no luck operating it, I know what I want to do, but also know I have to do something else.

I want to stay with Nate—make sure he's still breathing. I want to be there when he wakes up, to tell him I love him. And yet, I know I can't stay.

"I'm going to get help," I tell him. "Stay with me—just stay. You have to stay."

When I reach the bottom of the slope, I stand there, gasping for air, my entire body shaking.

"Hey, are you okay?" A guy—probably not much older than me—approaches me. "Are you hurt?"

I shake my head. Words. I need words. But all I can do is shake my head.

"May I?" He gently pulls the goggles from my face. "Tell me what's wrong, sweetheart."

I blink into his arctic-blue eyes. Nate's eyes are a shade or two darker—more like a deep sapphire. They are deep-set, and when he smiles, the edges of his eyes crinkle while the dimple in his left cheek becomes more prominent. I can't get what I saw up on the mountain out of my head. And I can't look away from this man's eyes.

I open my mouth.

Then close my mouth.

"You having trouble breathing?" Those blue eyes tinged with concern search mine.

Up ahead, I catch sight of the ski patrol. "My husband. He needs help," I croak. "He needs help now."

And then suddenly, as if a blanket is being pulled out from under me, I watch in slow motion as Blue-Eyes races toward the ski patrol, snow spraying behind him. I tip my head up toward the sky, my legs giving way beneath me. I fall to my knees. And there is nobody there to catch me.

I don't ask for the man's name.

He manages to extract some vague information from me about Nate's location and stays with me while the ski patrol activate their rescue. When the helicopter chugs overhead, we sit there in the snow, silently praying. And when it comes time to leave—to go to the hospital—he leads me to a car, presumably his, and distracts me with a convoluted story about climate change, which morphs into a story about electric cars, which morphs into a story about reality TV shows. I mostly sit there and nod, all the while trying to convince myself that Nate will be okay. He's a good skier—an exceptional skier—capable of doing black diamond runs, and this is not going to be the way he leaves me. There is simply no way I can accept that the thing that Nate loves the most is the thing that will change everything.

Later, I'm told the crew lost Nate during the flight to the hospital. His injuries were, to put it simply, too extensive. They said the most likely explanation for his fall was the result of him hitting an ice patch. He ruptured a vertebral artery in his neck, and the bleeding in his brain as a result of that caused him to go into cardiac arrest.

I never got the chance to say goodbye. I never got the chance to give him my definitive answer. Because suddenly, it's a firm yes. I want us to start a family. I want it more than anything I've ever wanted before. Those unspoken words are like a present that will never have the chance to be unwrapped. That's the thing about losing someone and the rest of your life in one swoop. It isn't just the person you lose; it's all the other things.

CHAPTER EIGHT

Isla

Loretta Hoffman, the vice principal, sits to the left of Beth Raynor, with me opposite them both. This has everything to do with the three-page letter I penned to them at midnight after my mother left and I couldn't sleep. In what I can only describe as a report not dissimilar to a persuasive essay I had to write in my university days at Monash, I tried to diplomatically put forward all the reasons I felt genetics should not be a topic covered in the school curriculum for children Reese's age.

I wrote an incohesive mess that did little else but alarm these two poor women into inviting me in for a "chat."

As Loretta politely explained moments earlier, learning about genetics isn't part of the school curriculum per se. In fact, it isn't even the focus of Reese's project at all. It is a personal identity project, for which Mrs. Raynor has spoken about genes and inherited physical and personality traits in passing. Her general reference to genetics was meant to be engaging and fun, and not an aspect of the teaching she expected Reese or the rest of the class to latch onto in the way they did; Reese's curious mind turned it into an investigation with a scientific slant.

"Isla, I can see you're upset by this. Is there anything we can do?" comes Loretta's voice, all sincere and calm.

"No, but it would have been helpful if the whole topic of genetics had been avoided in the first place, especially for someone like Reese." I rub my temples. "She doesn't know she's donor-conceived and I'd have preferred not to have to answer questions about hereditary traits for some school project." After I speak the words, I hold my breath. I haven't admitted this out loud to anyone. *Ever.*

Loretta and Beth nod.

"I understand and I apologize for bringing the topic up at all," says Beth. "This is the last project before the end of term, and I'll make sure we focus only on the personal identity aspect of things."

"If Reese needs some additional support with some of the recent playground events—if you think she could benefit from talking to one of our well-being coordinators—we can work something out for her," says Loretta, chiming in.

"I'll keep it in mind," I say, picking up my handbag.

"Great. If there's anything at all we can do to support you or Reese through any challenges you might be facing, we can help."

Only they can't.

Nobody can.

I created this mess. I'm the one who has an issue anytime anyone brings up the topic of genetics. After all, I'm the one who all those years ago decided to break a promise, and nobody can fix what I have broken.

That evening, my mother calls me while I'm at the supermarket trying to wrestle my way to the last roast chicken. I beat the mother with twin toddlers to the counter by a couple of seconds, and when I see her shoulders slump, the haphazard pieces of oatmeal in her hair, I don't have the heart to put it in my basket.

"Here," I say, handing it to her with a smile.

"What's that, Isla?" comes Mom's voice down the line.

"Nothing, Mom. Just a cooked chicken." To the lady, I say, "I just realized I already have a chicken." The woman eyes my empty basket, but that doesn't stop her from hugging the bagged chicken to her chest and making a beeline for the self-service checkouts. As a mother, I've been there and fully appreciate the life-changing benefits of a cooked chicken at the end of a long day.

"From the *supermarket*?" says Mom.

"Where else does one get a roast chicken from?"

"The only place a roast chicken should come from, darling. The oven."

"My oven is broken."

"It seemed to be working perfectly fine last night."

"It has a problem with roasting chickens."

"Maybe if you finished work earlier, you'd have time to look into the problem."

I silently count to three and toss a package of tacos and some mild sauce into my basket. There is no problem. Not unless you count the fact that my mother hasn't caught up to the reality that these days, resorting to a supermarket roast chicken at 6 p.m. on a Wednesday night is well within the realm of normal for the average middle-class suburban family. The only reason she has a problem with it is because the one thing she wants from me is the one thing I don't want to give her. Sure, having Mom pick Reese up from school, help her with her homework, take her to tae kwon do, would be convenient—a blessing, actually. But not at the cost that would come with it. I've worked hard to keep my mother at an arm's length, and I have no intention of tearing down the barrier she's forced me to put up. The arrangement—dinner at my place once a month, lunch at hers every two weeks—is ample.

"I need to go, Mom. Was there a specific reason for your call?"

"Yes, actually. Did your father happen to leave his reading glasses behind?"

This is a lie. Dad never leaves the house with his glasses. The only time he ever wears them is when he reads the newspaper, which he still has delivered every morning. What can I say? He's a creature of habit. A glass of orange juice, a plate of scrambled eggs and cooked mushrooms, and then he starts reading the paper.

"I don't believe so, no."

"Well, if you find them."

"I have your number," I say, deadpan, as I drop four cans of tuna and a box of crackers into my basket.

There's a pause before she continues. "So did you talk to her? The teacher?"

"Yes, I did."

"And?"

"It's handled. It was a misunderstanding."

"As long as she knows not to bring it up again. You know how it is, darling. If you keep shaking a piggy bank, eventually the coins will fall out."

I smile into the phone. "Bye, Mom." And then I hang up.

As it turns out, even Reese has a problem with the chicken, or lack of it.

"Give me strength." I heap a spoonful of beef into my taco shell.

"You said you were getting a *chicken*."

"Thought you *loved* tacos."

She crosses her arms. "Not anymore, I don't."

"Stop crossing your arms like that. You're turning ten, not two."

"And you're the worst mom." She scowls at me and uncrosses her arms. That's something at least.

"How was school today?" chimes in Ben as he heaps a dollop of sour cream onto his taco. "Did Mrs. Raincoat bore you to tears?"

Reese's face breaks into a smile. "Daddy! It's Mrs. Ray-nor."

"Ah," says Ben. "But does she own a raincoat?"

He starts singing "Singin' in the Rain."

Reese laughs. Even I laugh then. And it's enough for Reese to forget about the roast chicken entirely. Ben always has a way of averting tears and tantrums and I love him for it. It comes naturally to him. Me, on the other hand? I need some work in that department. He and Reese share the same sense of humor. Maybe that's it. Maybe my brand of humor doesn't chime with them. Maybe I'm too serious.

"Why were you at school today?" asks Reese as she heaps a fistful of grated cheese into her taco, half of it spilling onto her plate. "Talking to Mrs. Hoffman and Mrs. Raincoat."

Out of the corner of my eye I sense Ben's head turn toward me and then back to Reese. "Button? Another fight with Mitchell?"

"No, I just needed to sort out..." The words won't come. "Suggestions for the concession menu."

Reese makes a face as if to say, *Bor-ing*, and bites into her taco, which literally collapses onto her plate. "Ohhh," she groans.

Ben screws up his nose. "The concession? Since when are you involved in the concession? Or anything school-activity-related."

I try not to appear hurt. I stand up to get another napkin for Reese, and Ben starts filling another taco shell for her before going back to singing.

"Why were you really at the school?" asks Ben an hour later. His head is under the kitchen sink trying to find the cause of a leaking pipe. He's been on his back for almost thirty minutes. Plumbing tasks aren't exactly his forte. I step over his legs and grab a dishwasher tablet.

"All done," says Ben, sliding out from the cupboard. He stands up as I close the dishwasher with my hip. I go to walk away. I have an inbox full of unopened emails and need to send the Section 32 by 8 p.m. to a red-hot client I'm sure is going to make an offer on a home.

"Isla?"

"Mmm?"

"The school meeting?"

I pretend to check the calendar on the wall by the fridge. "I went in to talk about the school project," I say casually.

Ben raises a brow. "Are we concerned about that?"

"After the 'fake baby' comment? Yes. I'm concerned about it, Ben. It's not right that our daughter has come home asking us about genetics."

"Does this have anything to do with what you and your mom were talking about last night?" he asks knowingly.

I don't need to answer him because he already knows this has everything to do with that. This is what fourteen years of marriage does—it gives you an innate sense of knowing when your spouse is glossing over things.

"Maybe if we explain the whole 'fake baby' thing properly, it won't bother her so much. Especially if we help her understand this is a common thing." Ben fills Peaches' bowl with water and pauses, blinking a few times. "Why don't we just talk to Mitchell's parents and explain things to them? Maybe they could have a good talk with him once they know where we're coming from?" suggests Ben.

"No way. It'll make things worse!"

"Isla, come on. They're adults. They'll understand."

The last thing I want is for our business to be aired out on the school playground, and that's exactly what will happen if we loop Liesel and Sam into our private business.

"We need to let the school deal with it. Hopefully by the time she goes back to school next year it'll all be forgotten."

"Fine. But sooner or later, we're going to need to explain that she's donor-conceived, and I don't think we should wait for things to escalate at school for us to do that. I think we should tell her soon."

My skin prickles. "After what's been happening at school, I think we need to give Reese a breather," I reply. By this, Ben knows I mean we should *not* tell Reese anytime soon.

"Isla—"

"We're not ruining Christmas for her."

"We won't be *ruining* anything. Why can't you see that?"

"Ben. Please."

He shakes his head in defeat but I know it's only a temporary defeat. I can tell from his expression that I'll only be able to bide my time for so long before he puts this back on the table for discussion.

"I'll go tuck Reese in tonight." He puts a hand to his mouth and calls out, "Tooth fairy wants to know if your teeth are squeaky clean, cricket!"

"I'm bwushin dem wight now!" she calls from the bathroom.

"We need to figure out what we're going to do about Frostie," I say as he goes to walk away.

Ben takes a second to register what I'm saying. "Oh. Yeah. The West Park letter. I'll write a check tomorrow."

"You didn't read it, did you? There's no more mailing checks back. This is crunch time."

We are going to need to decide whether to use our last frozen embryo, or else it will be statutorily disposed of.

I'm in my late thirties, I stay in shape, and financially we can afford to have another child. The question—the one I ask myself every year—is do we both want what I think I want?

"I'm ready for you to tuck me in!" calls out Reese from her bedroom.

"Coming!" replies Ben. "We'll talk about this later," he says, squeezing my shoulder.

But as I suspect, later never comes.

CHAPTER NINE

Lucy

The first person I call after the accident is Nate's mom. Janet is a semi-retired watercolor artist who spends months at a time traveling the world alongside Terry, her husband, who is fascinated with European architecture. Only Janet doesn't answer, and neither does Terry, so I call my mother. My mother, who I haven't called in months. She always calls me.

"Aha! So you do have my phone number."

I take a deep breath. I am not going to cry. "Hi, Mom."

"Two months, three days, and four hours, give or take," she says.

"I spoke to you two days ago."

"Yes, but I always call you. And I haven't seen you in over a year. For all I know you could have gotten pregnant and had a baby, and I could unwittingly be a grandmother."

"You are not a... grandmother."

It hits me.

She will never be a grandmother.

"Lucy?"

I scrunch my eyes closed and push the words out. "He's gone. Nate's... gone."

"Where'd he go?" There's a scraping noise in the background. "Sheila, let's move the couch over there, by the window instead," she says. "The pub? Tanzania?"

"No, Mom. I mean he's *gone*. There was an accident."

The line falls momentarily silent. "And he's not...coming back?" asks Mom, her tone serious.

Saying it out loud hurts so much I don't know how I've managed to stay standing upright.

"No."

"You mean like, not *ever*?"

I sniffle into the phone and wipe my eyes with the cuff of my sleeve. "Never ever. The funeral director—he's organizing Nate's repatriation. He's getting us on a flight that leaves on Wednesday night."

"Oh, shit. Hold on. Sheila! I need you to call Victoria and cancel this week's classes unless Loredana can cover for me. I'm going to Melbourne. Once you're done, come upstairs and help me pack! You can have the rest of the week off."

And then, "Lucinda, don't you worry about a thing. I'm coming."

"No, there's no need. Really, I'll be fine. I just...needed to tell someone."

But there's no answer. She's already hung up the phone. Shirley Livingstone will be coming. For the first time in years I realize that maybe I truly do need my mom.

Mom swoops in and makes sure that everyone—me, Terry, Janet, and Lysa from two doors down—has enough Kleenex and Long Island iced tea, her specialty. Everyone on our street, a wide cul-de-sac, has been briefed on the news because Mom door-knocked them all as soon as I jumped in the shower once I got home from the airport. She delegated the role of cooking to my neighbors, who turn up one by one that afternoon with their best Corning Ware dishes replete with hearty casseroles and nutrient-dense soups even though we are close to the thick of summer.

The moment Nate's parents arrive from the airport to my place that afternoon, a numbness overtakes me. It's like I'm here, but the scene unfolding in front of me isn't real. Nate's brother, Liam, is on a flight from the U.S. and won't be here until tomorrow. Janet starts pacing the kitchen, firing questions at me like, "Would Nate have preferred to be buried or cremated?" and, "Does he have a will?" and, "What kind of flowers were his favorite?" to which I answer, "I don't know, probably not, and I have no idea." As I already explained to Ian, the oddly upbeat yet compassionate funeral director who competently dealt with Births, Deaths, and Marriages, the consulate, and Department of Foreign Affairs to get Nate home, the two of us never spoke about anything like this—not even after Nate had his scuba diving accident.

My father-in-law, Terry, normally as calm and collected as a Navy Seal, sits on the kitchen stool, the color slowly draining from his face.

He clears his throat. "Lucy?" he says.

My eyes flick up from the stack of papers I'm flipping through.

"Water?"

"Yes. Course. Are you feeling okay?" I go to open the fridge. Mom puts her hand on the door to stop me.

"I'll handle this," she says. With that, she helps herself to Nate's twenty-five-year-old whiskey—the bottle he got for his ten-year anniversary at work last year. She proceeds to concoct a double-shot whiskey highball, which she commands Terry to drink. Like an obedient dog, he does as he's told. Mom then pours herself a glass, throws back a shot, and pours herself another, but before she can down that one, Janet swoops in and helps herself to it. For a woman accustomed to fine wine and nothing stronger than a nice Bordeaux, she impressively consumes three highballs by the time Ian finishes running us through the finer details of Nate's farewell—his choice of words, not mine. Janet makes the call for cremation, so I don't have to decide, and I settle on white roses and purple hydrangeas.

Later, Mom and Janet relieve me of the task of searching the filing cabinet for anything that resembles a will since I can't seem to get my hands to work properly, and there's a puddle of paperwork at my feet.

"Aha! I think I might have found something," Mom says half an hour later, brandishing an envelope. She taps it on the counter. "It's got your name on it and I'm guessing if he wanted you to have it while he was alive, then he would have given it to you already."

She holds the envelope out for me. A small, sealed, pale blue envelope with Nate's unmistakable bold type font that spells my name out in felt-tip marker.

Nate wasn't the type of guy to plan ahead, let alone leave a will tucked into a legal-sized envelope in case of death. So when I take it from Mom's hand, I stand there blinking at the words:

CONFIDENTIAL
For Lucy. You'll know what to do with this and when.
Love, Nate xo

"Are you going to open it?" asks Mom expectantly.

"I'm pretty sure I know what it is. He was going to surprise me with tickets to see *The Lion King* for my birthday, but I pretended I didn't know." The truth is, I don't know what this is.

Mom and Janet exchange a look but refrain from saying anything more. I tuck the envelope into the back pocket of my jeans and signal to Mom to pour me some whiskey.

"Nope, none for you. I don't want you turning to alcohol to solve your problems." She says this right before she drains whatever is left in her own glass. "If you need someone to go with you to the show, I could come," she adds before reaching for one of the sandwiches my neighbor Lysa brought over earlier this morning.

Janet throws me a sympathetic look. Mom is trying a little too hard.

"I think I need to lie down."

Janet extends a hand and rests it on my arm. "Lucy, darling, Terry and I will take care of contacting everyone. Where's your phone? You won't have to worry about a thing."

Of course I do worry. About everything. About how I will lie down tonight alone. About how I will manage to keep breathing when I wake up tomorrow morning without Nate beside me when it's already so hard to breathe.

I give my phone to Janet and then take Nate's phone from the coffee table, punching in his password—our wedding anniversary date—as a photo of us drinking cocktails at the Six Senses villa resort in Bhutan flashes before my eyes. We hiked vertiginous mountains and valleys and never once did it cross our minds that in a year Nate would be gone. I mean, who lives their life preparing for the worst like that? It's unfair. No, it's worse than unfair, and I am moments away from falling apart. This house—our home— was meant to be the start of something. A new chapter. Part Two. Only he slipped on a patch of ice and now there is only me.

"Lucy?" asks Mom from the hallway when I'm seconds away from entering my bedroom.

"Yes?" I say, glancing back at her.

"What about Isla? Do you want . . . Janet to call her?"

I stand there, blinking, a sour taste rising in my throat.

Isla. My eyes start to sting.

"No," I say finally, my words betraying me. I'm seconds away from bursting into tears.

"She deserves to know," says Mom quietly, and her tone in that split second is one that is completely foreign to me.

I don't have the willpower to debate this. "It's actually not my problem." I haven't seen Isla in almost ten years. The last time Nate and I heard from her and Ben was five years ago, via a brief and direct email. Even if they try calling her, she probably won't pick up the phone.

I step inside my bedroom and lean against the closed door, the pain rising up, up, up, until it all spills out.

If there's anyone I want here with me in this moment, it's Isla.

It's nine o'clock by the time Janet and Terry leave. Mom orders Thai for dinner, and I eat no more than a spoonful of coconut rice before heading back to my room. When I can't resist a moment longer, I open the envelope.

Dear Lucy,

This whole letter-in-the-envelope thing is probably throwing you for a loop, because if you're reading this, it means I'm not here anymore. Before you go any further, I want you to know that you'll be fine. You can do this without me, I promise. I know you can, even if you think you can't.

The scuba diving incident made me rethink a lot of things, but most of all it reminded me I'm not invincible. I know I'm not usually one to plan ahead or think of the worst but this is something I had to do. Just in case…

There's a blue USB stick in the garage. It's in my toolbox. I know you'll make the best decision about what to do with it and when. I trust you with everything, Lucy.

Love you to bits and beyond.
Nate

P.S. Tell Mom she can stop looking for a will because you won't find one. We both know I'm not that organized. You get everything.

I finish reading, grief washing over me in waves. It's as if I've floated out into the ocean and am merciless to its power.

You can do this without me, I promise. I know you can, even if you think you can't.

He's wrong. Completely wrong. There is no possible way to do this without him. In this room there are reminders of him everywhere. His pajamas, a quirky printed T-shirt covered with fried eggs with matching shorts, are still bunched up under his pillow. They smell of the Hugo Boss fragrance he wore—a scent I can only describe as his. Our bed, far too big for the two of us, its springy mattress and overstuffed pillows that take me forever each morning to put back, with the hand-knit chunky wool throw I picked up on a trip to Sweden. This is where we spent lazy Sundays, eating breakfast, making love, drinking rosé, working out our next travel plans, exchanging birthday gifts. Nate will never, ever be here again in this bed, spooning me from behind, whispering that he loves me, ever again. I roll onto my stomach, press my face into the stupid eiderdown pillow, and will it to absorb every last bit of sadness I can expel.

I can't do this without you. I don't want to do this without you.

We were thinking of starting a *family.*

Just when I let out a muffled moan, Mom barges in with a tub of Nate's favorite ice cream and two spoons. She maneuvers herself onto the bed and tucks her legs underneath her, holding the tub between her knees as she pries the lid off it.

"Come on now. Sit up." She hands me a spoon. "The house is beautiful, kiddo. You two did a great job with this place." She pauses. "You made a great life for yourselves, didn't you?" She reaches over, and I sense a hint of apprehension. Or maybe it's a twinge of sadness. Maybe that's why I don't move. She sweeps some stray wisps of hair away from my eyes and smooths my hair back. My mother hasn't touched me like this since I was a little girl. "Just like you said you would." She smiles, like she's reminiscing. "You had a good life. With him. I'm glad you made the most of your life. I'm . . . I'm proud of you, Lucy."

I nod as I dig my spoon into Nate's last tub of double-chocolate, but I don't have the energy or willpower to bring it to my mouth.

"I saw the swatches of fabric in your studio. Did you design them yourself? The lemons?"

I nod again. I've been experimenting with fabric design since I stopped work. Those prints took me weeks to get right. The only person who'd seen them was Nate.

"Impressive," she whispers. "Janet took Nate's phone home and she'll keep making calls. She got through to most of your contacts." She pauses. "Isla didn't answer."

That doesn't surprise me. Not one bit.

"Not that it's any of my business, but I think you should try her again yourself."

I pretend not to hear her.

"People change, Lucinda. Time changes us. People make mistakes. Sometimes you need to give the ones you love a second chance."

Leaving me with that thought, she gets up, draws the curtains, flicks the light off, and heads upstairs, leaving me completely in the dark.

CHAPTER TEN

Isla

"We really need to make a decision about this," I say to Ben the next morning, holding up the letter from West Park.

He turns the coffee machine on and takes two mugs from the overhead cupboards.

"Double shot, please." He knows to use my favorite mug—the one with the marker on the brim that says, *Don't talk to me until you reach this line!* which sits above another marker that says, *Keep pouring!* Ben chose it for Reese to give me for a Mother's Day gift six years ago.

He double-taps the button on the coffee machine, which grinds into motion, sending a satisfyingly bitter odor into the kitchen.

"They're basically saying we have three months to let them know what we want to do with it."

I notice Ben's hand hovering over the toaster before he drops a slice of bread into it.

Up until now, we've made the same decision each year. The timing to have another baby never seemed to be right. First there were finances to consider, then our careers, and by the time we managed to reach a point of stability where we could afford to have another baby, Reese was almost six years old. We'd long ago packed away the baby furniture—her nursery morphing into a little girl's room with bunting and watercolor prints, a telescope in the corner, and glow-in-the-dark stars on the ceiling. She graduated from kindergarten and started wearing a school uniform, and our conversation never quite progressed from not being able to have another baby to actually making room for one. The unspoken decision to not do anything about it simply faded into the background, dropping to the bottom of the priority list—the same way chores like cleaning out the heating ducts or sorting out the linen cupboard do.

"What happens if we want to keep it on ice?" he asks.

"We already got permission to extend storage for five years, and we hardly have a good enough reason to convince them we should have an extension now." The limit the law allows for is ten years and our time is up—plain and simple.

"Okay, so what are we going to do? What do you want to do?" says Ben, heaping a teaspoonful of sugar into his coffee.

In four years we'll be parents of a teenager. Could I go back to sleepless nights and diaper changes while running a business? I remind myself of the bigger picture. The way I only need to look at Reese and my heart fills with indescribable love and joy. I'm nearing forty. This could be—is—our last chance to have a baby. Yet the way Ben goes around the kitchen getting breakfast ready tells me he's not on the same page as I am. Even if we do decide to have another baby, there's no guarantee a transfer would even be successful, but there's a difference between not wanting to try and at least giving it a go.

"What do you want to do?" I ask him, without first answering his question.

Ben pours Corn Flakes into two bowls—one for him and one for Reese, who is still asleep in bed. By the time she gets up, the Corn Flakes will be soggy, she'll refuse to eat them, and he'll have to make another bowl, but sometimes one has to pick their battles, so I don't say anything at all.

"I think that under different circumstances it might be time to let the idea of having another baby go," he says. "But those embryos were created for us to use."

The idea of letting our embryo *go* leaves me feeling uneasy.

"Are you saying you've decided? You don't want another child?"

"I suppose I'm thinking about it now. In a way it feels like we missed the boat." There's a tinge of sadness in his voice that hints at a sense of mourning for something we could have had but lost.

"Yeah, three years ago," I say morosely, staring at the now-pudgy Corn Flakes. The year we finally reached a point of financial stability where it might have been possible to have another baby.

"I'm sorry," says Ben, and when he looks up at me I can tell he means it.

Only sorry can't send us back in time. Sorry can't change anything. That one mistake—that one bad judgment call—almost cost us a marriage.

I'd just taken a pregnancy test when I made the discovery. I thought I'd surprise Ben by changing the wallpaper on his laptop to a photo of two pink lines on a plastic stick. Ben's password was easy enough to guess: my name, all lowercase. The screen popped up, countless browser tabs all open at the same time—one of Ben's habits that irked me. I was a one-tab-open-at-a-time kind of girl. Ben was also the kind of guy who never cleared his inbox, whereas I regularly performed housekeeping to keep my emails to a manageable number—always fewer than fifty at any given time. My mouse hovered over the button to minimize the browser when one of the tabs caught my eye. It was a government website—an information page of the Australian Financial Security Authority—and the heading, staring back at me in clean purple font, said, *Am I eligible for bankruptcy?*

Bankruptcy.

My mouth went dry. And sticky, like I hadn't had a drop to drink in days. I flicked to the next tab. Maybe he'd been sorting out his quarterly Business Activity Statements and clicked on a random link from the tax office website that had got him there by mistake.

But no. The rest of the tabs were equally damning.

I can't pay my debts.

Paying unmanageable debts.

The rest of the tabs brought up web pages. Banks. Commonwealth. HSBC. ANZ. Westpac. Bendigo...

There was no mistaking things. This was bad. I was pregnant. Pregnant! We were finally having a baby and we were...poor? Destitute? How bad was it? More importantly, how had the man I'd lived alongside for years managed to keep this from me?

My body flushed with heat. There was another pressing question. How did this even happen? We'd gone through round after round of IVF without Ben so much as batting an eyelid. We'd traded in my car last year for a new one. He'd told me that despite the hiccups last summer when the winery suffered fire damage, we were solid. Our lifestyle hadn't changed. We still ate out at restaurants and booked weekends away. My credit card was never declined. Ben still kept up his gym membership.

I slammed the laptop closed, pulled out my phone, and opened my banking app. Password. What was my password?

Our day-to-day expense account seemed healthy enough—no strange withdrawals or transfers to be seen. My heart revved a little when I recalled a day about eight months ago, or was it ten? I'd tried to access the banking app on my phone but had been logged out. I'd complained about it to Ben over a glass of freshly squeezed orange juice and a piece of burnt toast. I'd told him I'd have to call the bank, but he'd told me he'd take care of it, handing my phone back to me twenty minutes later. Only then I could no longer see the mortgage account or the redraw sum that most couples like us could be proud of. It hadn't bothered me because I could still see the daily transaction account my weekly pay went into, and that was the account I usually checked.

My hands were shaking as I dialed the number for the bank.

"Could I please have the balance of my mortgage?"

The chirpy customer service representative asked me to confirm my details.

Isla Louise Sutherland.

54 Peacock Court...

Secondary account holder Benjamin Matthew Sutherland.

"Just one moment, please."

After a couple of moments, she answered.

And that's when I dropped the phone.

Ben's password for the business bank account was something far more complicated than my name, and after an entire day of searching the filing cabinet in the study, there was no paper trail or bank statements to be found. Not even in his inbox, which housed a cringeworthy 2,946 unopened emails.

He got home just after six o'clock, carrying a bunch of flowers—coral peonies, which he knew to be my favorite. He bought me an armload of blooms every week from the florist a few doors down from his office, two if it was an IVF week. For those weeks he'd throw in a chocolate bar too.

"Hey, beautiful," he said, extending them my way. Standing there with my arms crossed, I gave them no more than a cursory glance. He deposited them on the counter in response.

"Is... is everything okay?" he asked, tentatively.

I shook my head.

"You've been crying. You took a test?"

He wanted a baby as much as I did. We both knew that if the second embryo didn't take, we'd be left with our last, only one more chance to have a baby before we resorted to Plan C—adoption, which could take years or not eventuate at all—or Plan D—no kids.

"Where's all our money, Ben?"

Ben's head jolted up then, like he was a puppet on a string.

"Just give me an answer."

He rubbed a hand over his cheeks, his eyes trained on the flowers. "Isla...let's sit down." His eyes were suddenly misty. "I screwed up."

"To the tune of..." I thrust toward him a copy of the bank statement I'd managed to get hold of after my phone call. In hot-pink highlighter I'd marked the balance of what we now owed on the house.

"It's *all* gone. Everything we worked for, Ben. Everything! We almost had the house paid off!" My hands curled into tight fists. "Now we can barely meet the repayments!"

Ben wasn't looking me in the eyes. He was staring at the bouquet positioned on the edge of the kitchen counter. "Give me some time...to fix this." He raised his hands. "I'm going to fix it."

"Well, before you attempt to do that, I'd like an explanation at least."

Ben winced and closed his eyes for a brief moment before opening them again.

"Ever since Edward left—he took my best staff with him—and the fire...you know how tough it's been to come back from that. We lost the majority of our overseas orders—the canceled functions and events..."

The fire had whipped through the winery, taking with it half the vineyard and the events hall—a renovated shed that was the envy of most of the wineries in the Red Hill region. I knew this had made things tough, but Ben had reassured me on multiple occasions that the business was in a good position to be able to endure this. Evidently, he'd been lying.

"You told me insurance took care of things."

"It did, but..."

A pause.

"We were underinsured."

"Why didn't you talk to me?"

"I didn't want to worry you."

"What, so you pretended everything was normal? That I wouldn't eventually notice?"

The thing was, I *hadn't* noticed. I hadn't noticed a thing. Should I have?

"You were already so worried about having a baby. I didn't want to add to that stress. I didn't want the business or our finances to impact you."

"Well, guess what? It has! I'm not worried. I'm angry. And that's much, much worse. Want to know why?"

He clenched his jaw.

"Because you lied to me. You've been lying to me for months! You've been using our life savings to keep a business—a *business*—afloat! For months! You burned through hundreds of thousands of dollars and not once did it occur to you that you should have told me, or that maybe it wasn't the right thing to do!"

"Isla, please. I'm trying to get things under control...I found a way...I can—"

"You're looking into filing for bankruptcy! Enough with the excuses!"

"Okay. Okay," he repeated. "What I mean is, I may have someone who's interested in coming on board as a partner."

I didn't want to hear it. There was nothing to say a partner would save us, and even if it eventuated, there was no way it would fix our financial problems overnight. "We're having a baby! We are starting a family and I'm going to be home on maternity leave!"

"I'm sorry. Wait, you said…we're having a baby? You're… you're pregnant?"

I nodded, slowly. This was not how I'd imagined things would go. A baby was everything we'd ever wanted—and we had tried so hard to get here—and now, all the financial stability we'd had in our lives was completely gone. A crib, a car seat, diapers, clothes, and school fees. Sports coaching, swimming lessons—how would we even begin to cover the costs of having a child? This wasn't the kind of debt a couple recovered from overnight. This would take *years*.

Ben's face crumpled and he started crying into his fist.

I wanted to hold him. I wanted him to hold me. But instead I replied, "Yes. I am. And I'm putting the house on the market first thing tomorrow morning."

It was the only thing to do.

Now, a decade later, we're talking about having a baby in the same kitchen of our home—the one we were able to salvage after my mother spotted the two-page spread in the local paper advertising the very same house she contributed a deposit toward three weeks before my wedding. Perk of being a real estate agent is that you know where to find the best stylists and photographers to optimize a listing. Downside to having a mother with a penchant for scouring the local paper for idle gossip and real estate prices despite her distaste for my chosen vocation is that she immediately called the agency and put an unconditional offer in before we even had the Section 32 off the press and inked. Somehow, in the space of hours, she managed to put the puzzle pieces together when she tracked down the number for Ben's ex–business partner in Hong Kong—his stepmother was a previous member of the country club but still close friends with one of the golf shop attendants. He told her exactly how underinsured the business was, and then she showed up at the winery with a checkbook. Of course, Ben initially refused to accept her help, until he realized that without it, we'd have no chance to resolve the situation. We needed to keep the house and both of us were prepared to work hard to pay it back—all of it. I suppose at the time, I didn't know what the true cost would be. I underestimated the cost of losing someone I loved in the process, and it also cost Ben and me the chance to have another child. Repairing a marriage and regaining trust in my husband was one thing, timing and financial stability another.

I stare at the letter in my hands, and when I look up at Ben, he's standing there, waiting for me to step into his arms. I throw myself around him and press my face against his chest. "I want another baby. I'm not ready to let go."

CHAPTER ELEVEN

Lucy

The following morning I oversleep. Mom makes breakfast using more crockery and pots than a normal breakfast should ever require. Then again, this is my mother, and the kitchen is not her usual place to flourish.

"Ta da!" she says proudly, holding up a plate of now-cold rubbery eggs with a smattering of mushrooms that I plan on tossing into the compost the moment she turns her back. I give a small smile and head straight for the coffee machine. Mom beats me to it, extending an arm with a mug of what I hope isn't cold coffee. She's making an effort and I should be grateful, but what I want most is to be alone.

I take a sip of the sickly sweet, milky coffee—I take mine black, no sugar—and try not to grimace.

"What's the matter? Is it cold? I heated it up in the microwave when I heard you get up."

"You did?"

"Yep," she responds, seemingly proud of herself.

"I might make another one. It's fine, I'm sure, for whoever takes their coffee white." And with as much sugar as a pavlova, I think.

"Oh, yeah, sure," says Mom, sounding slightly wounded.

I make myself a fresh coffee and flick my eyes up to Mom, at last noticing her perfectly styled hair, her recently manicured hands, and a blouse that looks familiar. This is a stark contrast to the mother I remember from my younger years.

"Is that my shirt?"

"Yes, fits great, don't you think?" She smooths her hands over the fabric and grins.

"I need some fresh air," I say, heading outside with my coffee and laptop.

No less than five minutes later, Mom pokes her head outside. "Janet wants to know what time she should come over tomorrow morning."

I quickly shut down the browser tab. I can hardly tell her I'm sidetracked with thoughts about pastel bunting, tiny one-piece terry-cloth jumpsuits, and bottles of baby shampoo.

"Um, nine should be fine, I guess."

"What's on the USB?" she asks, noticing it sitting atop the envelope Nate left for me.

"Just some photos we took on our trip to Peru last year," I say coolly.

"You went to Peru?"

"Yes, Mom."

"I don't remember you telling me about a trip to Peru. Is that where Chichen Itza is?"

"That's Mexico. Machu Picchu. We went to Machu Picchu." We didn't make it all the way up because I sprained my ankle on the way. Nate said he didn't care but we still vowed to go back someday and now . . . now we will never get the chance to.

"I've always loved *The Lion King*," she says casually, eyeing the envelope.

The closest my mother ever came to taking an interest in anything to do with Disney was when she parked me in front of the television while she went to play the slot machines at the local gaming venue. She would have no idea whether I liked any Disney movies, let alone *The Lion King*.

"There's a lot you don't know about me since I grew up," I reply.

"Mmm, funny you say that. Maybe if I saw you more often, I'd know more about you."

And maybe if you had been the mother I needed you to be, I'd want to be around you more often. Of course I don't actually say this, but the look on my face obviously speaks volumes because Mom retreats into herself and stares into her coffee cup.

"I deserve it. I was a shitty mother to you when you needed me most."

I want to tell her it's okay. That I forgive her. That it's fine because "I turned out okay," but it isn't how I feel—not by a long shot.

"I'll leave you to it," says Mom when I don't answer, slowly closing the door behind her.

The last time Nate and I had any contact with Isla and Ben was via email. Five years ago—almost to the day. No picture, no news—just a request from Ben to Nate, which was granted and then promptly forgotten about. Would we consent to keeping our last donated embryo in storage for another five years?

> *Nate: Yes, no problem. Consent form attached.*
> *Ben: Thank you so much. Really appreciate it.*

As I sit in the middle of the spare room, my mind wanders back to the day Nate and I decided we'd give Isla and Ben the chance to become parents.

Isla was sitting on a picnic blanket under a tree near the seashore, with an oversized straw hat on her head and a laptop on her legs. For weeks, since she and Ben had been told they needed help in the fertility department—outside help, which had to be altruistic since offering payment to donors for gametes was prohibited by law in Australia—she'd been scouring fertility websites obsessively.

I sat down beside her. "Can I take a peek?"

"Look at all these ads," she said, tilting the screen so I could see it. Most of the donor recipient profiles on this website read the same—a heartfelt introduction, an explanation of why a donor was required, and then an appeal for anyone able to assist to get in touch. All of them were heartbreaking in their own way.

"Look at this one," Isla said. "Margaret from Ocean Grove clearly doesn't know how hard it is to get an answer to one of these ads because she wants proof of IQ from her potential donor and they must be bilingual."

"We're talking about babies here. Human beings. Aren't you just supposed to get a surprise? It kind of feels a little like engineering."

"I guess so. If you're lucky enough to get matched with a donor from the clinic, they do give potential recipients some information about the donor's hobbies, personality, and appearance. But honestly, I don't care about any of that. I just want my email to ping."

"The clinic can't help you?"

"We're on a waiting list. It could take forever. So I wrote to the Minister for Health and got an ad approved. It's online but I also put it in here." She picked up a copy of a parenting magazine and handed it to me so I could read it.

Everything we ever wanted was to become parents...
Our doctor advised us recently that this is our only option...
If you think you could help us achieve our dream to welcome a child into our life, we would dearly love to hear from you...
This advertisement has been approved by the Minister
for Health as per the requirements of Section 40 of
the Human Tissue Act 1982 (Vic).

"We had to do something. It's basically our only option. Ben thinks it's pie-in-the-sky and that we shouldn't be pinning our hopes on the off-chance someone might actually answer our ad."

"Tell me something. How many of these ads actually end up being successful? Do people really respond to these things?"

Isla was quiet as she took the magazine from me. She folded it and tucked it into her tote. "The chances are there. But they're slim."

"How slim, exactly?" After I asked this question, I wasn't sure I really wanted to know the answer.

"Last year in Victoria there were just over a hundred embryo recipients, and only a little over fifty of them resulted in clinical pregnancies. That's from over forty thousand embryos that are actually kept in storage to begin with. There's probably a higher chance of winning the Sunrise Cash Cow jackpot."

"You really want to become a mother, huh?"

"More than anything." She closed the laptop. "I mean, don't you? One day you're going to settle down and start a family, aren't you?"

"Mmm, yeah, I guess?" Who was I kidding? "Actually, no."

"What about Nate? Doesn't he want kids someday?"

"As I recall from our first date, that's a no."

"He might change his mind. You might change your mind," she said. "Don't you worry you'll change your mind down the line and it'll be too late?"

"No," came my answer, plain and simple. "I'm happy, Isla. Everything is great and I'm not ready for it to change by starting a family. I love my life. Nate and I—we love our life as it is."

"Then I guess that makes you both lucky."

"I guess it does. Now hand it over. I want to write you a new ad no couple out there will be able to resist."

I never ended up writing the ad. It made little sense to do so when Nate and I were sure—so sure—that we didn't want children. Isla was my best friend. I could give her what she longed for.

That night, I came home and told Nate about Isla and Ben's situation.

"She really wants to carry a baby. They need a donor *couple*. An *embryo* donor couple. This is their last resort. Do you know that there are plenty of embryos out there on ice—in storage, waiting for couples to decide what to do with them? Only a small number of them actually get donated to couples who might want them. There's a big chance this isn't going to happen for them. Not without help from another couple."

Nate took a second to register what I'd told him. "Another couple," he repeated.

I nodded.

"Is that...? Are you really thinking...? *You* want to donate?"

I shook my head. "I couldn't give her what she wants anyway. An egg isn't enough. But *we* could give them what they want."

"Did Isla ask you for this?"

"No, but think about it." I folded my legs and twisted my body to face his. "It makes sense, doesn't it? It's not like we want kids. And if we're going to do something like this, it may as well be for them, right?"

"We don't have any embryos in storage last time I checked."

"I know. And I know this isn't exactly a common thing, but I spoke to someone at a fertility clinic to see if it would be allowed and—"

"You already called them?"

"Yes, but just to see if it would be possible. *If* we decided we could do this for them."

"And what did they say?"

"They said yes, it would be permitted, but we'd need to agree to counseling—on our own, as a couple, and with the recipient couple."

*

Nate took a few days to think about things, and just when I thought he was about to shut the entire idea down, he turned up in the bathroom one morning when I was brushing my teeth and said, "Okay."

"Okay? As in the donation?"

He nodded. "He...she...they would be our biological children. So I think we need to be sure that we can take a step back and accept that they'd be Isla and Ben's kids. Not ours."

"Right. I totally agree with you."

"If there's a chance you ever want to have kids, then I don't think we should do it."

"Does this mean you're not sure?"

"No. You?"

"No. So you're sure."

"Yes," he said. "She's like a sister to you. The way I see it, we can't *not* do this for them. They deserve it."

I threw myself into his arms and it was like falling in love with him all over again. Everything I knew to be true about Nate showed itself to me again that day—his generosity of spirit, his love for others. Seeing him so on board and ready to help made me realize just how special he was. It was perfect. Together, we were going to give Isla and Ben the most precious gift of all. I couldn't wait to tell her.

At the time of donating, we were told by a fertility counselor that leftover embryos are usually donated by couples once they're done with IVF and their families are complete. Yes, leftover embryos they don't know what to do with because they don't like the idea of allowing them to thaw out. Couples who don't have children don't usually go around donating embryos. Who could have known that, years later, I'd end up wanting the very thing I gave away?

I pick up the phone and dial Isla's number. There's every chance she'll ignore the call or hang up on me. There's every chance that the passing of time hasn't changed anything. Either way, there's no easy way to say it. No easy way to tell her: Reese's biological father—the one she never got to meet—is dead.

CHAPTER TWELVE

Isla

"I've been thinking about what you said," says Ben, hitting the snooze button on the alarm clock. He turns onto his side to face me. "I think we should have another baby."

I prop myself up onto my elbow. "You *do*?"

"I do. I think it's something we might otherwise regret, and I think the right thing is to use the embryo as intended."

Hearing this is a relief. I can't bear the thought of it not being used either.

"Our lives will change," I tease.

"Duh." He grins and shifts his body closer to mine and kisses me.

"Sleepless nights. Diaper changes. Tantrums."

He laughs. "This isn't working. I'm on board. Fully on board. The timing's right."

"I'm happy," I whisper. "This makes me happy."

"So, what do we need to do to get the ball rolling?"

"We'll need to make an appointment with the clinic, and I guess I'll need to get a preconception check-up."

"Yeah," he says, smiling. "I guess you will."

Ben left the house early to take Reese to her tennis lesson, and I'm outside deadheading the roses in the garden. Somewhere between venturing into the kitchen for a pink lemonade and making my shopping list, I get around to checking the emails on my phone.

After that, I check for texts and voicemails in case the Pinketts have decided to make an offer on the seaside beauty on Elixir Drive they'd be crazy not to snap up since it checks all the boxes—outdoor shower, huge patio, and a butler's pantry that would make Jamie Oliver envious. But no, there are no voicemails waiting for me, but there are two missed calls, both from the same number, one of them from last night that I haven't gotten around to calling back yet. There's also a text message from this number and it isn't from the Pinketts.

It's me. Lucy. Please call me. As soon as you can.

Lucy wants me to call her.

As soon as I can. Which, in my mind, can only be a disaster waiting to happen. Naturally, I do the only appropriate thing: I drop a few ice cubes into my glass of lemonade, delete the message, and go back to deadheading the roses.

Over the years, I've imagined all the sorts of things I would say to Lucy if she called. Or rather, I've explored all the ways I could apologize. None of them ever fit—there simply isn't ever going to be the right kind of words to convey what I should have said years ago.

I'm sorry, but I didn't feel like I had a choice.

I'm sorry, I'm an idiot.

I'm sorry, you have every right to hate me. Now can we get on with our lives and pretend this never happened?

No. Nothing would cut it. Nothing could justify my actions. I sometimes dared to imagine how Lucy might react to an apology. I envisaged her firing words back at me—ones I'd already told myself. Words that confirmed what a terrible friend I am, and how my selfishness hurt her. Or worse still, I saw her staring back at me—steely-eyed, confirming that she hated me for all the reasons I hate myself for doing what I did. I don't know which would be worse—the words or the silence.

It's not like I made an effort to right the situation. It was easier to walk away and stay away. What would an apology be worth without any meaningful action to right things? Maybe that's exactly what it comes down to. Apologizing to Lucy would mean making room for Lucy in my life again, and deep down, it's entirely possible that I don't *want* to make room for her. After all, how can I make room for something I've tried so hard to pretend never existed? If it doesn't exist, it can't worry me.

Ben and Reese get home around four o'clock. She is buzzing from too much sugar and the excitement of the impending annual pre-Christmas sleepover at my parents' that Mom insists on each year. Reese literally skips down the hallway singing a song I don't recognize, with a Smiggle shopping bag in her left hand that bobs against her legs. She has two angry grazes on her knees from when she tripped in the driveway on her rollerblades last week. Despite this, she drops to the floor in front of the coffee table and tips the contents onto it—more scented erasers than I can count and a rainbow collection of pencils she'll probably lose by the end of the day.

"Look what Dad got me!"

A glittery star on her T-shirt casts tiny rainbows onto the surface of the table. It has what I can only imagine are gelato stains splotched on it—shades of pale brown and pink. She is, after all, predictable. Raspberry and chocolate chip are her go-to flavors. Cones, never cups, but she never makes it to the end and Ben usually ends up consuming the soggy waffle cone by the time she's done.

I uncross my legs and close my laptop, depositing it on the sofa beside me, while Reese practically clambers into my lap and shoves an eraser that smells faintly reminiscent of grape or something equally fruity toward my nose.

"Mmm, delicious." I poke her in the sides and make her giggle.

"Sleepover at Grandma and Grandpa's, hey?"

She nods enthusiastically.

Ben ruffles Reese's hair. "Go pack your bag, Button. I'll drop you off on my way to the hardware store." He turns his attention to me. "Do you need anything while I'm out?"

"From the hardware store?"

"In general."

"Nope. I'm good, thanks. By the way—the West Park appointment we were talking about? I booked a time for after Christmas."

"Oh, for the *dentist*." He winks at me. "Excellent."

Reese grabs my hands and turns them over so my palms are facing up, and she starts counting the erasers by placing them into my palms one by one.

My phone starts ringing. The Pinketts. The offer on the house.

"Would you mind answering for me?" I say to Ben. "Offer."

He glances around for my phone until he spots it on the edge of the kitchen counter near the fruit bowl. He scoops it up and accepts the call. He walks toward me and holds it against my ear.

"Hello, this is Isla."

I tip Reese's erasers back into the Smiggle bag, and Ben relinquishes his grip on the phone as I take over.

"Come on," he whispers to Reese. "Let's go pack."

"Isla? Thank goodness you answered," comes a female voice, filled with relief.

"Yes. Who am I speaking with?"

I ask the question even though I already know the answer. The voice on the phone is unmistakably Lucy's—melodic, like sunshine and honey...but weighed down by something. She sounds *defeated*.

"It's me...Lucy. I'm sorry to be calling out of the blue after all this time, but—"

"Lucy," I whisper. Maybe I expected her to sound...different... distant and bitter. Not like regular old Lucy. "How long has it been?" I say, suddenly aware of how clammy my hands are. I loosen the top button of my shirt and make my way down the hall to my bedroom, where I close the double doors for privacy. "It's nice... to hear you—your voice—it's nice to hear *from* you." I cringe.

"Um, I'm calling because I have some news."

She sounds slightly breathless.

I sit on the edge of my bed and wait for the news, which doesn't come. The line goes completely silent.

"Lucy, are you...are you still there?" I check the phone to see if the line has dropped out.

A few moments later, her voice comes down the line, only it sounds strained now. That's when I feel it—a curdling in the pit of my stomach.

"I...uh...there's been an accident. A skiing accident. In France. We—Nate and I—were there...we were skiing...we went off-piste...and—" Her voice cuts off, and it's like hearing glass break.

"What happened? Is he...? Is he okay? Is he in the hospital?"

She snivels into the phone, and somehow I manage to make out something to do with skiing, a patch of ice, and a funeral.

A funeral.

Nate is gone.

I inhale sharply. It doesn't sound remotely believable. This isn't a pet goldfish. This isn't an indoor houseplant that didn't survive a hot summer. It's *Nate*. Lucy's *husband*. The love of her life. Ben's best man. The guy who had known Lucy for six and a half minutes before she agreed to go out on a date with him, the guy she knew all along she'd end up marrying. This is the guy who lived every day as if it were his last.

"I'm so sorry," I whisper.

"I can't believe it," she says at last. "What...am...I...going to do?" She starts crying again. "I know it's been so long and you probably don't want to hear from me but I had to call you. I wanted to hear your voice..."

No matter what's happened between us in the past, I have to be here for Lucy. I can't leave her alone in this state.

"Tell me where you are. I can come and stay with you before the funeral," I blurt, without thinking about what I'm committing to. All I know is that if Lucy needs me, then I have to go. That's what the agreement was. That promise we made to each other all those years ago...

Always and forever here for you.

No matter what.

Pinkie swear?

I'll do you one better...

"Are you...are you sure? What about Reese? Will you bring her with you?"

My hands are shaking. Taking Reese with me...it's too much to think about right now. "She's with her grandparents."

"Oh," she says quietly, and I can sense the disappointment in her voice.

"Text me your address," I say. "I'll be there tomorrow after-noon."

As soon as I hang up the phone, it's as if the tightly wound ball in my chest starts to unravel. After all these years, Lucy has called me. I still remember the look on her face when we had the conversation that changed everything. The worst part was that she looked at me as if she never actually knew me at all. What nobody knows is that I've spent months—*years*—wondering whether I really know myself. Deep down, part of me is relieved that I did what I did, while the other part can't bear to even think about it.

"Isla?" says Ben when he enters the bedroom. "Are you okay?"

"That was Lucy. Nate's . . . *dead.*" The words hang limply in the air, as if I haven't grasped them yet.

Ben shakes his head. "*Your* Lucy? Nate? *Our* Nate? What? Dead?" He sits down next to me. "How?"

My eyes start watering. "Skiing accident in France. She's a mess. Lucy's a mess."

Ben inhales deeply, and exhales slowly. Nate was, at one point in our lives, one of his closest friends.

"What else did she say?" Ben asks.

"She gave me details of the funeral. It's in two days and I told her I'd go there to be with her before it. I'll head to Melbourne tomorrow afternoon."

"As in stay there?"

"She needs me," I say and I know this needs no further explanation. Ben knows exactly how close Lucy and I used to be.

"I'll cancel the photo shoot."

The winery has been selected for a magazine spread that involves a styled photo shoot and interviews with staff; it's been in the making for months. There's no way Ben can have someone else fill in for him.

"You can't do that," I say.

"I think it's important that I go," he says quietly. "What if I ask them to reschedule?"

We both know this isn't an option. "I know you want to go but there's no way they'll be able to do that."

He shrugs in defeat. "Well, you'll take Reese with you, right?"

"It's her Christmas sleepover with my parents this weekend. We can't interrupt it." We both know this isn't true, but taking Reese with me...this would be a huge step—one we haven't planned.

"She should go with you." There's a firmness in his voice that instantly makes my skin prick with heat.

"I can't take her with me, Ben. She's too young to take to a funeral and she...doesn't even know him."

"She went to your Aunt Brenda's funeral when she was three years old!"

"That was different. She can't even remember being there. I don't feel comfortable taking her. I haven't seen Lucy in so long. It's going to be awkward enough as it is without having Reese with me to complicate things."

"You can't *not* take her with you." He says this in a tone that indicates he's serious about this and that it's not something he has any intention of letting go of.

"This is not the right time for something like this. She doesn't need to be dealing with the death of—"

"A stranger," he says, and I can tell he's annoyed. He has every right to be. I'm the one who has insisted on our silence. "We need to tell her the truth."

"Are you serious? You want to dump this on her *now*? No way."

"Tell me something. Have you ever asked yourself how comfortable you are about the decision we made?"

"What? How is that question even relevant?"

"She was a decision. Reese was a decision."

"Most children are. What's your point?"

"Our decision was to conceive via embryo donation. If we're honest, it wasn't our first choice."

"I love our daughter, Ben!"

"I know you love her. I'm not doubting that at all. But how comfortable are you with the fact she isn't your biological daughter but your best friend's?"

"This has nothing to do with Lucy," I say, shaking my head.

"Actually, I think it has everything to do with Lucy. And it has everything to do with your insecurities too." He rolls up one of the cuffs of his sleeves. "This is something you need to face, especially if we're going to have another child who's going to be in the exact same situation. We can't sever Reese from her biological heritage. Lucy and Nate gave us a *child*. They gave us everything we ever wanted, and now he's gone. She's reached out to you."

Ben rubs his temples. "Knowing your heritage—your biological identity, where you come from—is the most basic level of information about a person's existence. You know this. This isn't something you're hearing for the first time. Maybe it's about time you realize that it's our job to make sure she isn't robbed of the opportunity to know who she is and where she comes from because I can almost guarantee we'll regret it later if we don't."

"That's not true. You don't know that for sure."

"Really? Read up on the papers that exist out there and get back to me. There's no good reason that we shouldn't tell her. The longer we keep it from her, the worse it'll be." With that, he rolls up the cuff of his other sleeve, picks up his baseball cap, and scoops up his car keys. "We can't engineer Reese's life to avoid pain or discomfort, Isla. We're parents. We're human. Part of our job involves letting our child get hurt and being there when she falls. None of this is going away, no matter how much you want to wish it to, unless you deal with it—unless you *let us* deal with it."

What did my mother say about sweeping things under the carpet—eventually, you find all the lumps.

"Fine," I concede. "I'll take her with me but the rest we deal with another time."

Ben lets a momentary beat of silence hang in the air. "You're doing the right thing by taking her," he says.

I chew my lip. It doesn't feel that way at all.

"I know you miss Lucy," he continues. "Who knows? Maybe this could be the start of repairing the friendship."

The thought of this fills me with hope, but at the same time I know there's so much that is broken between us.

"I owe this to Lucy, but I don't think I can expect anything from her as far as reconciling is concerned."

"It was just a thought," says Ben dismissively.

His response isn't intended to hurt me, but it does. It tells me that even Ben would be surprised if Lucy could find a way to forgive me after everything I did.

CHAPTER THIRTEEN

Lucy

Once I hang up the phone and manage to take a few deep breaths, I let things sink in. Isla is coming to see me. Not only that, she's coming to *stay* here. To *be* here. With me. After almost ten years of not hearing from her, of wondering what it might take for us to ever meet again—I could not have imagined that Nate's funeral would be the event that would bring us together. But if I cast aside the hurt and disappointment, out of all the people in the world, despite all that has happened between us, I want her here. Nobody knows me like Isla does. Nobody will know how to sit with me during the discomfort and pain the way Isla will. I've missed her through every Christmas, Easter, and birthday since the day she cut me out of her life. I haven't thought about it in years—Nate always said we should put it behind us. After all, there was nothing we could say or do to change things. No matter how much I tried to reassure Isla that things could be different, that this decision wasn't necessary, she didn't want to hear it.

It was in the days leading up to Isla's first ultrasound that things started to go wrong. Plans had suddenly changed and now the sonographer apparently only allowed the two people in the room, which I knew was a lie. Instead, Isla had proposed brunch for later that morning, after the scan, and she asked if Nate could be there too.

The moment Isla and Ben arrived, Nate and I sensed something was up. The two of them sat down, their movements robotic, the tension in the air so thick I couldn't help but feel nervous.

"How was your ultrasound?" I asked.

Isla sat there, clutching her handbag like a security blanket.

Ben cleared his throat. "Uh, guys, this really isn't easy for us to say. It's...well..."

Nate got straight to the point. "Just come right out and say it. We can handle it. Is there something wrong with the baby?"

Neither of them answered. I held my breath.

"Let me ask you again. Is there something wrong with the baby?" Nate asked, this time more firmly.

Ben took a deep breath and looked around the room, completely avoiding Nate's gaze.

"Hey, look at me. Answer the question."

I tried to make eye contact with Isla but she kept staring at the jug of water on the table.

"Did you guys change your mind?" said Nate. "Is that why you're being so evasive every time we talk about the pregnancy?"

"Yes," piped up Isla.

"Yes there's something wrong with the baby or yes you changed your mind?" I said, interjecting.

"The baby's fine," said Isla, only she was looking at Ben, not me. "The baby's healthy."

"Then what's the problem? You don't want to keep the baby?! You want to give it back? To us? Is that it?" said Nate, who was becoming impatient now. He was never one for avoiding confrontation or skirting around difficult conversations.

I stared at Nate, wide-eyed. Us? Parents? Of a donated-returned-to-its-original-owners baby?

Nate reached out and clasped his hand around mine.

"It's...we've changed our mind about the arrangement and the level of contact between us all," said Ben.

"What the heck does that even mean?" exploded Nate. I couldn't remember the last time I'd heard that kind of tone in his voice.

Ben honestly looked as if he needed a stiff drink. "Isla feels that—"

In my mind, Ben had done enough of the talking. "Why doesn't Isla be the one to tell us how she feels, then?" I said, feeling the burn in my cheeks amplify. "Last time I checked she didn't need a spokesperson to talk on her behalf."

The skin from Isla's neck to her chin had broken out in angry pink blotches, the way it always did when she got worked up.

I knew what she was going to say before she even said it. A conversation from our first compulsory counseling session together at the fertility clinic rang in my ears.

Couples sometimes change their minds about involvement once the child arrives or as the pregnancy progresses.

Did Isla feel threatened? By me and Nate? It was unfathomable. We were like *sisters*.

"I've—we've—given it a lot of thought. And we think maybe it's best if we take our time in deciding exactly how much contact she has with you both."

"Wait? *She*? It's a girl? When did you find out? How long have you known?"

"I had a blood test. I was going to tell you—"

"When? Once you'd given birth?"

Nate spoke up. "How much contact are you thinking?"

Isla shook her head. "I don't know yet. It's too overwhelming. I think we need to take a break for now."

"A break? What does that even mean? And since when are you so cryptic!"

"Let's keep it down," said Ben, glancing around the room.

"You want us out of your lives? Is that what you want?"

Isla started crying. "No...but..."

"I expected so much more from you." I stood up. "I thought I knew you. But maybe I never really knew you at all."

When we got home, Nate pulled me into his arms. "Remember this. Baby girls grow into little girls, and little girls become teenage girls, and one day she'll grow up and there is every chance she'll reach out to us then."

In the meantime, we would become invisible.

Nate told me he'd seen her once. He'd been surfing in Portsea on a rare weekend we spent on the Peninsula about four years ago, which incorporated a Sunday lunch at the clubhouse with my mother. On the way back to his car, he saw them—Ben and Reese. She'd been carrying a mini surfboard—turquoise, he said; it matched the color of her eyes. She was standing by the trunk of the car, waiting for Ben, who was nearby rinsing a pair of sandals under a faucet.

"She saw me, Lucy. She looked right at me and smiled before she said, 'I like your surfboard.'"

Nate told me he returned a "thank you" and then spent five minutes in the car, all choked up. He watched them drive away with the windows of the car down, music playing. She was smiling. She looked happy. That was the one and only time he ever laid eyes on her.

She will never get to meet him—never get to ask him questions about his life; she'll never get to witness the way his dimple appears before he starts smiling—like a little warm-up.

An ache, reminiscent of a deep longing, starts building in my chest. Nate and I were close—*so* close—to having our own baby. I was finally ready to push aside all my doubts and fears about becoming a mother. I know I shouldn't but I let myself imagine what our baby might have looked like. Aside from a picture of her as a newborn, I don't have any other photos of Reese. My desire to meet Reese is something I've worked hard to push to the side. I know now why Nate was always hesitant to bring her name up in conversation. Instead, we quietly wondered about her in our own minds. Because now that I'm thinking about Reese—*really* thinking about her—I desperately want to meet her. I want to meet the little girl Nate and I helped bring into the world. I realize there's one thing that bothers me about Isla coming: the fact she said Reese was at her grandparents'. It tells me what Nate and I suspected all along.

Reese has no idea who we are and she probably doesn't even know we exist. It makes me wonder whether I really want Isla to be with me after all.

CHAPTER FOURTEEN

Isla

We call the sleepover off, and Reese takes the news slightly better than my parents, who've no doubt made plans to spoil her to bits.

"We're going to have to tell Reese about Nate and Lucy," says Ben, pulling the pillows off the bed and onto the floor. I pick them up and put them on top of the armchair in the corner of the room. "*Before* you leave for Melbourne."

"Ben. We're leaving tomorrow afternoon."

"I know," he says coolly. "But I've been thinking about it all evening. We can't let her go without some understanding of what's happening in her life. Besides, I think we need to explain things better so she can deal with the schoolyard teasing anyway."

"We can leave it until we get back," I say, knowing Ben won't buy this. I can tell from his tone he's more serious about this than he's ever been.

Ben pulls his T-shirt over his head and tosses it into the wicker basket in the corner of the room. "In the hope that maybe it'll all go away? That I'll somehow forget and you can buy more time?"

"Oh, come on! Be reasonable here. Will you look at the timing? Nate just died!"

"Yeah, and if everything goes the way we hope, we're going to have another baby soon." He folds back the comforter and slides into bed. "And just so you know, we are going to be up-front from the start with the next kid." He mumbles something about the whole situation becoming an absolute joke. "Nate didn't deserve this. He should have had the chance to know her."

By this he means it's my fault. And it is. I can't deny it. I let this happen.

"I think we've exhausted all the reasons to put this off for a moment longer." He turns onto his side and flicks the lamp off, leaving me to crawl into bed in the dark. "I don't want to have to tell her on my own but I will, if that's what it comes to."

"Okay," I whisper. "We'll tell her tomorrow morning." As I speak the words, my body floods with dread. I don't want to do this, yet I don't know how it can be avoided. I'm not ready to deal with what will come in front of us once we tell our daughter we aren't her biological parents.

"Good," murmurs Ben.

"Ben?" I say, after a while.

"Mmm."

"Will she be okay? After we tell her?"

"Course she will be," he replies, his voice already thick with sleep.

I want to believe him, but I can't push away the niggling thought that makes me wonder: *What if he's wrong?*

We promised Reese pancakes for breakfast. I'm jittery, made worse by the fact I've barely slept and have had two cups of coffee already.

"Guess what?" says Ben, flipping the last pancake onto a plate, which he slides in front of Reese. "I have something cool to show you."

I don't know how he can be so calm about this when I can barely manage to function. He hands Reese the science kit we bought as part of her Christmas present.

Her eyes light up. "Science kit!"

"Open it up; there's something in there I want to show you."

Reese opens the box with Ben's help, and he wrestles a small plastic dish from the packaging.

"Is it for soap?" asks Reese, screwing up her nose.

"No, it's something you normally find in a science lab. It's a Petri dish that scientists use. Sometimes they use them to make babies, remember?"

"Then why is it in my kit?"

"Because you can use them for other science-related things, sweetheart," I say.

Ben steers the conversation back to where he needs it to go while I take another sip of coffee. I can't believe this is the moment Reese will find out the truth. We are sitting in our kitchen, surrounded by splotches of pancake batter on the Caesarstone countertop, a sink full of dirty dishes, and a pancake stack in front of us from which drips too much maple syrup. It's a normal morning like any other pancake morning, only it's the morning that will change everything.

"You know how the kids at school have been making fun of you for all the 'fake baby' stuff?" says Ben casually.

She nods.

"Well, I know Mom and I told you a bit about it, but we wanted to explain it properly so that we are one hundred percent clear on something."

She nods again.

"So one way babies are made is with the help of science. A scientist called an embryologist can make the baby or babies—at that point they're called embryos—in a dish like this one. An embryo is so tiny you can only see it with a microscope. The doctors can then take an embryo and put it in the mom and the baby grows that way. So you see, it's not really fake at all."

"Did they do that with me?"

"Well, Mom and I, we tried for a baby—wished for a baby . . . for you—for a really long time."

"How long?"

"About two years."

"Two *years*?"

"Yeah, that's like over seven hundred days' worth of wishing."

"Whoa, that's a long time."

"Super long time. So Mom and I, we were spending all this time wishing for you but things weren't...happening. So we, uh, we decided that because we really wanted you, we would get science to help us. And that's how you came to us."

"Okay." I can see Reese struggling to process this, but she attempts a smile. My brave little girl. "That's pretty cool."

"It also means you aren't a fake baby, Reese. Lots and lots of babies are made this way—not just you. We don't always hear about it. Want to know why?"

"Why?"

"Because you're here now, and *how* you got here doesn't really matter, does it?"

"I guess not."

"That's right. When I go to work in the morning, nobody says, 'Morning, Ben, how did you get here today?' "

"That would be dumb."

She laughs but I can't even manage to crack a smile. I just want Ben to stop talking. This is too much. The moment we open this door, we'll have to have the same conversations with the people close to us who don't know the truth—Ben's family, our close friends. My mother. Once she finds out...My heart starts racing.

Ben continues talking to Reese. "Exactly. Now, those kids making fun of you at school? They're not worth getting upset over."

"It's just Mitchell."

"Well, maybe Mitchell needs to be ignored for a bit. You love science and science helped you get here," says Ben.

"Maybe that's why I love science."

"Yeah," he says. "It is pretty cool, isn't it? So now, if anyone like Mitchell or anyone else makes fun of you, you know exactly how you got here and what the truth is."

Ben picks up a pancake and tears it in half. "Does it make a bit more sense now?"

"Yeah, kind of."

"Kids like Mitchell, they don't always mean what they say. They're just words. There's nothing to make fun of here. Got it?"

"I know. I have one question, though," she says.

"Fire away," says Ben.

"Why didn't I come when you and Mom wished for me?"

"Well," he says, and his smile disappears. "Sometimes you can't always get what you want, so you have to find another way to help get what you want. Sometimes if you're very lucky, you can end up getting what you wish for."

"Like how I didn't get a scooter for Christmas last year and I got a basketball hoop instead and now I have to save up for a scooter if I really want one?"

"Yeah," he says. "Kind of like that. So now that you've got that, there's something else I want to explain—"

"Speaking of Christmas!" I say, interjecting. I stand up so quickly I spill my coffee onto the counter. "Santa Claus wants to know if your list is finalized."

Ben fires me a look.

"If you have more questions, you can ask me on the way to Lucy's, Button."

"Isla..." pleads Ben. "We need to—"

"Reese, finish your breakfast, and then we'll get going," I say, reaching for the dish sponge to mop up the coffee.

"Do I have to go?" asks Reese.

"Yes, Button," says Ben. "Lucy is a very special person and it's important that you and Mom go. And when you get back, we can finish this conversation," he says.

Only he's looking at me, not at Reese, and he doesn't look happy. He doesn't look happy at all.

CHAPTER FIFTEEN

Lucy

Isla looks the same as I remember her, only she's almost a decade older with a more sophisticated haircut and color. She's gone a gorgeous ash-blonde that works beautifully with her peachy skin tone. She's wearing fake eyelashes and her skin is flawless. Around her neck she's wearing a chain, and on it are two charms, one of which I recognize. It's a white-gold daisy. She must notice me staring at it because her hand, as if by instinct, travels to it and covers it. Her favorite perfume used to be Jo Malone's English Pear and Freesia, but today she's wearing something different—a fragrance I don't recognize. She makes eye contact with me and smiles—the kind of smile you flash at a stranger in the supermarket. Suddenly, the memories of all the years of friendship we shared together come flooding back—during all the major milestones of my life Isla was there, right beside me.

I smile back at her but there's a wrestle going on inside of me—joy at seeing her again mixed with hurt I can't easily sweep to the side. The ache I've tried to ignore all this time for what could have—should have—been is still there. We haven't lost weeks or months. We've lost years.

"Hi," she says, jolting me from my thoughts. She extends both arms and then hesitates before I step forward and feel her body close to mine. She lets go and steps back.

"It's good to see you."

She nods. "I'm so sorry about Nate," she says, swallowing back her emotion. Then, as if we've both almost forgotten her, she grabs her daughter by the shoulders and gently encourages her to move forward. And there she is, right in front of me.

My biological daughter.

Reese is standing on my front porch with a pair of bright blue headphones around her neck. She's wearing a pair of white denim cut-off shorts and a black T-shirt with silver foil letters of the alphabet scrawled over it. She's taller than I expected. Our eyes lock and I forget to breathe. Her eyes. They're the exact same shade as Nate's. And the tiny vein, visible just above his eyelid? Hers is the same.

She's chewing Hubba Bubba and blows a bubble that almost covers her face before stopping right in her tracks to pop it.

Isla patiently waits for Reese to peel the bubblegum off her face and then sticks a hand under her mouth for her to spit it out.

"Reese," she says finally. "This is my friend Lucy. Say hi."

"Hello!" she says, and I can do nothing but stare at the smattering of freckles dotting her nose and spreading out to her cheeks.

Isla puts her hands on Reese's shoulders and gives her a not-so-discreet nudge forward, prompting her to stick out her hand for me to shake. Elinor instilled good manners into Isla from the moment she could talk, and this has clearly rubbed off on the next generation.

"It's nice to meet you, Reese," I say. Her hand fits into my palm. It's soft and small and the contact sends a rush of warmth through my body.

"Is your house near the beach?" asks Reese, jolting me from my thoughts.

I hold the door open for the two of them.

"No, but I love the beach."

"Mom said you grew up near the beach together."

Isla smiles, but Reese doesn't notice the awkwardness. Reese obviously knows this detail about our friendship, but I can't help wondering how much Reese knows about me in general.

"That's right. I used to live in Sorrento. My mom still lives there, actually."

Mom told me she'd bumped into Isla at one of the local craft markets years ago when Reese was still in diapers. She'd reported that Isla looked a little worn out, albeit the happiest she'd ever seen her, which was not a surprise because the baby was cute as a doll! "Smiled the moment I picked her up, and the minute I put her back in the stroller, she closed her eyes and dozed right off. What a dream! Complete opposite of how you were at that age."

"Do you like fishing, Reese?" I ask, when Isla doesn't speak up.

"I love it. So does Daddy. Mom not so much."

Isla's face flushes.

"Your mom used to like fishing," I say. "In fact, she won an award for fishing once."

Isla waves dismissively. "Oh, I did not."

"She did too. It was an elephant fish, actually."

Reese laughs all at once, revealing two gummy spots, and then it fades into a small giggle before it ends, and it gives me butterflies. It reminds me of Nate's laugh. He was never truly done with a joke and had to milk it for everything he could. I want to hear it again.

"You never told me that," she says to Isla.

"It was a long time ago, Button. I forgot all about it."

"Come inside," I say, holding the door open. Mom's in the kitchen, where she's started setting herself up to bake. She pulls open a kitchen drawer, throws on an apron, and lines up a set of baking canisters on the counter. This, of course, is something I've rarely seen her do. Even Isla, who hasn't seen my mother in years, does a double take.

"Now, before I get to work, let me meet your daughter properly," she says to Isla.

"Reese, meet Shirley," says Isla, guiding her toward Mom.

"Welcome!" she says, brandishing a ceramic rolling pin that sends a burst of flour particles in the air. The wonders of a flour shaker and rolling pin in one.

Reese beams at her while Isla shifts her weight from one foot to another. I know this is uncomfortable for her—she barely said a word while we were unpacking the car.

"Hello, Shirley, I'm Reese." She extends her arm. "It's lovely to meet you."

Mom's eyes literally light up. She crouches down so she's at eye level with Reese and takes her in. "It's lovely to meet you too, Reese. Tell me, how old are you?"

"I'm nine."

"And I bet you like school."

"I *love* it. I'm going to be a scientist one day."

Mom's eyebrows shoot up. "Wow. What kind of scientist?"

Reese shrugs. "I don't know, but I'm doing a big investigation at the moment."

"You are?" says Isla.

Reese looks at her as if she should know what she's referring to. "Yes, I'm investigating my family genes but not the ones you wear. Because I have blue eyes but my mom and dad don't, so I need to investigate it. Mom got her eye color from my grandma."

"It's a personal identity project, actually." She coughs discreetly. "But Reese picked up on the genetics and...well...she's..."

"Obviously very curious," I say. At this point I'm guessing Reese has no idea who I am.

Reese looks up at me. "Where'd you get your blue eyes from?"

At first I find it hard to find the words to reply. I didn't see this coming. And judging by the color of Isla's complexion, I'm pretty sure she didn't either. "Um, I got my eye color from my mom." I point to Mom, who smiles politely. "Your eyes are beautiful, Reese."

She giggles. "That's what Mom always says. But I don't know where I got my blue eyes from so that's why I have to do the investigation. My best friend, Bailey, is doing an investigation too because she's adopted and she doesn't look like her mom and dad and she doesn't even know where they are."

"Oh…" I reply.

"Yeah, but she knows where her grandma lives. She's in Adelaide. She met her once."

Isla smiles awkwardly.

"I know the periodic table by heart."

Mom makes a face that shows she's impressed. "Ahh, but do you know how to bake?"

"I actually love baking but Mom, well, she doesn't really like it." At this point, she stands on her tiptoes to get a better look at what's on the counter. "What are you baking?"

"Sugar cookies. Would you like to help me?"

Reese flashes Isla a look of uncertainty, her eyes seeking approval.

"Yes, that's fine, Button."

"Now, come on over and let me look at you." Mom motions for Isla to come closer and then practically flings herself into her arms. "You haven't changed a bit, have you?" She presses her hands on the top of her shoulders and looks her up and down before pinning her with her gaze. "How are you, sweetheart?"

"I'm good, thanks, Shirley. It's good to see you again. Life is obviously treating you well. I love your apron. Have you been blonde for long? It suits you." Isla has always had a way of making people feel special and can pass out compliments in a way that always comes off as sincere and genuine. When she was eight, her mother made her spend the summer attending etiquette classes. When Mom turns her attention back to Reese, she looks her squarely in the eyes and smiles like a miniature version of her mother.

"Now, I'm sure you and Lucy have a lot to catch up on. Why don't the two of you go for a walk or something while Reese and I get these cookies done. Would you like that, Reese?"

She nods eagerly.

Isla and I exchange a glance, the whole experience vaguely reminiscent of the time I was grouped with a stranger at school camp and told we needed to spend some time getting to know each other.

"Oh, come on, girls, it's not like you're strangers. Outta here! Isla, your daughter will be fine with me, won't you, Reese?"

"Mom, please don't push. She barely knows you."

But Reese is already wearing an apron and doesn't seem bothered by the flamboyant woman in the colorful apron who insists on baking cookies with her.

"Lucinda, stop overcomplicating things," says Mom.

"Maybe we could bring back some pizza for an early dinner?" suggests Isla.

"Great idea. Tell me something, love, are you still a fan of Pecorino's?"

"Well, yes, I suppose so."

"Excellent. Grab my purse on the hallway buffet before you go. Pizza's on me." With that, Mom shoos us away with her hands. "Off you go, now. We've got cookies to bake, and we can't afford another moment of interruption, can we, Reese? On the side of the refrigerator there's a step-stool, sweetheart. Go grab it for me."

Reese laughs and obediently retrieves the stool. "Bye, Mom!"

As I hold the front door open, I overhear Mom whisper to Reese, "Did you know that Pecorino's in Sorrento is where your mother had her first kiss? I know this because I went to pick up some takeout lasagna one evening and there she was sitting at one of the outdoor tables kissing a boy!" Mom screeches with laughter.

Reese, on the other hand, screws her nose up and looks positively horrified. She is, of course, barely a tween.

Isla appears momentarily stunned before looking at me and holding back a smile. In that split second I forget about what happened in the snow. I laugh. Mom laughs. Reese laughs. And then Isla bursts out laughing too.

"Sorry about Mom," I say, once we're down the street.

"I wouldn't expect anything less from Shirley Livingstone," she says, smiling to herself.

"What was his name?" I ask. "The guy you kissed at Pecorino's. Was it Alex Winters?" It was so long ago the details are hazy.

"Nope. Joe Menezes."

"Ha! No way."

"Yeah, well that lasted about five and a half minutes. He'd broken up with me by the time he walked me home, remember? Said he was more compatible with Heidi from three blocks away because her dad installed an in-ground pool that year and it was going to be a hot summer."

Now I remember. She was devastated.

"'Compatible.' Wasn't he like... fourteen years old?"

"Fifteen and yes, those were his words. He probably watched too much *Perfect Match*." She guffaws. "Probably turned out for the best anyway. You do know they ended up getting married?"

"No!"

We're smiling at this point and it feels strangely like old times.

"They also got divorced a few years ago. She broke the news, poolside actually, Club Med in the Maldives. Told him she'd met someone else."

"Oh, that's kind of sad."

She shrugs. "Happens, I guess. We're at that age where marriages sometimes fall apart and people have to start over." She literally stops walking and looks at me. "Lucy, I'm so sorry. That was insensitive of me. I wasn't thinking."

"It's fine," I say. I will have to start over. There's no avoiding the truth.

"No," she says firmly. "It's not fine. Not fine at all. You lost Nate." She says it like she still can't believe it.

"I know it's not fine—I don't know how I'm going to . . ." I tilt my head up to the sky and squint at the sun. "Live without him." Tears pool in my eyes. "How do I do that? Where do I even start?"

Isla reaches for my hand and looks at me sincerely.

"You start here, and every day you take one step forward, and one after that . . ." She stops herself. "Scrap that. I sound like a self-help guru. I actually don't know how you do it. But all I know is that you start here, in this moment."

My face crumples then, my body shuddering as I try to keep the sobs from erupting, and then all I can feel is Isla's hand rubbing my back, her breath against my ear as she whispers, "It's okay. Let it out. You can let it all out, Lucy. I'm here."

"He left me behind," I say. "It's just me now, with a house full of his stuff and nothing else."

"You have the memories."

"They'll fade away. With time they'll recede into the distance and I'll start forgetting things." Like the way he always put Vegemite in his scrambled eggs instead of salt or the way he pulled his socks off in bed and tossed them on the floor. We took turns opening doors for each other because it was fun—a nod to our level playing field. Nate made me a better person—a stronger person. Someone who inspired me to take risks, and aim high and then a little bit higher still. He'd come on set sometimes and watch me, and when my workday finished, he'd say things like, "You did good work today. Think of how many people are booking tickets to Banff right now thanks to you. They'll be out on Lake Louise making memories that will last a lifetime all because you inspired them to book a plane ticket." There's no doubt about it. Nate believed in me, more than I believe in myself. He wasn't only my sidekick, my best friend, the guy who brought me coffee in the morning just the way I like it. He was the guy I trusted implicitly, the man who taught me to ski and skydive and hike mountains.

We sit on the park bench outside the pizza shop waiting for our order when I take the USB stick out of the pocket of my dress and hand it to Isla. "This belongs to you. Actually, it's for Reese. From Nate."

Isla stares at it like it's something dangerous to touch—like something might explode if she clasps her fingers around it.

I continue, "A while ago, Nate was involved in an accident—a scuba diving accident where he almost lost his life. After that, he decided to take some time off work, and eventually he quit his job and decided on a career change. We both did, actually. Long story, but we recently finished renovating the house. Anyway, the accident—it made him reassess a few things in his life and I suppose he decided that he didn't want to die without his biological daughter knowing who he was. In case she ever came looking for him."

Isla flinches at the words *biological daughter*.

"What's on it?"

My voice quavers. "It's a video. For Reese. Like a digital journal he'd been keeping for her. Things about him, his life, our life. I didn't know whether you'd want it, but it's not my place to decide that. It's yours, and you get to decide what to do with it."

Isla lets out a breath. Her hand trembles as she takes the USB and tucks it into the pocket of her handbag.

"He wanted a baby, but he told me only weeks ago, and now…" My voice breaks. "It's too late."

Isla's body stiffens. "He…wanted to become a father?" she says. There's a wobble in her voice. Only slight, but it's there, and I've known Isla long enough to know this moves her. I also know that as soon as I uttered those words, I opened a door that can't be closed.

"I thought you didn't want to have kids."

"Actually," I tell her, "that's what I thought too, but I guess things can change. We were in the process of…planning…deciding… talking about it…" My mind momentarily flicks back to my last conversation with Nate—those plans that will never be realized.

Isla nods, understanding. "That must make this all the harder."

"Yes," I say, letting out a sigh. "It does."

CHAPTER SIXTEEN

Isla

On the morning of Nate's funeral, I get up early and check on Lucy. She's lying in bed, but she's awake, staring at the ceiling, tears streaming down the sides of her cheeks. Her face looks like it used to when she'd fall asleep at night at my place, wondering where her mother was. From the moment we first met, Lucy and I became inseparable. We met every day of the summer holidays outside the Milk Bar on the corner. I brought spare change from the crystal dish on my father's bedside table—coins he tipped out of his pockets every night before he went to bed.

Lucy never brought spare change with her. That's because her mother never left anything lying around except for mess. She blamed it on being busy—Shirley was always flitting in and out of the house; one minute she was off to call bingo, and the next she was delivering ironing to Mrs. Lopowski down the road.

Lucy's dad had died the previous summer, and between all the flitting her Mom was doing, which involved long stretches of time at the hotel pouring money into slot machines that would never, ever be able to fill the void in her heart, Lucy started spending more time at my house. Mom announced she'd arranged things with Shirley, who had no problem with Lucy spending her days with me. Lucy told me once that her life changed the summer she met me. The truth is, mine did too.

"Lucy? Can I come in?"

She doesn't reply, but despite the long interruption to our friendship, I do the only thing there is to do. I crawl into my best friend's bed and hold her.

"I'm here."

"I don't think I can get out of bed."

"I know. That's why I'm here." At these words, she scrunches her eyes closed.

"I missed you so much."

Now I'm crying too. Words can't describe how much I've missed her. "Me too."

"You were always there. When I needed you, you were there."

I know what she's referring to. She's thinking about the summer we met. When Mom staged what can only be described as an intervention. One morning, Lucy tapped on the front door. It was 10 a.m., around the usual time she'd been showing up over the holidays. She was holding a plastic bag and wearing the same clothes as the previous day. I knew this because her overalls had the same pink stains from the popsicles we'd struggled to finish before they dripped over our clothes. Sometimes I wondered if Shirley even had a washing machine. If she did, it wasn't getting much use, that's for sure.

Lucy held the bag out for Mom to take. She accepted it from her and peered inside.

"Ice pops. Mom brought them home last night, only she forgot to put them in the freezer."

Mom didn't seem too impressed. "What time did she get home, Lucy?"

Lucy shrugged. "Same as always. I think it was ten. Or eleven. I'm not really sure."

"Was she working?" I asked. Lucy's mom seemed to be working a lot.

Lucy nodded, but Mom, she let out a noise—not a laugh, a kind of suspicious "hmm" sound that she makes whenever she thinks someone is lying.

"Elinor, could I get a hand in here, please?" called Dad from the kitchen.

Mom turned around, her long skirt flowing side to side as she walked down the hallway. Lucy and I went into my bedroom. We put empty tomato cans against the wall and overheard Mom saying that the reason Shirley was never home wasn't because she was always working; it was because she was always losing money. Mom said it started when Lucy's dad died.

"What's she buying? Does she buy clothes?" I asked, only that didn't seem to fit. According to Dad, my mother was always spending money on clothes, which always seemed to be getting dry-cleaned, washed, or pressed. A new dress for this occasion, or that. Nope, that couldn't be it. Lucy almost always wore the same clothes.

She didn't answer, just sat there, knees to her chest, shaking her head. "No," she said. "Not clothes."

Mom's voice carried through the air. "We all know she's not calling bingo numbers while the slot machines are ringing."

"Regardless, it's not your place to interfere."

"The poor child needs someone to look out for her, Lewis! What happens when her mother burns through all her husband's money? What happens to her then?"

Lucy clamped her eyes closed.

"It's not healthy. I'm going to have to find a way to fix things."

"Stay out of it, Elinor. How other people live is none of your concern."

At the sound of Mom's heels click-clacking down the hallway, Lucy and I split apart and leaped onto my bed. Mom appeared at my bedroom door.

"Girls?"

"Yes," we both said in unison, our heads shooting up.

"We're going to Lucy's."

Our adventure that day involved a tidy-up of Lucy's place and a visit to the grocery store. And so began several months of my mom checking in on Shirley every Tuesday. Soon, things started changing at Lucy's. For starters, Shirley stopped putting her money in the slot machines and she got a job. A real job, in a school office. And she started doing yoga. She turned her life around. In many ways, for Lucy, it was too little, too late. I wonder if the same stands for me.

Later that morning, Lucy enters the church with Shirley and Janet by her side. Nate's brother, Liam, walks alongside Terry. Liam bears a striking resemblance to both his dad and Nate, only his hair color is lighter and his eyes a darker shade of blue. Lucy stops in front of the casket, Shirley's hand resting on her back as if she's helping to hold her daughter upright. Lucy presses a hand on the casket and bows her head for what feels like minutes. When she turns around her face is blotchy and wet. Imagining the pain Lucy's going through, as I watch her alongside the crowd of mourners who've turned up to say goodbye, brings tears to my eyes. I fight them because I know once I start properly crying I won't be able to stop.

Reese tugs on my blouse. "Mom, you're crying."

I slip my hand into my pocket for a tissue to dab my eyes. "Remember when I told you I might be a bit teary today? You don't need to worry about me because we all have sad days sometimes, especially when we have to say goodbye to someone once they go to heaven."

She nods and doesn't loosen her grip on my free hand.

As Lucy approaches the front pew, she notices Reese and me. Her eyes plead for me to sit beside her. I point to the spare seat she's referring to and she nods.

"Come sit up here, sweetheart," I whisper to Reese as I lead her toward the front.

Shirley smiles at me even though her eyes are downcast. "Reese, why don't you sit here next to me?" she says, patting the empty space next to her.

Nate's mom notices us and briefly surveys both me and Reese. "Isla," she whispers. I can't recall the last time I saw Janet and Terry but a vague recollection of a family barbecue at Lucy's pops into my mind.

"Janet, I'm so sorry for your loss," I say. I lean in to embrace her before passing on my condolences to Terry and Liam.

"Your daughter's beautiful," whispers Janet before sitting down.

Throughout the service Lucy grips my hand while Shirley provides a steady supply of tissues. It's unfathomable how Lucy's life has changed in an instant, how one moment Nate was here and now he's gone. As Liam stands up and delivers the eulogy, Reese keeps her eyes locked on him, listening intently as he recounts tender stories of the much-loved, wonderful man who helped give Reese a life. The man she will never have the chance to know because of me.

Later that afternoon, Shirley offers to take Reese out for ice cream. Lucy flicks off her shoes and takes two beers out of the fridge. I don't drink beer, and to my knowledge neither does Lucy, but I accept it anyway.

"It was Nate's favorite," she says. "May as well use it up."

We trail outside and sit on the loungers.

"I'm glad you brought Reese with you," she says pensively. "It would have made Nate happy. She's beautiful. I mean, I'm not surprised...I just...I don't know what I was expecting. She's bright and bubbly...and so smart. She really knows the periodic table by heart?"

Lucy doesn't know much about Reese aside from her love of all things science-related, the day of her last haircut, and the item at the top of her Christmas list after the bike—a snow globe, of all things, which I haven't factored into my shopping at all.

"She does. There was this song she learned on YouTube. She's amazing, actually. I barely even know the difference between acids and bases."

Lucy takes a slow sip from the bottle and stares ahead. "She doesn't know about Nate and me."

I run my finger around the rim of the bottle. Even though Lucy's not asking a question, there's no easy way to admit what she already knows is true. "No. She doesn't," I say quietly. "We're trying really hard—to give Reese a good life," I add, inwardly cringing. The fact Ben and I can reassure Lucy about the kind of life we're giving Reese doesn't justify our silence.

Lucy takes another sip of her beer. "I can see that. I never once doubted you'd be a wonderful mother."

"It's actually the hardest job ever. Most of the time I feel like I'm getting it wrong. Like someone forgot to give me the memo with the 'how-tos.' " For a moment I feel like I've said the wrong thing. Reese is a gift she gave me, and here I am admitting my imperfections. Who am I kidding, though? Parenting is *hard*. Would Lucy understand?

"So I hear, but like I said—you're a great mother. She's so happy."

"I know it probably doesn't seem like it after what I did...but I'm so grateful. Ben and I...we are so grateful for what you and Nate did for us."

Lucy nods. "I know you are." She sets her beer down on the small table between the loungers. "So when *do* you plan on telling her?"

"I don't know." My cheeks flush with shame. This is not what we'd agreed on all those years ago. Not by a long shot. Ben would be furious if he could hear me right now.

"So you're never going to tell her about us? Is that the plan?" she asks, her voice slightly accusatory. She shifts in her chair.

"Ben and I decided she should attend the funeral but...we haven't figured the rest out..." My voice fades.

"Nate just died," she whispers. "She didn't get a chance to know who he was before he died. She didn't get to say goodbye to the donor parent she will never get to know because she still doesn't know he was her donor parent. Now you're here, but it sounds like you're still not ready to tell her the truth." Lucy shakes her head in disbelief. "You've had *years* to think things through, Isla."

"I'm sorry," I say, standing up. "The last thing I want to do is upset you. Especially today."

"Wait! You don't get to walk away like that." Lucy stands up and rests a hand on her hip. "Whenever anything gets awkward, this is what you do. You walk away."

"Maybe coming here wasn't such a good idea. There's too much history between us. Too much that can't be fixed."

"The only reason it feels that way is because of the decision *you* made. Things could have been different between us." Lucy lets the heaviness settle in the air for a moment. "What are you scared of? That I'll swoop in and try to be her mother?"

"No. Of course not." But I kind of am. In a way. I'm scared of how things might change. Of how the truth might somehow result in losing a part of Reese.

"I don't know Reese, but I do know that children do not like being lied to. And you know what I think? I think this is going to come around and bite you. Maybe not now, but someday."

The words are ones I've heard before, only in a different context, uttered by my mother.

"The thing that hurts the most is that I'm not a stranger. I was your best friend."

"You've every right to be angry with me, and for what it's worth, I really am sorry. I don't go a day without regretting what I did." I shake my head. My brain feels foggy, like I can't make sense of things.

"I don't think I believe you," says Lucy.

I understand where she's coming from. On the one hand, I desperately want Lucy back in my life, but the potential cost of that feels too great. To have Lucy back in my life means being up-front with Reese, and even though we've come close to telling her the truth, we're miles away from working out what delivering it will mean for our family.

"There's more to this than you know. I know it might make little difference but there's something I need to explain. Something that doesn't excuse any of this but..." I take a deep breath and stop myself. I can't admit this to Lucy—and it won't make a difference to the outcome of things anyway.

"But what?" she asks.

"It's not worth mentioning. I don't think it's helpful for me to bring up what's already happened," I say, hoping she won't press me further.

"So this is it? You go back home and life goes on as normal?"

"I'd like to see you again."

"But how can that work if I'm not prepared to lie to your daughter? I'm willing to forgive you, but I can hardly be a part of your life as long as Reese doesn't know the truth. That wouldn't be fair to her, would it?"

"No, it wouldn't," I say quietly.

"I think it was a mistake," she says finally.

I bow my head.

"Calling you to come here, I mean. That was a mistake."

I want to plead with her—to ask for a chance to right this. But there's no point. Unless I can agree to telling Reese the truth about her relationship to Lucy, there's simply no way we can even start to fix what I broke. This is the cost of my silence.

Walking away from Lucy once was bad enough.

Walking away from her in her time of need is worse.

CHAPTER SEVENTEEN

Lucy

No matter how hard I try to sweep the conversation with Isla to the side, it keeps replaying itself in my mind. I wish Nate was here to talk about it. He'd be angry about the situation, of course, but he'd eventually come around, and in the process he'd end up finding a way to help calm me down. In a way, what's happened doesn't surprise me. I called Isla in a moment of need—of weakness—without fully thinking about the consequences.

"You know what this place needs? It needs a freshen-up," says Mom, interrupting me from my sulking, with a wave of her arm. "I think we can start by getting rid of the flowers. Gerberas are so nineties."

Trust my mother to put a trend on blooms.

"Nate's funeral was less than a week ago and you already want to get rid of the flowers?"

"We'll donate them. There's a retirement village on the corner. I'm sure Betty and William will love them." So now my mom is on a first-name basis with the residents of the local retirement village?

"Betty and William?"

"Yes, I met them at the local café near the village. You should consider donating your excessive collection of loungewear to Betty. She walks every morning and still does aerobics three times a week."

"Pardon?"

"The DVD collection is right up William's alley."

"Nate's DVDs, Mom."

"Clutter. Be honest with yourself. You'll probably never watch them."

I clasp my palms together and place them in front of my mouth. "Mom, I know you mean well, but this is—"

"We have streaming services these days, Lucinda. Speaking of which, I think you should cancel yours today," she continues. "It'll only encourage you to waste away hours of your life feeling sorry for yourself."

"Where's all the wine?" I ask, noticing the empty rack.

"Trunk of my car," she says, winking. "We'll smuggle it in with the DVD collection."

She's already carrying out the boxed arrangement of offending gerberas. Despite her distaste for them, they make me feel happy. Correction: flowers made me feel happy before my husband lost his life. Happiness now seems like something that is elusive—out of reach and unavailable—at least for the foreseeable future, and if I'm honest, binge-watching Netflix in my loungewear with a bowl of popcorn and a bottle of wine is exactly the kind of thing I want to be doing.

I have to give it to Mom. In a way, she's right. There are way too many flowers that only serve to remind us of what a sad time this is. Nate would have hated them. He would have said they were a complete and utter waste of money which could have been put to better use—like saving monkeys in Tibet, or helping some other cause.

I sigh. "Fine. But keep the peonies. I love the peonies."

"What, so they can remind you of your wedding day and you can wallow down memory lane for another afternoon?"

She yanks the arrangement of peonies from the vase and deposits them at the front door. Once she's made three trips to the car and back, she wipes her hands on her jeans and switches the TV off.

"I don't need to tell you I was watching that," I say.

"Get up, Lucy. We have work to do."

"Nate and I almost finished decorating this place. The house doesn't need a freshen-up. The house needs some quiet time. To settle."

"It has the rest of its life to settle. And you have about ten minutes to get some shoes on or we're going to be late." She gives me a stern look that says there'll be no arguing.

Inexplicably, I do what I'm told. I get up, I put a pair of sneakers on, and one of Nate's favorite hoodies despite the fact we're in for an eighty-three-degree day, and meet her in the driveway.

Mom surveys me from top to toe, unimpressed by what she sees. "Well, if that's how you really feel about life, then I suppose we'll have to work with what we've got," she says.

I slink into the passenger seat, slide on a pair of sunglasses, and lean back.

"Is there any way you could tell me where we're actually going?" I say to Mom as she reverses out the driveway.

"Not a chance," she replies.

Thirty minutes later, I'm squirming in a black, wicker, Parisian-style chair while my mother orders cocktails for us at a swanky café I don't know the name of.

"Really? This is your idea of fun? This is you helping me get my mind off the fact that I just said goodbye to my husband?"

"Yes. As a matter of fact, it is."

"I suppose you're going to tell me the day spa across the street is our next stop."

Mom doesn't say a word.

"Mom, you're joking, right?"

"You'll feel like a million dollars once Beatrice is done with you. I have it on good authority she has a gift that rivals even the very best therapists our country has to offer, and you'll get an amazing massage."

I fold my napkin. "I'm sorry. But I can't do this. I need to be at home. With Nate, Mom."

Mom leans forward. "Sweetheart, Nate is in a jar on your mantel. He's going to be fine without you."

I hold my breath. *One, two, three...*

"You can still love him if you drink the cocktail."

"I don't want the cocktail. I want to be with him."

She pushes my glass forward. "Go on, honey. Take a sip."

"I'm going home." I go to stand up.

"You forgot your handbag, darling." She dangles the car keys in front of me. "And I have the keys. Sit down. Drink."

She waves over a waiter. "Could we please have another? Double shot for my daughter. And a bowl of nachos, please?"

"Mom...not the..." Nate always ordered nachos. Always.

"I know, I know. Why else do you think I ordered the nachos?"

After my massage, I meet Mom at the car.

"I got you something," she says, handing me a gift bag.

"Swimwear?" I side-eye her suspiciously as I lift the bikini from the bag. It's a sixties-style navy and turquoise halter with a cute bow knot, and if I'm honest, I kind of like it. But I have no use for it. I will not be spending time by the pool this summer.

"Thank you," I say, jamming it back into the bag before fastening my seat belt.

Mom puts the car into reverse, glances into the rearview mirror, and says, "Come home with me, Lucy. Just come home."

Oh, no. There's no way I'm going home. I run the possible excuses through my mind but I know she won't buy any of them.

"I can't come home with you," I say in the most patient tone I can muster.

"And why not?" This is delivered more like a demand than an actual question, as if the mere proposition of it being outside the possibility of a yes is inconceivable to her.

"Because I have a life here. I have friends. This is my home."

"You don't have friends."

"I have friends. You met them at the funeral."

She gives a theatrical roll of her eyes. "Thelma and the minions?"

"Mom!"

"They're not your friends, darling. Anyone worth their salt could read their body language."

"They came to pay their respects."

"Bet they don't even remember your birthday. Or your favorite meal." This is true. But Sandra, Josie, the women I recently started lunching with on Fridays—they'd miss me. Or at least I like to think they would. The thing is, Nate and I spent so much time traveling, our friends are dispersed all over the globe. Up until recently we spent so little time at home, we actually didn't have all that many friends in Melbourne. And since I'm between careers, I'm not exactly tethered here either. If I really want to, I can go back to the town I grew up in.

"All I'm asking is for you to come down to the beach for the summer. The sunshine will do you good. You could catch up with Isla again—I'm sure she'd love to reconnect properly. Sort out whatever fell apart between the two of you."

"Isla has her own life, Mom."

"But she came to the funeral. She stayed with us. You were getting along swimmingly as far as I could tell."

"Well, things aren't always what they seem. Besides, I can't go because this place reminds me of Nate. His things are here."

"It's not like you're not going to be reminded of him irrespective of your surroundings. Which is exactly why you should get away."

"Coming from a woman who loves to run away from her problems," I counter, unable to help myself.

"I am a mature woman now. I have learned from my mistakes. Which is why I don't want you making this one."

"No, Mother, I am not coming home. I have to make plans. Decisions. I have a life here. I need to think about work, too."

"Mother," she repeats, ignoring my comment about work. "What is this, 1943?"

She rolls the car into the driveway and cuts the engine.

"You can think about work while you're back home in Sorrento. With me."

Before I know it, Mom is wheeling a suitcase into my bedroom.

"Not happening, Mom."

She gives a well-practiced sigh that oozes exasperation and all the hallmarks of patience wearing thin. "Don't make me pack it for you, Lucinda."

"I can't come, and I'm serious this time. I have work to do. Here. The house."

She gives me a look that says, *C'mon, you know you want to come with me.*

By now, she's rifling through my drawers. She picks up a blouse and holds it against my cheek. Her nose turns up.

"No, not that. I hate that color on me."

"It's the Pantone color of the year but honestly, sometimes I don't know what they're thinking. Coral is an impossible hue for even the best complexions."

In some inexplicable way, I do want to go with her. This isn't a side of my mother I see often, the "I'll look after you" kind of side.

I open my closet, pull a couple of tops off their hangers, and toss them to her.

She claps her hands together. "Yes! That's the spirit!"

"This is going to be fun," I say, unable to hide my sarcasm.

And then, my mother does something she hasn't done since she arrived—something she has not done in years.

She hugs me.

Mom lives in Sorrento on Victoria's Mornington Peninsula, walking distance from the main street with its cute little boutiques and their sandstone facades that make window shopping a delight. Up on one of the hills stands her house, a white-gabled home with jaw-dropping views of the beach. Her home is not what I expected. It's vastly different from my childhood home, a testament to how hard Mom has worked to rebuild her life.

She motions for me to follow her as she gives me a tour of the house. "Your room's here across the hall." She pushes open the door, revealing a large room with a double bed, its stark, embroidered white coverlet, and pastel-blue throw rug. There's a distressed timber wardrobe painted in a dusty-blue, a large desk with a white chair, and a scented candle that hasn't ever been lit. On the nightstand is a photo of me and Mom together on the beach, the sun setting behind us, and next to the photo is a large keepsake box I remember from my teenage years.

"All yours," she says.

Mom pauses in the doorway before leaving my room. "I kept that box for you. Figured you might want it someday."

Late that afternoon, Mom walks to the local Coles and returns with a roast chicken and an assortment of plastic tubs containing things like olives and roast peppers filled with cream cheese. She tips the contents out onto the counter and hands me a head of lettuce before starting to shred the chicken.

"With any luck you might bump into a friend while you're down here."

"I thought you said I don't have any friends."

"Want to talk about what happened before Isla left your place?" Mom asks.

I finish rinsing the lettuce. "Do you have a lettuce spinner?"

Mom chortles and hands me a clean tea towel instead. "So? Want to talk about it?"

"Not really," I say quietly as I press the lettuce leaves dry. "But thanks," I add quickly.

"You know, I bump into Elinor every now and then. Her women's group meets at the beach club once a month. Never talks about Isla. Ever." She pops an olive into her mouth. "I've never seen the woman sport a shirt without perfect creases. If only she had the courage to embrace her imperfections, she'd probably start to feel a lot better."

I raise an eyebrow. Elinor and my mother have a long history, and I know Mom holds a deep sense of gratitude toward her, even if she doesn't outwardly show it.

Mom stops shredding the chicken and wipes her hands on her apron, her expression turning serious. "She's yours, isn't she?" she says softly. "I mean, not yours exactly—but she's your biological daughter?"

I hold my breath before letting it out slowly. "Yes. She is. Mine and Nate's."

Mom gives me a small smile of understanding.

"You've a heart of gold, Lucy. I don't know what I ever did to deserve a daughter like you."

"How did you know?"

Mom lets out a soft chortle. "She's the spitting image of you, Lucinda, right down to the freckles on her nose."

"I spent years thinking about her, wondering what she was like and...she's wonderful. I can't even find the words to describe what it feels like to look at her and see what came from the gift we gave Isla and Ben all those years ago. We helped them become a family...Seeing her made it feel so much more...real." I would love nothing more than to see Reese again—to have a relationship with her—but it's clear that won't be happening anytime soon.

"In all these years, you never met her? Not even once?" asks Mom.

"Never. And if Nate hadn't died—well, I'd still be waiting to meet her."

"So this is why you and Isla haven't been a part of each other's lives all these years? Because if I remember correctly, it's been about ten years since you stopped talking about her."

"Yes," I say, remembering the day like it was yesterday.

We'd been so sure we didn't want to become parents then—despite all the counseling and the gentle suggestions that it was entirely possible that with time we'd change our minds.

"Hey," says Mom softly, pressing a hand over mine. "Are you okay?"

"He wanted a baby, Mom. Nate wanted to be a dad. We talked about it right before he died. Now it's too late. Nate's gone and I have nothing left of him."

"Oh, sweetheart, I'm sorry."

"Reese...she's so beautiful. I see him in her, Mom. I see Nate."

That's the moment it dawns on me. We donated three embryos, the first of which didn't take. My mind jumps to the third one.

CHAPTER EIGHTEEN

Isla

Ben and I are on our way to my work Christmas party. I've been tasked with the job of selecting this year's staff gifts, which I'd nearly forgotten about after coming home from Lucy's. I was meant to confirm twenty-four jade money plants in ceramic bowls from the local nursery but by the time I remembered I'd forgotten, all they had left were small olive trees in jute bags that I've been trying to keep alive for the past five days and which will probably end up being regifted or left to die.

"So I had a doctor's appointment this morning," I say as we stop at the traffic lights. All I could think about during my appointment was what Lucy had told me about her and Nate wanting a baby. In her moment of grief and loss, how could Ben and I be thinking about having one?

Ben glances over at me. "Are you feeling okay?"

"Yeah. I'm fine. I'd booked in the preconception check-up with Dr. Shields, remember? I had a blood test. He wants me to start taking prenatal vitamins."

"I forgot all about it. Sorry."

"It's fine. I kind of wish I'd waited until after Christmas. There's so much going on right now."

"Yeah, there is. And we should probably talk about it. What you did with Reese before going to Lucy's—stopping me right before I was about to tell her the truth…what were you thinking?"

I let my window down, at this point not really caring if it messes up my blow wave.

I don't answer him. Instead, I opt to behave like a mature adult and pretend to plow through my clutch for something important. All it contains is my driver's license, my debit card, my phone, a container of Tic Tacs, and a lipstick.

"I've changed my mind about telling her. It's not necessary."

"School's almost finished for the year! There is no sound reason to keep the truth from her, and you know it. She's met her biological mother, Isla. We can't run from this. Not anymore."

"It's not like they'll have ongoing contact."

"Wait. What? You went and saw her, stayed with her after all these years—and that's it? You walk away again? I thought..." Ben and I have held differing views over the way we handled the ending of our relationship with Nate and Lucy, something Ben was never fully supportive of, even if he did go along with it.

"You thought wrong."

"Did something happen while you were there that I should know about? Because you've been moping around since you got back and you haven't said more than a couple of words about it. Reese hasn't stopped talking about how great Lucy and Shirley are, but what did Lucy say to you when she saw you? Surely you spoke about things."

I drop a couple of Tic Tacs into the palm of my hand.

"Here, take one—they're orange-flavored," I say, offering one to Ben.

Ben waves my hand away, despite the fact he loves orange Tic Tacs. "Just tell me what she said to you."

"Things got a bit awkward before I left." I feel myself getting agitated, and I turn the radio up.

Ben is quick to turn it down. "Mmm, she hasn't seen you in years, she made an effort to invite you to the funeral, and then things 'got awkward,' " says Ben, his voice dripping with sarcasm. "What does that mean, exactly?"

"She was upset that we haven't told Reese about her and Nate."

"Of course she's upset! Which is why we should have been up-front before the funeral. That was the whole point!"

"That wasn't the plan, Ben! I took her to the funeral. We can leave things as they are."

"But how can you think we could leave it at that? I mean, surely you agree that a door's been opened now? We need to take the next step!"

"I can't do it, Ben! I can't deal with telling Reese the truth—it's too hard!"

Ben shakes his head. "You need to look at this from a different perspective. Reese deserves to know."

"I don't *need* to do anything," I say, my irritation getting the better of me.

"Isla..."

By now we've reached the restaurant car park. My colleagues Tim and Monica wave as they walk past the car. They live in apartments. If anyone is going to rate the olive plants as the worst corporate Christmas gift in history, it will be them.

"You owe it to Lucy to patch things up. Reese is her biological child. Imagine what she must be thinking. After all this time she calls you after a devastating accident and you show up for her, you let her meet Reese, and then you disappear again." Ben pulls the handbrake and angles his body so he's facing me. "Seriously, how do you think that's made her feel? She didn't have to call you after everything that happened. But she did. And despite all that, you're still acting selfishly!" he says. "This is crazy, Isla. You're better than this."

"I wish you'd understand! I'm not like you. I can't just pretend it's all going to work out for the best. You might be prepared to lose Reese but I'm not."

Ben inhales. "We aren't going to lose her!"

"You don't know that!"

"Think about it. Nate is gone. He's *gone*. There's no chance to wind back the clock, and we have no idea how much damage this could cause for our daughter. She never got the chance to meet her biological father! Somehow, I don't think you've caught up with this, and if I'm honest, I'm starting to feel like I've had enough of keeping secrets. Nobody in our immediate family knows the truth. Reese has already started asking questions about genetic traits for no other reason than it came up in school and she's a curious kid. We have to tell her."

My eyes burn. "Ben...no...please. Just let me sit with this. I need to talk to my mother first."

Ben frowns. "What does your *mother* have to do with this?"

I stare out the window. How can I admit this to him?

When I don't answer him, he turns the ignition on and puts his hands on the wheel. "Okay, fine. Play it that way, but I'm heading back home. Let me know when the party's over and I'll come and pick you up."

"They're...expecting you."

"Tell them what you want. You're good at hiding the truth. Make something up. You'll think of something." He puts the car into reverse and fixes his eyes on the windshield, waiting for me to get out. "This is not just about you," he says before driving away, leaving me standing there, blinking away the tears.

Ever since our disagreement last night, Ben's been quieter than usual. He barely spoke during dinner and answered Reese absent-mindedly when she asked him how to solve a math problem; usually those kinds of questions animate him. This is unusual for Ben—he loves chatting over dinner more than eating itself. I see how much this is weighing on him and I know I need to be up-front about how I got us into this whole mess in the first place. It's finally time to be honest with him.

"Ben, there's something I need to tell you," I say to him once I finish reading to Reese and she's tucked into bed for the night. "About the house—about my mom." I sit down on the sofa beside him.

He turns the volume down on the TV and turns his body to face me. "Yeah, I've been wondering about that, because I can't figure out for the life of me why you feel you need to consult with your mother about something that concerns Reese."

"Let me explain. She...she wasn't happy about the arrangement. She didn't want us to go ahead with the donation..."

I cast my mind back to the crossroads moment—one I've spent years regretting.

My mother wanted none of it. To say she hadn't taken the news well regarding accepting an embryo from Lucy and Nate was an understatement.

A huge one.

There were plenty of times in my life I'd done things to displease my mother. Like the time I chose a Mazda over a Mercedes, and a house on what she considered the wrong street in the right neighborhood. I married Ben when she much preferred William Bradford, the most stuck-up, full of himself, narcissistic goof I'd ever laid eyes on. She turned a blind eye to the Mazda and was bothered for a year and a half over the house, and while she was for the most part quiet about it, she didn't let me live down my marriage choice, as evidenced by the fact William Bradford's name popped up in conversation—usually every summer when my parents were invited to William's parents' house for New Year's Day lunch.

My mother was concerned with money and manners and what other people thought of her, and it was exhausting.

"You have no idea what you'll be getting yourself into," said Mom as soon as I entered the restaurant and sat down, making me instantly regret my decision to tell her in the first place. We'd chosen an outdoor table in the courtyard, bordered by overflowing pots of petunias in every imaginable color. "Having someone else's babies... Having Lucy's babies probably sounds like a good idea because you think there's no alternative, but it will only serve to complicate your life."

"The way I see it, it'll be less complicated because of the fact we know them. They'll be involved in our children's lives anyway."

"You'll be forever comparing yourself to her. And her mother might have put herself together in the end, but we all know the family history."

"Really, Mom? I'm telling you that this might be my only chance to become a mother and this is your response?"

Mom picked up her napkin and placed it on her lap.

"Let me ask you something. Did Grandma Connie actually teach you to become such a judgmental—"

"Isla! Close your mouth before you regret what you're about to say," she snapped.

I pushed my chair back in response and stood up. "Fine then. Have it your way."

I left early, in tears, leaving my mother to foot the bill and explain to the waiter why her daughter had spilled a pitcher of iced tea and wasn't coming back.

As expected, Mom did not let up. In fact, she staged what I could only describe as an intervention. Over the course of the next month she left countless messages, telling me she wanted to clear things up. Eventually, I relented to a request to pop around to her place after work for dinner. Dad was out with friends and she wanted to have another chat. I went into it prepared—or as prepared as a daughter in my situation could be.

"Come in," she said, holding the door open.

Inside, Mom had been busy arranging posies of flowers for the local nursing home she visited every Friday morning.

"You look tired, dear. Have you been getting enough sleep?"

"Eight hours. The usual." This was a lie. Before my mother had planted a seed of doubt in my mind about the donation, I'd been sleeping fine.

Mom headed toward the doors to the patio and garden, where she'd set two places at the outdoor table for us. She helped herself to a rissole while I piled some Greek salad onto my plate.

"I've been thinking about what we spoke about last time I saw you and I realize I may not have made my reasons clear," she said as she filled my glass with sparkling water.

"Your reasons?"

"For why I think you should potentially wait for another opportunity."

I rubbed my temple. "Mom, I've had a long day at work, so if you want to 'clear things up,' then all you need to do is apologize and then we can move on."

"Darling, this is not about an apology. This is about me showing you something you most likely haven't even considered, purely because you're far too emotionally invested in this entire saga."

A saga. Mine and Ben's fertility issues summed up in two words.

"I thought you should see something," she said, picking up a piece of paper from the seat next to her. She handed it to me. "Go on, read it."

I scanned the page. This was a printout of a news article.

FAMILY LAW IMPLICATIONS OF EARLY CONTACT WITH DONOR PARENTS

"What is this?" I asked, failing to hide my frustration.

"It's something I would like you to read very carefully. It says that early contact between donor parents and a donor-conceived child can create some problems."

I held up my hand for her to stop talking, and scanned the article. "Mom, this is talking about a sperm donor trying to assert legal parentage of a child being raised by a single mother. That's a completely different situation from mine and Ben's. Besides, our donors are Lucy and Nate. We *know* them."

"All I'm saying is that you need to be aware of any family law implications. These clinics—they have rules and regulations and papers to sign, but it's the law that hasn't caught up with the reproductive technology."

I inwardly sighed as I stabbed my fork into a tomato. "I'll be sure to look into it," I mumbled.

"There's something else we need to talk about."

I slowly inhaled, rubbing my temple. My mother had an uncanny knack for bringing on a headache. "And what's that, Mom?" I asked, reaching for my sparkling water, wishing it were wine.

"Your inheritance."

My head snapped up. "My what? Mom, are you sick?" I sat up straighter. This was something I'd never heard my mother speak about. Ever. So naturally, it could only mean one thing.

She waved her manicured hand in a kind of dismissal. "How positively morbid of you! No. I'm fit as a fiddle. And it's not your father either. Even though he really needs to bring his cholesterol down."

"So what does that have to do with anything?"

"I meant what I said about Lucy."

"Pardon?"

"You heard me, Isla. I don't recommend you go down that path. Find another donor couple—one that you and Ben won't constantly be comparing yourselves to because they are privy to every element of your future child's life."

I set my fork down and inhaled. "This might be our only chance to become parents, and your only chance to become a grandmother. We are at the end of the road here whether you like it or not. And if I'm completely honest, there is nobody else in the world that I would rather accept help from. You might have your prejudices against Lucy and her mother because of how you were raised, but I don't. And quite frankly, I couldn't care less about your money."

Mom sat there, somewhat frozen, but as expected she kept her composure, and if she was offended, she didn't show it.

"Really?" she said, lifting a brow.

"Yes, Mom. Really. The decision was made without your input, and for all we know, I could be pregnant now."

It turned out I wasn't pregnant. Lucy and Nate's donation had resulted in three embryos but the first transfer was unsuccessful. Little did I know that when the second transfer resulted in two pink lines on a stick, and I was days away from losing our house, my mother would show up, checkbook in hand, ready to save the day.

There was one condition, though.

Silence.

Ben goes completely quiet after I tell him the story.

"Are you going to say something?"

"You mean to tell me that we have kept this from our daughter, our wider family, and friends not because you felt it was the best decision at the time, but because your mother blackmailed us?"

"That's partly why, but it's not the complete truth. She kept telling me stories about relationships between parents and children that had fallen apart once children found out—"

"Yeah! They probably found out by accident and discovered their parents had lied to them their whole lives! I mean, wouldn't you be angry if that happened to you?"

"Of course," I whisper. "You're right. Maybe it was easier for me to let her convince me that she was right. Part of me was—*is*—scared that she's right."

"Why didn't you talk to me about this?!"

"I guess we had a lot of stuff going on in the early years. We needed the money; there's no denying that fact."

"There is no way I would have accepted your mother's help if I'd known she'd placed this condition on you. No way! What about your dad? Did he have any input in this?"

"He knows Reese is donor-conceived, but he goes along with Mom's expectations."

Ben shakes his head. "You should have come to me. I'm your *husband.*"

"Things weren't great between us back then, Ben. This isn't your fault but you lied to me about the situation we were in. We were having a baby, everything was in upheaval—our marriage, our finances. This was a lifeline and I took it. I've carried this with me for all these years...but I don't know how to let go."

"Oh, Isla." He shakes his head and slips his arms around me.

"The worst part is that I went along with it. I'm *still* going along with it. I'm scared of telling Reese the whole truth. On one hand, I know it's the right thing to do, but my fear of what it'll do to our family—it's overwhelming. And it's been easier to set it aside and try to forget about it but that's also meant I've lived for years with this sense of guilt."

Ben shifts closer to me and puts his hand on my knee. "Look, we know what research tells us. Most donor-conceived kids are going to react positively to the news. Reese is not going to reject us because of it. She can handle it."

"There'll be so many questions from everyone. They'll think we're horrible people for keeping this a secret from them...It will blow up into this huge drama and I don't know if we'll be able to shield Reese from it."

"That's the whole point, Isla. We *have* been shielding Reese from it. The longer we continue to do this, the harder it's going to be. If we wait until she's an adult, there is every chance she'll question why we kept it a secret her whole life. What if she equates the secrecy with shame? That's what I don't want for her because there is nothing to hide here. If other people have a problem with the way we started our family...well, quite frankly, that's their problem."

"The way I've handled this. It makes me a terrible person, doesn't it?"

"No," he says, his eyes full of sincerity. "I think it makes you human."

CHAPTER NINETEEN

Lucy

Nate always told me that in life we have no second chances—that you have one chance to get your life on track. I never knew what he meant until now. He didn't mean that you don't get a chance to start over. He meant that you get a chance to do your best every day to chase the things in life that hold meaning. I know what this points to for me but can I really do it? Can I actually have a baby without Nate here to hold my hand—to help me raise a baby?

I sit outside watching the summer tourists walk past after their long days out on boats and on the beach. Not too far away is a street filled with food trucks and music playing for one of the summer twilight festivals.

"There's a salad in the fridge for you," says Mom, carrying out her yoga mat.

"I ate not long ago but thanks."

"Want to go to the drive-in tonight?"

"People still visit drive-ins?"

She pushes her glasses up onto her head and gives me a look that says, *Duh, of course they do.*

"Would you prefer to go to the twilight market?"

"I would prefer to stay home."

"You've your whole life to relax, Lucinda. Now is not the time." Her voice softens. "Why don't we go join them?" says Mom, referring to the people on the street.

I lean into the recliner and uncross my legs. "Don't feel like it. It reminds me of Europe in summer." What I really mean is that it reminds me of summer nights, with Nate, in Europe. I close my eyes and remember the way his hand felt pressed against mine, how our palms fit perfectly together—how our last trip to Europe in summer had been to Puglia and we stayed in one of those white-and-gray trulli houses and we spent our evenings dining at the same clifftop restaurant overlooking the water every night.

He hadn't wanted to become a dad then. I know exactly what he'd tell me—he'd remind me that life doesn't always turn out the way you plan it. I could go back to traveling; I've spent years seeing the world. But I don't want to see more of it without him. I need to move forward in my life. Never did a day pass without Nate wanting me to be happy. I know that having a baby would make him happy.

Mom pulls the other recliner next to mine. She sits on it so she's facing me and takes a few moments before speaking. "I know it reminds you of him."

"I miss him, Mom. I really miss him."

"I know you do. I was thinking about what you said the other day. Feel free to tell me to mind my business, but I was wondering... were you trying for a baby?"

My attention fixes on the ice-cream van at the bottom of the street with the line that snakes all the way around to the back of the cinema.

"He only said he wanted kids not long before he died, so no."

"You said he."

"I meant *we*. I was... in the process of deciding."

"You never wanted them before?"

"No," I say quietly.

"Because of me?" Mom chews her lip and watches me, waiting for a response.

I slowly turn to face her. "Yes," I admit, closing my eyes. "That had something to do with it."

"Oh, Lucy. What did I always tell you? Don't let my actions from the past put you off becoming a mother. You're nothing like me. You're *so* much better."

Mom gets up, presumably to get some tissues, but returns carrying a padded shield and a set of boxing gloves.

"Get up," she says, tossing me the gloves.

"I went for a jog this morning, and I'm about five minutes away from putting on my pajamas."

"Put the gloves on, Lucinda."

I cross my arms. Mom walks over, takes one of my wrists, and shoves a glove on it.

"You're unbelievable."

"Yeah, and I want to hear all about it. Other hand."

I get up and she helps me get the other glove on. She steps back and holds the shield up.

"Jab!" she commands.

Hesitantly, I punch the pad.

"Again," she instructs.

I punch, first with my right fist, then my left. After a few seconds my body swerves into motion, like a gear has changed, and suddenly I'm pounding at the pad, unable to stop.

"Tell me how you feel about me, Lucy."

I wipe the beads of sweat collecting on my brow.

"What? No." I shake my head. I don't want to do this. Not now. Not ever.

Mom moves forward with the shield. I press my gloves against it to stop her.

"Keep going and tell me how it feels to have a mother that let you down." She holds my gaze.

"Mom," I say, my arms hanging loosely by my sides. "I'm not going to do that."

Mom moves toward me again. "Why'd you get on the plane, Lucy? Why'd you leave me, Lucy? You got on a plane and you left to travel the world—"

"I didn't leave you, Mom! I left to start my career, to live my own life!" I punch the shield.

"What if I needed you?"

"Well, maybe it was a little too late because *I* needed *you*. Maybe *you* should have thought of that before you packed me away and disappeared from my life!"

"You loved Elinor and Lewis, didn't you?"

"I loved you too!"

"That's right. Keep going."

I pummel the shield with my fists and then grab either side of it and knee it.

"You left me. You took all our money and you whittled it away until there was nothing left! And then you started to fix things—you got better and then..." Tears stream down my face. "Then you left! And by the time you came back it was too late!" I kick the pad and follow with a series of punches. "You were a shitty mother and I hate what you did!"

"That's right. Keep going."

I have nothing left in me. Resting my mitts on my knees, I bend over, gasping for air.

"Tell me about Nate now," says Mom.

I drop to the ground, knees pressing into the lawn.

"I hate it! I hate that he's gone and I'm all alone!" I pummel the grass before falling into a heap.

Mom lowers herself onto the ground beside me and throws her arms around me. "Let it out," she says, patting my back as I moan into her shoulder. "I'm here for you. Your shitty mother is finally here for you."

*

Later, after Mom points me to the shower and pours me a glass of straight vodka, we make our way to the street market.

We haven't eaten dinner but both have a craving for the Nutella crepes from Luciano, the guy who owns the Italian trattoria up the road. We take our neatly packaged desserts to the beach, where the sun is setting. We walk on the sand, barefoot, the gentle waves still warm from the sun washing over our ankles.

"I'm sorry about what I said to you," I say.

"You don't need to apologize. In fact, I'm the one who needs to do that. Only I . . . find it hard to talk about. Your grandmother was never great at communication and I suppose . . . maybe that rubbed off on me."

She stops walking. "Lucy, I really am sorry for everything I did to hurt you, for all the mistakes I made, for the times I put myself and my problems—my way of dealing with those problems—ahead of you and your needs."

"Mom, it's okay."

"No, it's not. It's not okay at all. I'd like to explain it to you. It started after your father died. I . . . He was my world. He was everything I ever knew about love and family. And then he checked out and suddenly I didn't know who I was anymore."

"I wasn't enough for you."

"That's not true. That has never been true. I found it very difficult to cope. The gambling—it was a silly way of trying to escape my grief rather than deal with it. It was the most horrible time in my life, Lucy. I couldn't sleep at night—I didn't know how to ask for help. I was ashamed. I couldn't tell you. I could not bring myself to tell you or anyone."

"Elinor and Lewis knew." In fact, Elinor had intervened. She helped Mom. She helped *me*. She made sure the house was clean, the fridge was stocked. She even bought me a new school uniform. Elinor and Lewis went above and beyond, taking me in when Mom eventually left.

"They did," says Mom. "I'll always be grateful for what they did for us—for you."

"You eventually got better and then you left. I still don't understand why you did that. You could have stayed. I needed you."

"When the job teaching yoga in Fiji turned up, I took it. I made the best decision I could at the time but I know now that it was wrong. I made a mistake. It was only supposed to be for six months—enough time for me to have a deep rest and deal with my grief and my problems. Elinor said she and Lewis would be happy to look after you during that time and I knew you'd be safe... and happy."

"Mom, I was convinced you were never coming back. It felt like years."

"Oh, no," she says, her face crumpling. "I would always, always have come back to you. That was never not part of the plan. Ever. The truth is, I don't even know who I was during that time. It's no excuse but I never intended to hurt you or make things hard for you. I just... This was bigger than me."

Mom did return home, and while she'd gotten her life back on track, I never managed to forgive her. At least not until now.

"I forgive you, Mom."

Her face softens. "You do?"

"Of course I do," I say, my eyes damp. "It would have been hard for you. I understand that now. Nate was right—he was always right. He said I needed to get past all of this." I've been pushing Mom away for years—keeping her at arm's length—but maybe now is the time to allow things to be different between us.

"I suppose he was a wonderful man," says Mom. "You know, nobody talks about it. Nobody wants to talk about things like money and gambling, especially when there are problems."

"There is nothing wrong with putting up your hand and asking for help, Mom. Ever."

Mom's brow lifts. "I know that now." She lets out a deep sigh. "I don't want to lose you again, Lucy."

Our eyes lock and that's when I feel it, a reversing. I don't want to lose her either.

The following afternoon, I fall asleep in Mom's outdoor hammock in the garden. I've never pegged Mom for a gardener but I have to give her credit. She's created a relaxing haven in the backyard. On one side, she's set up a barbecue area, and on the other, a running water fountain and a patch of beautifully manicured lawn for her yoga class, bordered by flowering escallonias. The moment I close my eyes I'm out. It's always the same—the last image I see in my mind before I drift off is Nate's face. Ever since I lost him, I dream the same dream. The two of us, in the snow, holding hands, getting ready to ski down the mountain. Me, pressing my face against his chest, trying to remember the feel of his strong arms slipping around my body, holding me close. Him, whispering into my ear. He always says the same thing—*You'd make the most amazing mother*—right before he releases me from his embrace and gives me a gentle nudge. And as I push off the mountain and feel the cool air whipping against my cheeks, I realize I am alone, and that's when I wake up.

"Lucy!"

I'm still gasping for air when I open my eyes to see Mom's face hovering above mine.

"You were dreaming."

I rub my eyes. "Just dozed off." I want to close my eyes again, to see Nate—feel him one more time. It makes sense. I want to have a baby. *Nate's* baby. I want it more than anything. The idea of it seems perfect—it's what Nate wanted. And it's what I want too. Yes, there's the issue of whether the remaining embryo is still available. If it is, I'll need to talk to Isla about it, but surely she'll understand.

A gaggle of women wearing yoga pants are helping themselves to a jug of lime-and-mint-infused water in the far corner of Mom's garden.

"We just finished a class on the beach. I invited them back here. We're having a cook-off. You don't have dinner plans, do you?"

"A what?"

"Good, you can be on Glenda's team. She's in charge of dessert. I think you're making a pavlova. I'm in charge of the salads and Fran is trying to decide between a grilled octopus dish or paella."

"I don't know how to make a pav."

"You can whip the cream. Get up."

"We've decided on the paella!" calls out a woman, who I can only assume is Fran.

Mom flashes two thumbs-up. "Why don't you invite the girls?"

I give her a blank look.

"Isla and Reese."

"Mom, you know that's not possible."

Mom puts her hand on her hip and smirks. "You miss her. She misses you. She'll come around. Eventually."

"She's had a decade to 'come around,' Mom," I say, standing up.

Mom ignores me and turns to face the women. "Ladies, I'd like you to meet my daughter, Lucy. She's very excited about learning how to make a pavlova for the first time."

It takes every bit of energy to wave back at their beaming faces. Then Mom, as if I'm a five-year-old, takes me by the hand and leads me over to the group. She points to each of them one by one and reels off their names: Glenda, Alina, Josie, Sally, Prue, Malinda, and Fran.

"I'm Glenda," says one of the women. "You'll be on my team with Alina."

Alina, a stocky woman with red hair and a warm smile, waves. "I heard you won't be on that travel show anymore," she says.

"But your Mom said you're launching a new linen brand," says one of the other women who I *think* is Sally but could well be Josie.

"*Might* be launching a linen range," I say. "I have a few things I need to sort out before I throw myself back into work."

"Oh?"

"Yes. I'm thinking about having a baby," I say. Or should I say, *blurt*. This isn't something to announce to a group of strangers. My cheeks instantly bloom red.

Mom, who's carrying out two jugs, stops in her tracks. Malinda, who's trailing behind her, comes to an abrupt stop, sloshing iced tea on the two of them in the process.

"It was just a thought I had," I reply to the women, whose eyes are suddenly all on me.

A thought that is open to discussion about making a decision.

Nothing is ever just something.

Mom places the jugs on the table and takes a step closer as my face crumples, and I drop my head into my hands. Someone—Josie?—pulls a chair out, and before I know it, I can feel the touch of a stranger's hands holding me as I let everything out, all at once.

"What's all this business about having a baby?" asks Mom later that night once everyone has left. "I'm guessing you're not pregnant."

I had three cocktails and whatever was in the jug with the berry-colored liquid. No, I am not pregnant.

"It might not even be possible."

"Might it be possible for you to fill in the gaps so what you're saying makes sense?"

"I told you that Nate wanted a baby, Mom. Right before he died."

"You did tell me that. But how...?"

"There's an embryo. In storage. The last one of the three Nate and I donated to Ben and Isla. Or at least it *might* still be in storage. I don't know for sure."

Mom sits there silent and unresponsive.

"I don't even know if they'd allow me to use it."

"They?"

"The clinic. The law." Then, of course, there's the question of Isla and Ben. Would they be on board with this?

"You want to do this on your own?"

"I can do this, Mom. Nate would be happy about it—I know he would be."

"Raising a child on your own, honey. It's not..." She stops herself.

"What?" I whisper. "What were you going to say?"

She gives a small shake of her head. "I was going to tell you that it's not easy. But since when is parenting easy? Family looks different for everyone—if this is how you want to start yours, then I guess my only question is... what's the next step?"

I blink at her. The next step would involve me finding out exactly where I stand. For the first time since I lost Nate, I feel something stir inside of me. It feels a little like hope.

CHAPTER TWENTY

Isla

The following night, once Reese is in bed and Ben is asleep on the couch, I take out my laptop and finally muster up the courage to look at what's on the USB Lucy gave me. There are two files on the stick. A video and a Word document: *Donor Legacy Video* and *For Isla and Ben*. I open up the Word document first.

Dear Isla and Ben,

I know what you must be thinking since I'm usually not this sentimental. The thing is, I came close to dying not so long ago, and it jolted me into thinking about things in my life I hadn't ever considered before. One of those things is my biological child. Reese. It feels strange typing her name out. Lucy and I never say it out loud. I think it's been easier not to. In saying that, we think about her every now and then, and don't doubt she's living a great life, and that's everything we ever wanted to come of this.

Anyway, after my accident, I started wondering how Reese would have felt if I'd died without her knowing me. What if she found out about me one day and started asking questions about me—about the kind of person I was, or what was important to me, or why I decided to become a donor for the two of you. Hearing these answers from other people surely couldn't compare to hearing them from me?

Lucy and I completely respect your decision about keeping a distance from us, but I can't help wondering about whether one day Reese might come looking for us. That's why I made this video diary. Lucy doesn't know about it—I think the idea of it would unsettle her. But it's important to me, and that's why I'm doing it. As Reese's parents, it's obviously up to you how you handle this, but I hope you find a way to get it to her at some stage. I also hope it helps.

Nate x

Oh, Nate.

I reach for the tissues and dab my eyes before opening the video file. I plug my headphones in and press play as Nate's body comes into focus. He's wearing a powder-blue sweater with a V-neck. His hair is a little shorter than how I remember it and he's clean-shaven. He's standing in the kitchen behind a white marble countertop with a fruit bowl bearing Granny Smith apples and a handful of bananas. Before he starts talking, he checks whatever device he's recording with, clears his throat, and gives his nose a quick pinch. He always did that when he was nervous. The expression on his face brings tears to my eyes, and before I can stop myself, I reach out a hand toward the monitor.

Oh, Lucy. How can he be gone?

Just as my fingers touch the cold surface of the screen, I pull them away and hit pause. Part of me wants to watch, but it feels like an invasion. This video is for Reese, not for me.

With the laptop still open, I run a search for donor legacy projects. One of the websites I land on talks about how donors sometimes choose to leave videos like the one Nate made, explaining a bit about who they are and why they donated, and other information like their hobbies and personality, medical information, likes and dislikes, philosophies on life—information that a donor-conceived child might like to one day know about them. Some people make memory boxes while others make scrapbooks, and as I click through the pages, it dawns on me how important information such as a donor's favorite song or movie could be to a donor-conceived child. Information that might seem insignificant to others has the power to provide connection in a relationship of this nature. One child commented on how important it had been to see his donor father walking in his legacy video—it was something he'd always been curious about.

Identity. It all comes down to a child's sense of identity. Of knowing not only who they are but where they came from, and no matter how much I wish for me and Ben to be enough for our daughter, we only form part of her story—we are not the full story, nor could we ever be.

As I continue scrolling through the website, I watch videos of donor-conceived adults talking about their experiences. One of them in particular catches my attention: a young woman in her early twenties who was told about her conception when she was around Reese's age. The girl—Chloe—talks about the lovely relationship she now has with her donor father, who she finally met when she was eighteen, after she started looking for him. He wasn't hard to find because he too had been looking for her. When they finally met, she realized they lived two suburbs away from each other. She has three other siblings she was able to form a relationship with.

I press a hand to my heart—the way this woman describes her relatively new relationship with her biological father is heartwarming and reassuring. I keep watching and hold my breath; her voice starts to wobble midway through the video once she starts talking about her younger years when she was initially told about her conception. She talks about it being the moment she realized she was different—how it led to being bullied at school. My stomach lurches, thinking about Reese and what she's been through this last term at school. I contemplate turning the video off and closing down the laptop, but I can't tear my eyes off this woman. I want to hear her story—*have* to hear her story.

"My shame around my identity developed because I was told to keep the truth about my identity a secret."

Chloe's parents told her the truth, but in doing so, they also encouraged her to keep it quiet between wider family and friends, including aunts, uncles, and grandparents. Some members of her biological father's family hadn't wanted to meet her. As a result, Chloe felt that not only was she different, she had something to be ashamed of.

I can't let that happen to Reese. I want her to feel proud, and special, confident and comfortable with her conception story. I can't do it until I reach that point first. The question is, can I ever reach that point?

I reach for the Kleenex.

I cry for Chloe, and I cry for Chloe's parents and the situations we find ourselves navigating without a compass, without a rule book, without enough hindsight to know what is right or wrong or in between.

I cry for Reese and Nate and Lucy.

And as I tear another tissue from the box, I cry for myself.

It's the last day of school term, and my car is sitting idle in the Kiss and Drop line, waiting for Reese to tumble out of the school gate. Christmas is around the corner. I've managed to finish my Christmas shopping, have officially set up an "Out of Office" response on my emails, and aside from two sales that need finalizing over the weekend, I'm ready for the holidays. But there's something I need to do first. I need to call Lucy.

Breathe, I tell myself. Just breathe.

"Isla?" she says.

"Yes, it's me."

"Sorry, could you hold on, I'm just going to go outside." Another pause. "Mom, I'm going for a walk. I'll finish this later."

I hear a click like a door is closing and then Lucy's voice comes through the phone again. "Okay, now I can talk."

"Your mom's still staying with you?"

"Uh, no, more like I'm staying with my mom."

"In Sorrento?"

"Hasn't changed a bit, only the shops on the strip keep getting more expensive."

"Oh, I know, but how gorgeous are they? Did you see Willow's Basket—the shop on the corner?"

"I've been there four times already. Mom approves because they don't sell loungewear."

"Loungewear?"

"Long story."

This comment reminds me that there are parts of Lucy's life I'm not privy to anymore—the mundane details of the everyday— and it gives me reason to pause. We slipped into conversation the way friends—old friends—do, and yet we aren't really friends at all anymore.

"Are you..." I want to ask whether she's okay, but even I know this is the stupidest question ever. Nonetheless, I need to know how she's doing. "How are you coping?"

"I don't know. It feels like he's away for work but he's going to get an Uber from the airport and walk through the door any minute...but, of course, he's not. He's never going to do that again. He's gone forever and I don't know how I'm going to live without him. How does *anyone* do this?"

I press my lips together and remind myself to breathe. "Your mom did it," I say, dabbing my eyes.

"And did a great job of messing up her life and mine in the process."

This is true but Shirley came out the other side eventually. She'd needed some help to get there. Okay, a *lot* of help.

"I'll be here all summer. With her. She insisted."

"You'll be fine," I tell her. "You're going to get through this."

The line goes quiet and then I hear her sniffle.

"It won't be easy but it will get easier. One day you'll wake up and you'll marvel at how it doesn't hurt as much as it used to."

"That's what Mom keeps telling me."

"Listen, there's something I need to tell you. A couple of things, actually."

"Go on..."

"Ben and I discussed things. I've made a complete mess of things, and as hard as this all is, I'm ready to tell Reese the truth. Really ready."

"Okay," she replies quietly.

This is all Lucy has to say? *Okay*? Part of me *wants* her to fly off the handle—to call me out for what I am. But she doesn't. She's too good for that.

"Do you have any...questions?"

"No. For what it's worth, I think you're doing the right thing for Reese. I'll stay out of your life until—"

"No," I say, quickly. "That's not what I meant. I...we...would like you to be part of her life...if you're still open to that."

"Of course I am," she replies. She leaves it at that. The lack of warmth in her voice is out of character for her.

"Great, well, we'll give her some time to process the news and then we can figure out how to go from there?"

"Sure," she says, leaving the words hanging limply in the air like stalks of droopy celery in a refrigerator crisper. A beat of silence lingers and then she clears her throat. "Is she...How is she?"

I rub my neck, which has flushed in angry pink patches the way it does whenever I find myself getting worked up. "She's great. She's wonderful, actually."

Lucy—the woman who gave me the greatest gift someone can give a person—deserves more, way more than a handful of vague, everyday words to describe how her biological daughter is. The two days Reese and Lucy spent together are nothing compared to a lifetime of knowing Reese. There is so much Lucy has missed out on. So much she doesn't know because I took the chance to know Reese from her. Of all the things I could say to describe how Reese is, I land on *great* and *wonderful*. I don't tell her how Reese aced her latest art project, which was showcased in assembly. I don't tell her how she's gone up two shoe sizes in the past eight months and how she's now reading at Year 6 level. I don't tell her how she giggles whenever she's embarrassed, or how she spent the last three months making slime and selling pots of it to raise funds for the Indigenous Literacy Foundation. Or how she and Ben spent six weeks building a Little Free Library which was featured in the local paper and which sat happily on the corner of Lively Drive and Cumberland Walk. There's no doubt about it—this new chapter for us is going to take some time to get used to, even if Lucy and I do know each other inside out.

"Why don't we meet up?" I suggest. "Or maybe…you and Reese could spend some time together after we've told her."

"She likes fishing, doesn't she?"

"She loves it."

"Well, how about you and I meet up tomorrow? Meet me at the marina, and once Christmas is out of the way, I can take her out on Mom's boat for a few hours."

"Great," I say. "Because there's also something else I want to talk to you about."

"Perfect. Why don't we meet for coffee first, then? Because there's something I want to talk to you about too."

CHAPTER TWENTY-ONE

Lucy

After I finish talking to Isla, I scoop up my car keys and drive to West Park Fertility Clinic. The waiting room, which has changed since I was last here, is now furnished with pale blue waiting room chairs and framed pictures of pastel-colored sunsets on the walls.

The woman sitting at reception, Dani according to her name badge, smiles as I approach her. "How can I help you?"

"My name's Lucy Harper. I don't have an appointment, but I...There's a few things I need to know...about an embryo my husband and I donated many years ago..."

"At this clinic?"

"Yes."

"And you don't have an appointment?"

I shake my head. "Would it be possible to have a quick chat with someone?"

Dani makes a face that indicates it probably won't be possible, but she's sorry all the same. "We really would need you to make an appointment. What's your query regarding? Maybe I could see if one of our counselors can answer it before her next appointment."

"My husband died, and I would like our embryo back because I would like to have our baby. I need to know what the process is."

Dani's eyes dart right and left as she takes in what is obviously not a run-of-the-mill type of inquiry for a Wednesday afternoon.

"Oh, um." She frowns. "Why don't you take a seat while I see if I can find someone available for you to talk to."

She emerges a few minutes later with a woman by her side—mid-fifties, with a heart-shaped face and a curly, angled bob with ash-blonde highlights.

"This is Charlotte, one of our counselors. She has a few minutes to chat."

Charlotte smiles and waves me toward the hallway. "Nice to meet you, Lucy. Let's see if we can find a free room down here." She motions toward a room on her left, waits for me to enter, and then gently closes the door behind her. "Take a seat. Anywhere is fine. Dani mentioned something about your husband passing away. Was this recent?"

"Last month."

"I'm so sorry to hear that. Do you have any children?"

"No. We never wanted...well, yes...but not really."

Charlotte patiently waits for me to elaborate.

"What I mean is that no, Nate and I weren't parents. Around ten years ago, we donated three of our embryos to another couple. They were our best friends. They now have a child—a daughter—Reese. She recently turned nine."

Charlotte takes a moment to register the information. "Right. So the embryos. They were all donated to the donor recipient couple. You and your husband don't have embryos in storage for yourselves?"

"No. We didn't want children. Or at least we thought we didn't until very recently."

"Okay," says Charlotte softly, jotting down some notes. She puts her pen down and leans forward.

"Lucy, can I ask what it is exactly you're wanting to do?"

"I'd like my embryo back so I can have a baby."

Charlotte slowly nods and clasps her hands together. "There are a couple of points to make here. Now obviously, I don't have your file or anything in front of me, so this is very general information. Firstly, you may or may not be aware that there are laws here in Victoria under the Assisted Reproductive Treatment Act that concern the posthumous use of gametes and embryos."

"Right...so could you explain what it is I might be dealing with here?"

"What this means is that it's not simply a case of a partner being able to say they'd like to have a baby once one of the partners in the relationship has passed away. Now, that is not to say you couldn't do this—but it does mean there is a process involved. It's not one I see very often at all, and to be honest I would need to look into things further, but usually this type of matter would involve obtaining permission from the Patient Review Panel."

"Does that involve an application of some sort?"

"Well, yes, it does. It's a legal process, and there are certain things they'd be looking at before making a judgment. One of the things they'd look at is whether your husband expressed his consent in wanting to have a child prior to his death, or gave what we call an advance directive for you to have his child."

I blink. "They'd need proof of this? In writing?"

"Yes, most likely." Charlotte smiles sympathetically.

"I didn't go around recording our conversations in case something like this were to happen."

"I know. It's just something to be aware of. Secondly, there is another significant issue at play here. Or rather issues."

The way she delivers this information makes me feel like I'm completely out of my depth. Not only do I need to think about what it actually means to want this, I need to consider the hurdles. Even if I do manage to get permission to use the embryo, there is no guarantee a successful pregnancy will come of it. There's no doubt about it: the odds don't sound like they're in my favor.

"Firstly, you mentioned you donated the embryos close to ten years ago?"

"That's right."

"The law states that the limit on embryo storage is ten years. So this potentially means that the storage limit has been reached. Usually the limit is five years and that means it is possible your embryo may no longer exist."

"The donor recipients—they reached out to me and my husband for an extension about five years ago."

"And it was approved?"

"Yes."

"It's likely the donor recipients will have received notice about the ten-year storage limit approaching. I'd need to check the status of this to see when that's due to expire."

My breath catches. "Could you...Would it be possible for you to check that for me now?"

Charlotte presses her lips together. "Let me look into things and make sure I have the appropriate information. I'll get back to you as soon as I've had a chance to check things and make sure there aren't any issues regarding privacy."

Charlotte asks me for my personal details and phone number, which she jots down.

"These situations can be quite complex, especially when it comes to the posthumous use of embryos and gametes." She pauses. "Are you still in contact with the recipient couple?"

"There's a bit of history there, but yes, at the moment I am."

"If things progress from here, we'd suggest counseling for each party." Charlotte picks up her pen. "Could you give me the recipient couple's contact details?"

I question her with my eyes.

"If the embryo is still in storage, the clinic will need to lock it down. This means neither party will be able to use it until such time as things are worked out. I wouldn't want it disposed of in the interim but I also need to make some inquiries as to how we as a clinic treat the situation since there's a statutory disposal issue here also."

I give her the details, which she scribbles down before standing up and extending a hand. "Good luck, Lucy."

I'm meeting with Isla tomorrow. I don't know how she'll take the news. I might need more than luck.

CHAPTER TWENTY-TWO

Isla

Every summer, Mom and Dad go on a three-week cruise to New Zealand, only this year Dad decided he needed to re-landscape the backyard. Since Mom is so bored—her social events begin in February each year, and never earlier—so far this month she's insisted on lunch, a rescheduled sleepover with Reese, and, of course, another lunch. So when I call her insisting to meet up this afternoon, Mom knows something is up. The conversation I need to have with her is one I simply can't put off any longer, despite the potential consequences. I don't want Reese to be the one to tell her she knows she's donor-conceived lest she react in a way that upsets her.

"Where's Dad?" I ask, noticing the backyard is extremely quiet.

"Fishing trip with Jim and Lionel. I think he's finally come to the realization he's not a landscape gardener and we should have gone to New Zealand. But now we can't find any tickets, and, of course, Richard, the gardener we want to do the work, is booked out until March." She lets out an audible sigh and passes me a mug of something that resembles instant coffee but tastes much, much worse.

"What is this?"

"Dandelion tea. Your father and I gave up the coffee months ago. According to my naturopath, Zoey…"

I zone out until Mom claps her hands together. "Right. You obviously have something on your mind. Out with it."

I clasp my hands around the mug and think about how to break everything to her.

"Lucy came back to Sorrento and she's living with Shirley for the summer."

"How's she coping after the funeral?" She gets up and walks over to the kitchen, where she starts arranging the fresh flowers on the counter that are delivered weekly.

"As well as can be expected."

"How much contact do the two of you have, exactly?" asks Mom, pushing a stem into the vase.

"Actually, that's why I'm here."

Mom steps back from the vase and eyes me. "You took your daughter to the funeral, Isla. If you see her again, you'll find it harder and harder to keep Lucy's anonymity from Reese."

"Have you ever stopped to ask yourself whether maybe I don't want to keep her anonymity anymore?"

"And what does that mean, exactly?"

"I'm tired of keeping it all a secret, Mom. Whether we like it or not, this is how it is because this is about Reese, not me, or you, or anyone else. It's about her."

"Isla..."

"It's too late. We've told her she's donor conceived. She just doesn't know who her donor parents are."

"This is ridiculous! You cannot go back once the truth comes out. We've spoken about this at length. We had an agreement—we agreed that the healthiest way for our family to approach this was for Reese to be spared from feeling different and now—"

"You imposed that on me! She's not your daughter, Mom! She's mine. You tried to convince me that this was the right thing to do. But it's not. Keeping the truth from Reese won't spare her from anything except a web of lies that will only cause her more pain down the track."

"Oh, please. You really believe that?"

"I can't let you do this anymore, Mom. I'm sorry, but it has to stop."

"Excuse me?"

"You have to stop interfering in my life! Telling me what to do, weighing in on all the major decisions I need to make and then suggesting I deal with them in a certain way. I can't do it anymore. So if you want to be a part of Reese's life, you'll have to accept my decision to tell her the truth. You'll need to support her. And that means accepting it yourself first. Because I don't want your preconceived ideas about things making her feel different or ashamed."

"Tell me something. After you tell Reese that Lucy is her mother, will you feel better?"

"Biological mother," I say through gritted teeth. "Yes…" I pause. "I will." I know I don't sound completely convincing because Mom turns back to the flowers and snips the bottom of the stem she's holding. "I wonder *why* you hesitated."

"I need your support, Mom. Once you're ready to offer it, come see me."

With that, I grab my keys and walk out the door, not bothering to look back.

Years ago, a counselor from West Park told us that there is no established way of telling a child they were conceived as a result of embryo donation. She also gave me a card for a local donor parent support group, and it's been tucked inside my purse for years. I make an appointment before heading to the kitchen. Today's the day Ben and I are finally telling Reese the truth.

Ben asks Reese if she wants ice cream for breakfast. He picks her up and sits her on the counter. "Chocolate-mint or vanilla?"

"Is that even a question?"

He tips his head back and laughs. "Let me guess? An extra drizzle of Magic Shell?"

She claps her hands together. "Now you're talking!"

With that, I open the freezer, take out a tub of Ben & Jerry's Mint Chocolate Chunk and hand it to Ben.

"Mom, I love your Christmas earrings," says Reese. The sincerity in her voice—the way she looks at me in total admiration—makes me weak at the knees. I sit down on a bar stool and watch as Ben scoops a ball of ice cream onto a cone. He gives the first one to Reese and then makes one for himself. He licks the drippy bits from his fingers while I sit quietly picking the stickers off the oranges in the fruit bowl, waiting for him to open up the conversation.

"Reese, we need to talk about something," he says. Whenever Ben needs to talk to Reese about something important, he always prefaces it by *telling* her he needs to talk to her. So, of course, she springs to attention.

"I got my letter in early enough. The elves should be able to get the bike parts."

"Huh?" I say.

"Christmas? My bike. Have the elves got things under control?"

"Yes," I say. "Of course they do."

"I FaceTimed Santa about thirty minutes ago," says Ben. He gives Reese the thumbs-up. "So yeah, we need to talk, Button."

Reese's eyes widen. "I'm sorry. I really love grape flavor and I wanted to make Bailey happy so I took it to school so I could show her what I could do. I shared it with her."

Ben rubs his forehead. Neither of us know what she's talking about.

Reese shrugs. "I gave her the biggest piece."

"What are you talking about, Button?" I ask.

"On the last day of school I took my Hubba Bubba with me so I could show Bailey my bubbles. I forgot to put the gum in the trash before class so I put it in the pocket of my school dress because everyone knows how much Mrs. Raynor hates bubblegum."

"Oh," is Ben's response.

Reese looks somewhat relieved. "Maybe the Hubba Bubba washed itself out of my pocket and went down the drain hole," she suggests.

"Mmm, maybe," says Ben. He clears his throat. "So yes, remember how we said we wished for you but you wouldn't come and then we needed to find another way?" he says, reminding her of one of our previous chats.

"Yep! I still have my Petri dish, and do you know that last week, I discovered that Alexander Fleming used one exactly like it to discover an important medicine that grew from bacteria because whatever was in it went moldy!"

"Really?" asks Ben, clearly impressed.

I give him a look that encourages him to get to the point.

"Yes! So I put the apple core that I found under my bed in it and maybe I'll be able to find the cure for whatever Larissa's dad died from. Maybe I can win a Nobel Prize like Marie Curie did!"

"That really is an excellent life goal, Reese. But just to go back to how you got here." He wipes some ice cream off her chin with his thumb. "Sweetheart, babies are made from a woman and a man. So in many cases, the baby's parents come together to form what's called an embryo. Mom and I—well, we needed some help, and that coming together is what happened in the Petri dish that made teeny-tiny you before anyone could see you without the help of a microscope. And the embryo was put inside Mommy and then you grew. You grew into what is called a fetus, and the fetus is what we eventually call a baby. Are you with me so far?"

Reese nods.

"But Daddy and I, we...we couldn't make our own embryo so another couple helped us. These lovely, very generous and kind people—a man and a woman—gave us three of their embryos and one of them became you."

"So you're my mom and dad, but not really?"

"Kind of," says Ben.

"No!" I say, interrupting. "That's not right at all."

"Isla," says Ben, putting his hand on my wrist. "Let me finish explaining it to her."

He turns back to Reese. "This couple—they gave you to us as a gift. What we call a selfless gift. They knew how much we wanted to become your parents and that is why they helped us."

Ben looks Reese in the eye. "You have your parents—me and Mommy. And the couple that gave you to us...they're your *biological* parents. All that means is that they helped make you. But Mom—she carried you in her belly, and she felt you kick, and then when it was time, she gave birth to you. Does that make sense?"

"Wait, so you and Mom are my parents but I have two other parents? They gave me to you?"

"Yes," says Ben, and I can tell he's starting to get emotional now.

I squeeze Reese's hands. "We are your parents, Reese. I don't ever want you to forget this, do you understand? We love you and this doesn't change a thing between us, okay?" I told myself I wouldn't cry but tears are rolling down my face. "Look at me, sweetie. I want you to remember this changes nothing between us. We waited to tell you the truth and chose today to tell you. But you can tell anyone you like, whenever you feel comfortable to, okay? This isn't a secret and it's nothing to ever feel ashamed about."

Reese sits there quietly. I can't tell if she's upset or simply letting the information sink in.

"What are their names?" she asks eventually, her tone flat.

Ben nods, encouraging me to tell her.

"Well, your biological dad recently passed away."

The moment Reese makes the connection, my heart sinks. "He's in heaven? My biological dad is in *heaven*?"

"Yes, he is."

"So how can I meet him if he's not here?"

I swallow the lump that's formed in my throat. "You can't, sweetheart. But he left a video diary just for you so you could know him a bit better. Whenever you're ready, we can watch it. But only if you want to. Okay?"

She doesn't respond and I feel the need to fill the silence.

"His name was Nate, Reese. The funeral we went to—when we said goodbye to Lucy's husband? That was . . . our goodbye to him."

Reese stares at me and for a moment I lose my footing. I can't help wondering if this is too much for her, but knowing I can't leave it at that, I continue.

"Reese, your biological mother is Lucy."

She cups her mouth.

"They're good people," I whisper.

"Very good people," chimes in Ben. "And we are very happy that Nate left you a special video so that you can find out all sorts of things about him if you want to."

Reese simply sits there and that's when I know we've done too much talking.

"Reese? Honey?"

"I don't care about a stupid video!" She drops her ice cream onto the floor and runs to her bedroom.

"Reese!" I call, about to go after her.

Ben reaches out a hand to stop me. "Give her some space—just a few minutes." He cups my face with his hands. "Breathe," he tells me. "It's going to be fine. She is going to be fine."

I fall into his arms, which wrap around me. It doesn't feel fine. It doesn't feel fine at all.

CHAPTER TWENTY-THREE

Lucy

Isla shows up at the boathouse, where I'm waiting for her with a hot coffee to go.

"How are things?"

The corners of Isla's mouth briefly turn upward and she shrugs. "Mmm, could be better," she says quietly. She sits down and stares out to the water. "Things didn't go the way we would have liked them to. Reese took the news badly."

I let out a sympathetic "Oh," feeling the weight of Isla's words settle on me. "So, um, what happened?"

"She got upset and went to her bedroom. Now she's refusing to talk about it. So I don't exactly know what she's thinking. I have a feeling she's processing things. But she's not asking questions and I wish she'd tell me what's going on in her head. Today would have been too much for her."

"Of course," I say. "This is huge for her."

"The thing is, I know Reese and I know she'll have questions. I just don't know why she's not asking them. She really warmed to you when she met you. She came home and didn't stop talking about you..."

"Hey," I say, reaching out for Isla's hand. "Maybe you don't need an answer to why she's not asking questions at the moment. I think she'll ask them once she's ready."

Isla shakes her head and wrestles the cap off her coffee cup. "In all these years, I kept trying to avoid the conversation, pretending like it was something I could sweep under the carpet. Now she knows and everyone was right—it is harder because she's older..."

"I could try talking to her... if you like? Just to let her know I'm here and it's safe for her to come to me for a chat—she can ask me anything. She can set up the terms around how she wants the relationship to go, assuming it fits with what you and Ben are comfortable with."

Isla sighs. "I don't know. I don't know what the best course of action is. I don't know if bringing you to her is the right way to go."

"I'm not a threat to you, Isla, and I never will be. I promise you that."

Isla meets my eyes. "I know you're not, but can I be honest with you?"

I make a face that says, *Humor me*, and she lets out a little laugh.

"There is a part of me that struggles with this. I'm worried about Reese seeing me differently—what if she resents me and Ben because of our decision and it changes our relationship with her? You know... when she was a baby and people used to say she looked like me or Ben, I had to stop myself from bursting into tears. At any medical appointments when doctors asked about family history and I had to explain things to them, I'd get so worked up that I couldn't even drive straight home afterward. Teachers sometimes notice things like her being good at something and they say, 'Does she get that from you or Ben?' and afterward, I sit in the car and feel this sense of... I don't know what it is... Loss? Yearning? Sorrow? Inadequacy? Whatever it is, I've wrestled with it, Lucy. I wish I didn't, but I do."

I take Isla's hand and guide her to stand. "Let's walk and talk." We slip our shoes off, grab our coffees, and walk along the sand.

"I think you're describing completely normal feelings. I think I'd feel the same way, especially since your mom hasn't exactly been supportive."

A pang of something—longing, maybe, for all the years I could have spent being some small part of Isla's life—sweeps through me. Just as I've had my own challenges with my relationship with my mother, she's had hers.

"Anyway, enough about me and Reese. How are you? How's life at home with Shirley?"

"Hmm," I say, thinking about the question. Where to start? "Well, things with Shirley are surprisingly getting better."

"Yeah?" says Isla, and she seems genuinely pleased to hear this.

"Yeah," I say, smiling to myself. I think of Nate and how much I know this would please him. He'd always encouraged me to get closer to Mom despite the wall I'd set up between us. "I think I'm in the process of forgiving her."

"Wow, that's . . . I'm happy to hear this. She always loved you, Lucy. Even when it seemed like she didn't care, I know she did."

I nod. "I think we expect our parents to be perfect."

Isla tips her head to the sky and laughs. "Oh, yeah. Spoiler alert!"

We laugh and then I turn to face her. "I want you to know that I forgive you too. I know you're carrying a weight with you, but Nate and I . . . As hard as it was, we understood."

"Thank you," she whispers.

I hug her and can smell the rose-scented moisturizer on her skin and the apple shampoo in her hair.

"I've missed you so much," she says. "So, so much."

"Me too," I whisper back. "Me too."

"Nate would be happy. To see us together today," I say, once we finish our coffees.

"Want to know something interesting?" says Isla. "Before Reese goes to sleep at night. Guess what she does."

"No idea."

"She pulls off her socks and tosses them on the floor."

"No way! That's genetic?" I say, surprised to hear that one of Nate's habits—one I used to moan about to Isla incessantly—has been passed on to Reese. What I would give to be able to pick up Nate's dirty socks off the bedroom floor again.

"I don't know! But it's what she does. I think about you all the time when she does that."

"What else?" I ask. "Tell me something about Nate. Is there anything else about Reese...that reminds you of Nate?"

"Apart from her laugh? She's totally into science."

"When we moved, Nate wouldn't let me throw out his science magazines from when he was a kid. Do you think...she'd want them?" For a second Isla goes quiet, like she's thinking about it, and I worry I've overstepped or made her uncomfortable. "Never mind, I don't think I remember where he put them anyway."

"Actually, I think she would really love them...so if you find them, I think she'd be happy to take them. You know, maybe one day—depending on how she goes with processing everything— she'd like to see some baby photos of you and Nate."

At the mention of the word "baby," my mind wanders back to Nate, and what life could have been like for us as parents.

When I don't answer, Isla flashes her palm in front of me. "You still there?"

I shake my head. "Yes, sorry. Of course. I'm sure Mom has loads of photos. I can ask Janet and Terry for Nate's down the road too."

"Did I say something wrong?" she asks, making me realize I'm the one that's gone silent. There's something else I want to talk to Isla about today but I don't know how to say it. How does one bring up the fact they donated an embryo and now would like it back, assuming it's still available? West Park still hasn't called me, and I was hoping they would have before bringing this up with Isla.

"No, not at all. I was just wondering…Did you and Ben ever try to have another child? Did you use the last embryo?"

"The emb…" Isla's voice trails off. She tries again. "Uh, no. We didn't. After Reese was born, I took some maternity leave, but not much. I threw myself into work so we could get ahead financially. That first year, there was no way we could have afforded another baby. I had to keep working. Same with the following year, and the year after that. By the time we got back on our feet, she was nearly six years old."

"It must have been really hard."

"It was. We got to five years and that's when Ben reached out to Nate."

"For permission to extend the storage limit. I remember that." I thought the reason they'd asked to renew the storage limit for the embryo was because they'd wanted to use it. They'd needed special permission from the Patient Review Panel.

"By that time Reese was starting school, and then it became more of a timing thing, and with each passing year it felt like it was never going to be the right time…" Isla bends down to pick up a shell and brushes the sand off it.

A sense of relief floods my body. "I need to ask you something."

"Sure."

"I want to have a baby."

For a second, I wonder whether Isla has heard me properly. She runs her fingers over the shell, eyes fixed on it. Eventually she looks up at me. "I think that's beautiful. Nate would have wanted to see you happy," she says. "Being able to look forward to a time where you meet someone, start a family—"

I shake my head. "No, uh, that's not what I mean. I don't want to meet anyone else. I want to have Nate's baby."

"*Nate's* baby?"

I nod. "If you didn't use the embryo, I..."

"Lucy, that's huge, but it..." She blinks at me, her eyes filled with something I can't quite pin. "It might not be possible."

My body stiffens. "The embryo is in storage. Of course it's possible." Sure, the odds of a successful pregnancy are a gamble, but it's not like it's impossible.

"You never wanted children," she whispers. "Nate isn't here to have a say, to tell you what he would want. I think it's natural for you to...I don't know...want a part of him back in your life, but...have you really thought about this and whether it's something you truly want?" Isla swallows and clears her throat. "You never wanted kids. You were never interested in having children. You said you wanted to travel and focus on your career and live this adventurous life that would leave no room for having a baby. That's what you said."

"I know. And at the time, that was all true. I'm not traveling for work anymore. For the first time in my life, I'm grounded. Nate had a wake-up call earlier this year. He changed his mind. He wanted to be a dad. We spoke about it before the accident."

"Oh, Lucy..." Isla sighs, and the pity in her voice makes me almost feel silly, like this is something I want but can't have, not only because Nate is no longer alive but because she obviously assumes it isn't a sound decision on my part.

"He changed his mind. We're allowed to pivot. We're allowed to change course. We are allowed to make room for what we never saw coming," I say, feeling the need to justify myself.

"I think you're grieving. Meeting Reese has probably brought up a lot of stuff for you too."

"You think I'm not serious about this, don't you?"

"That's not what I meant at all. I just think—"

"Nobody goes skiing down a mountain expecting to spend life alone from that moment."

"You're not alone. You have...me."

"Do I?"

Isla rubs her temple. "Of course you do. We're starting afresh, aren't we?"

"I just told you I want a baby and it doesn't exactly feel like I have your support."

Isla inhales slowly before talking. I know she's choosing her words carefully. "Lucy, I had a preconception check-up and I have an appointment booked for West Park in a couple of weeks."

"I'm sorry, what?"

"Ben and I...we would like another baby. Before it's too late."

"When were you going to tell me? I mean, you just said you waited all this time and you made it sound like you missed the boat..."

"You donated the embryos to us—I didn't know that came with a caveat to tell you the exact moment we would decide to use it."

"You know that's not what I'm referring to here. I told you Nate and I talked about this."

"Exactly! You said you talked about it, not that you actually wanted your embryo back to have a baby now that he's gone!" Isla raises her hands to her temple again and blows out a long breath. "I wanted to talk to you about this today—I wanted to let you know Ben and I are doing this...I wanted to make sure you knew ahead of time *because* you'd been thinking about things before Nate died. I didn't want an eventual pregnancy to be a shock for you," she says.

"Isla, you can't do this."

She stares out to the water, blinking in disbelief. "Lucy...I've been waiting years for this."

"I don't want this to be the thing that divides us. Not after you just told Reese the truth."

As I watch her walk away, sandals in one hand, arm raised to her face as she wipes tears from her eyes, I wonder if I can go through losing her again. Because if I do this, I might gain a child of my own, but I'll lose her and Reese in the process.

CHAPTER TWENTY-FOUR

Isla

My hands are trembling so much I can barely start the car. Just when Ben and I finally, after all these years, decide to try to have another baby, the opportunity is being pulled away from us. It takes me back to the endless cycles of IVF—the moments of hope followed by crushing disappointment.

Ben's car is in the driveway when I get home. I push open the front door, dump my bag on the hallway table, and call out for him. "Ben!"

"Up here!" he calls from the top of the staircase, where he's standing on a ladder changing a smoke alarm battery.

"I knew I shouldn't have let myself get attached to the idea."

Ben looks at me quizzically and makes his way down the stairs. "Isla, take a breath."

I start pacing the kitchen. "I mean, there's every chance a transfer could fail, but... *this*. I did not expect this."

"What are you talking about?"

"I've just seen Lucy. She wants the embryo back."

"Breathe," says Ben, holding me by the shoulders as he guides me toward a chair at the kitchen table. He pulls it out for me and motions for me to sit.

He goes to the fridge, takes out two bottles—a beer for him and a Coke for me—and nudges the door closed with his elbow. "Let me get this straight. She told you she wants it back so she can have a baby?"

I lift my hands in despair. "What else would she want to do with it, Ben?"

"Sorry, but it's not like it hasn't come out of left field. What am I supposed to think?"

"How do we feel about this?" I ask, trying to keep my voice even.

Ben twists the cap off my bottle and hands it to me. "Well, I suppose I understand where she's coming from."

"She never wanted to become a mother. Those embryos were never meant for her and Nate. They were intended for *us* to create a family."

"That's true. But something obviously changed?"

"She said she and Nate were discussing things right before he died."

"Okay, so then life dealt her a shitty hand and she changed her mind. People get to change their minds, Isla. She was twenty-seven at the time of donating."

"How can you be so calm about this?! You wanted us to have another baby, Ben! Do we have any rights here at all? If we want to use it because it was donated to us, where do we even stand?"

Ben perches himself against the table and takes a moment to reflect on things. "First of all, I did want us to have another baby. I still do . . ." He stops himself. "But . . . I actually don't know what our rights are."

"Does this mean we could actually lose the right to use the embryo?"

Ben pulls out a chair and sits down. "I think we need to take this one step at a time. We need to approach this calmly." Trust Ben to say this. The very fact he needs to point this out unsettles me.

The room goes quiet as he takes a sip of his beer. "Nate died," he says pensively. "There are laws about this kind of thing. Who knows if those laws might even apply to *us* using the embryo."

This is something neither of us has even considered.

"Assuming she does get permission to use it—the baby would be Reese's biological sibling."

"Well, yeah, that's true," he says, nodding slowly, like it's suddenly dawning on him.

"I didn't want Reese's life to be complicated like this."

"And it won't have to be."

"Oh. Yeah. Sure. It's taken us—*me*—years to get the courage to tell Reese the truth about things, and now we're potentially going to pile it on because in the near future we might also be dealing with Lucy having her biological sibling? Look at how she reacted to the news! She barely spoke to me this morning before your dad picked her up."

Ever since Nate passed away it feels like my body is a tightly bound spool of thread, unraveling, with no way to stop. "Would we even get a say? As to whether she can have it back?" I continue.

"I don't think we'd have a say," surmises Ben after a while. "It's her biological child."

"Potential biological child," I correct.

"Isla, I don't want to sound insensitive here but Nate's gone. Pretty sure you can't just waltz into a clinic, ask for an embryo back, and then do something with it. But even if she ultimately can use it, surely you don't *want* to have a say as to whether she does or not? I mean, it's not really our place to do that, is it?"

"I really want another baby." I know this doesn't quite answer his question, but it's the only response I can give him.

Christmas comes and goes, bringing with it a forecast of gloriously warm weather. I gather an armful of towels and take them out to the backyard. Reese is already in her bathing suit and Ben's tearing off the wrapper from a can of sunscreen. She extends her arms out in front of her, closes her eyes, and waits for him to spray.

"Are you getting in?" asks Ben as he adjusts the umbrella beside my recliner.

"Maybe later. I don't really feel like it right now," I say. I'd managed to get through Christmas Day without anyone suspecting I had other things on my mind, but now that the festivities are over I can't help but focus on what Lucy told me.

Ben eyes me and frowns. "Come on, it'll help get your mind off things."

Once Reese gets into the pool, Ben maneuvers himself onto a lounger so he's sitting opposite me and takes his sunglasses off. "I know you're upset and scared about what this could mean for us, but let's try to take it step by step. Does Lucy know we were close to using the embryo? Why don't you talk to her again and see if this is something she's serious about?"

"Of course she's serious about it. Why else would she mention it to me?" I stare up at the clouds and watch them drifting across the sky. "She's grieving Nate, right after they were deciding whether or not to have a baby. Part of me is worried that she's not thinking straight—that she's potentially making a life-changing decision based on her grief. She'd be raising the child without him, Ben. What happens when she realizes nothing—not even a baby—is going to bring him back?"

"Maybe we need to give her the benefit of the doubt." He shrugs. "If you try to convince her she's making a mistake, you'll just seem callous."

There's no way I can deny this, yet I'm not prepared to give up on the decision to have this baby.

"Remember what it was like when they told us we wouldn't be able to conceive naturally? That moment when we realized we would never be able to have a baby without help? It was like someone ripped away a part of my heart." I turn my head toward Ben. "And now... it feels..."

"The same," he says, finishing my sentence. He gets up and sits on the edge of my recliner. He moves the hair away from my face. "I know this is hard but we can talk to the clinic and find out exactly where things stand. Lucy's grieving. She might change her mind and realize this isn't what she actually wants."

"What if she doesn't? What if she's already decided and won't back down? What then?"

Ben sighs. "Like I said. Step by step."

"When my mom finds out about this new installment…" There's no telling how she'll react.

"What?" challenges Ben. "She'll sell the house out from under us? Withdraw her investment in the business?"

Ben stands up and throws a stray tennis ball across the lawn with such force that the thud against the fence disrupts a terracotta planter hanging from it. "Let her. If that's what she wants to do after she finds out, then so be it. I think she's done enough damage already, don't you think?"

The following day I keep my appointment with Diana, from the donor parent support group. We had a twenty-minute chat on the phone before the appointment and she made me feel at ease, but now that I'm sitting with her face to face, I'm almost lost for words.

"Start wherever you like, Isla," she says, obviously sensing my discomfort. "I'm all ears."

"Well, my husband, Ben, and I have a nine-year-old daughter who is donor-conceived. We accepted donated embryos from my best friend and her now late husband. We have one remaining embryo in storage. We're hoping to have another baby soon. The only problem is that now my friend wants to use it."

Diana tilts her head in curiosity. "You both want to use the same embryo?"

I nod, threading my fingers together. "I don't want to hurt my friend, but a part of me can't seem to let go. Ben and I waited a long time for this—we always said we intended to use all three embryos, only the timing was never right . . . until now. So I don't know how to *not* fight for this." I pause to take a breath. "I know we have a daughter but I've become attached to the idea of having a brother or sister for her."

"This is big," she says, tearing open a packet of sugar. She pours it into her tea. "I think the best thing would be for you all to sit down and talk about it together—the clinic can organize that for you. No doubt both your emotions are running high—it'll help you to have someone impartial guide you through this. You don't want it to get messy."

"That's a good idea," I say, thinking that it sounds terrible.

"You don't sound convinced."

Even though I know Diana's right, the thought of confrontation in front of a counselor isn't appealing. Time is running out, though—the embryo can't stay in storage forever. We need to figure things out, and the only way that can happen is if we find a way to talk about it.

"What's your daughter's name?" asks Diana.

"Uh, Reese. Her name is Reese."

Diana smiles. "Why don't you tell me a little more about Reese. You can start wherever you like."

I lift my mug and cup it with my hands. "Well, for a long time—up until very recently, in fact—Ben and I had been keeping Reese's conception story from her. Mostly on my insistence. Ben wanted for us to be up-front right from the beginning, actually. Every year he'd actively encourage me to agree to tell her about it, but . . . I always said no." I inwardly cringe, waiting for Diana to begin waxing lyrical about how the best way to approach these matters is to tell a child the truth.

To my surprise, she simply takes a sip of her tea. "So, Reese now knows?"

"She hasn't taken it well, and all my fears about this—it feels like they're all coming true." I swallow past the lump that has formed in my throat.

"Go on..." encourages Diana. "Take your time."

"When I was pregnant with Reese, my mother gave me some compelling reasons as to why she didn't believe it was a good idea to disclose the truth to her or anyone else—family, friends, and so on. I realize now that I should have done more—to challenge that, to look into it more—but it was easier, more convenient not to, because..." My voice cracks. "Because I think I need help dealing with it. I have... *feelings* about the donor conception that I don't think I've quite resolved after all this time."

I take a deep breath. "There were days, especially early on in Reese's life, where people would comment on how she looked like me or Ben and it would affect me for days. I shied away from mothers' groups and became adept at dodging comments about the similarities between us and our daughter. There were times I felt ashamed of my inability to conceive my own biological child, and other times that I worried incessantly about Reese rejecting me and Ben if she ever found out the truth. Because my mother made it into this thing that should be kept secret at all costs, I felt like there was shame in it—when clearly there shouldn't be. I adore my daughter but sometimes I still feel sadness about not being able to conceive her without help." I feel myself getting flustered, the conflicting emotions tumbling around inside of me like lotto balls in a machine.

"Okay," says Diana. "First of all, Reese's reaction? Normal. As her parents it'll be up to you to provide a sense of security and confidence about this. So how about we work on that together?"

The fact that Diana says this is something we can actually work on gives me hope.

"Let's take a breath." She raises a hand, takes in a breath, and then lowers her hand as she exhales, encouraging me to do the same.

"Great. Now why don't we start by acknowledging the grief?"

"But nobody died," I say, not understanding what she means.

Diana takes a slow sip of her tea and puts her mug down. "Sweetheart, let me explain it to you."

They say hindsight is one of those things that we wish we had. Coming out of my chat with Diana, I learned that we can't always spare our children from hurt. As for the grief, Diana explained that it is normal for parents in my situation to feel sad at times about the loss of being able to naturally conceive a child. I'd also lost a best friend—someone I was as close to as a sister. Diana helped me understand that I could still love Reese unconditionally while acknowledging the grief I feel about not being able to have a child in the way I had hoped for. I know she's right because when I look at Reese I know—beyond a shadow of doubt—that she is everything we ever wanted, and there is nothing that can change that. Ever.

CHAPTER TWENTY-FIVE

Lucy

Helen, the fertility lawyer, ushers me into a large Melbourne office offering views of the city. I've always loved the city—its trendy cafés and restaurants, the botanical gardens and City Circle trams. For so long, Nate and I never really had a place to call home. Now that he's gone, when I think of home, I don't automatically think of the house we renovated in the suburbs, but I think of Sorrento. The beach. The shopping centers. Ice-cream vans and flocks of tourists from Melbourne. Boats and jet skis and packages of fish and chips on the beach.

"How are things, Lucy?" asks Helen, motioning for me to sit down. "Why don't you elaborate on our phone call and give me an idea of how I can help you."

I bring Helen up to speed with the situation and wait for her response.

"Okay," she says, as if she's registering the information and filing it away somewhere. She raises her index finger. "Let's recap." She takes notes as she speaks. "You and your late husband donated three embryos to the Sutherland couple. One transfer failed, the second resulted in a live birth, and the third is still in storage but has almost reached the ten-year limit. The clinic has placed the embryo in lockdown since you expressed an interest in making an application for posthumous use of it."

"That's about it."

"So you don't have any other embryos in storage that were intended for you and Nate to use?"

"No."

Helen slides a pair of glasses off and pours herself a glass of water. "Okay, well, first of all, I'd like to review the consent forms and determine whether your husband—"

"Nate."

"Whether Nate allowed for the posthumous use of the embryos. Do you have the consent forms here with you?"

I do, and I've already checked them. "He didn't give his consent in any of the paperwork," I say as I hand the forms over for Helen to verify. She confirms that Nate and I had not left any written instructions about the use of our embryos after our eventual deaths.

"Things aren't as straightforward as what you would like them to be, Lucy," she says after a beat.

It isn't what I want to hear.

"An application to the Patient Review Panel would be your best course of action from here." Helen explains that the role of the panel is to review any applications regarding the posthumous use of gametes and embryos, or related assisted reproductive treatment requests, and it will likely involve a hearing. "There are some steps you'd need to take before lodging it, and that includes revoking permission for the Sutherlands to use the embryo, counseling with West Park, and having them provide you with a report. Now, that's the easy part."

"Then what's the hard part?" I ask, partly afraid of her answer.

Helen pulls a form out of the folder on her desk, pushes a manicured finger down the page to Section 7, and waits for me to read it. I feel a rush of cold whip through me.

"Do you have *anything* in writing stating that Nate consented to the posthumous use of his embryos in the event of his death?"

"It needs to be that specific?"

Helen nods. "In the state of Victoria, yes."

They want specific proof. Proof I don't have. All I have is a letter, expressing his desire to become a father. A letter he gave me the day before he died.

The question is, where is the letter now?

"So, that's it?"

"Well, there is one other avenue we could pursue," she says. Helen is to the point and I like this about her but I can't help feeling deflated. Of course I knew this wouldn't be straightforward—not by any means—but still, it makes me question whether I have the resolve to actually put myself through this.

"Here in Victoria, the Assisted Reproductive Treatment Act is very clear on the type of written consent that is required in order for the panel to be able to consider an application. However, if we were to request the transportation of the embryo to a clinic in another state or territory, like the ACT, we might be able to place an application there. As long as there's no evidence that says Nate did not consent to the posthumous use of the embryo, and there is some sort of material you can produce that demonstrates you were planning a family, there is a possibility it may be approved."

"I have a letter Nate wrote me. I don't remember his exact words but he said he wanted us to have a baby."

"That could be helpful," says Helen. "Shall we put the wheels in motion, then?"

My mind starts spinning. If I allow Helen to formalize things, can I ultimately find peace knowing I didn't at least reach out to Isla to see if there's any way she might accept this decision? There's no doubt in my mind that if I go through with this today without Ben and Isla's blessing, I risk losing both Isla and Reese forever.

"What are you doing?" asks Mom, as she traipses through the living room later that night with a watering can, moving from one indoor plant to another. I'm sitting on the rug in the middle of the room with two storage boxes filled with photos of me and Nate that I brought home from Melbourne. Earlier, I popped into our house to see if I could find Nate's letter but I had no success. I cannot for the life of me remember where I put it.

Mom comes over to have a better look. "Wow, you really got around, didn't you?" she says. Most of the photos are of us outside of Australia. On the back of each photo I've started noting dates and countries and a short reflection of what made our time there special. Some photos have captions like, *Nate tried the escargot and hated it!* and, *The Norwegian fjords were item 127 on Lucy's travel bucket list and we made it there in 2015! Her favorite was the Geirangerfjord.*

"I don't want to forget him, Mom."

She squeezes my shoulder. "So you went back home today?" she asks, picking up one of the photos.

"I went to see a lawyer."

"A lawyer?" She sounds surprised.

"For some advice about the embryo—to find out what's possible and what isn't."

Mom presses her lips together.

"You don't think it's a good idea?"

"I don't want to see you disappointed, that's all." She hands the photo back to me. "How does Isla feel about it?"

"She's upset. Obviously. The timing isn't great. They only just told Reese about me."

Mom cringes. "So how will that affect things between the two of you?"

"I don't know, Mom. She told me she and Ben intended to use it."

"*They* want another baby? And now you want a baby?"

I frown at her and nod. "Messy, huh?"

"Oh, Lucy."

"I didn't want to hurt her, Mom. I don't want to hurt anyone, but Nate and I—we *wanted* a baby and this is my only chance to have that. I don't want to fast-forward to a time years from now, meet someone else, and have a baby then. I'm approaching forty. I don't want to wait for things to *maybe* fall into place. I want Nate's baby and I know he would be on board with this. I just know it."

I stand up and stare out the window. "I just wish there was a way to not hurt Isla in the process. It's like I'm taking away something that belongs to her."

"Well, it's certainly not straightforward."

"Does this make me a horrible person? If I get permission to do this, and I go ahead with it, will I be able to find peace in that decision? I'm scared about what it means if I can't. I want her in my life, Mom. And I don't want to lose the chance to know Reese either."

"I don't have the answer for you, sweetheart. She's like family to you. It sounds like you need to talk to her. Sit down properly and have a chat. You love each other too much to walk away from each other again."

I agree with Mom but at the same time wonder how it can possibly work. I am the last person Isla wants to talk to right now. And it's not simply a matter of picking up the phone and talking to her—we both want the same, incredibly precious, important thing and no matter what, I can't let go—I won't back down.

The next morning, when Mom's at the studio teaching a yoga class, the doorbell rings. I don't recognize the car out front, a flashy black one, that's partially obstructing the footpath.

When I answer the front door, I don't immediately recognize the woman standing in front of me either. She's wearing a pair of linen pants with a blouse tucked into it, and around her shoulders

sits a thin, pale-blue sweater, fastened at the cuffs. This signature
style belongs to Isla's mom. Yes, Elinor Tippett is standing on my
doorstep and she doesn't look happy.

"Elinor…"

"Lucy, hello. Mind if I come in?" She steps forward anyway
and I watch her enter Mom's living room, where she slowly moves
her head, taking it all in.

"Your mother's done a wonderful job with her home. Lovely."

"Can I get you something to drink?"

"That won't be necessary. I won't be staying long."

I sit down on the sofa and watch her do the same opposite me.

"What brings you—"

"Let me get straight to the point," she says. "I'm here for Reese's
sake."

"Does Isla know you're here?"

Elinor presses her lips together and shakes her head. "Goodness
no. And nor will she find out." She pins me with her gaze. "I'd like
your cooperation with that if possible." She clears her throat. "Isla
informed me that she's told Reese that she's donor-conceived and
that you're her biological mother. Contrary to what Isla believes, I
don't think this is the right way for this to be handled. But what's
done is done, and to avoid any further upheaval to our family,
I think it's best if you don't pursue a relationship with either of
them from here on. It's the best outcome in what has become a
horrendously messy situation." She mutters under her breath,
presumably to herself, "As I predicted all along."

"Elinor, I've never pursued anything with Isla, Ben, and Reese.
When Isla came to Nate's funeral, she had a choice whether to
bring Reese or not. Now if Reese wants to know me—whether
now or down the line—she'll be welcomed with open arms, and I
won't be bullied into anything 'contrary' just because you think—"

"I need you to stay away from them, Lucy. I've warned Isla, and
when I came to her rescue all those years ago, it was conditional."

My heart starts beating furiously in my chest. "How can you impose something like this on your daughter?" I say in disbelief. "She's lived almost a decade carrying the unnecessary guilt and shame *you* put on her shoulders. I am not a threat and never will be. I know she's upset with me but she needs your support, especially now."

Elinor swallows, her eyes cast downward. But then she looks up and tilts her head. "She's upset with you," she says and I can't tell if there's an air of curiosity in her voice or if she's simply restating what I told her.

"Nate and I wanted a baby. I didn't know that after all this time Ben and Isla intended on using the embryo. She made it sound like their time had passed...that it was too late."

Elinor's expression hardens. "You want to use the embryo?"

"Yes," I whisper.

"Hmm. So you gave her a gift and now you're taking it away," she says.

"It's not like that," I reply, but her comment disarms me. Putting it like that makes it sound so clear-cut, black and white, when in truth the situation is anything but.

Elinor stands up and makes her way to the front door. "I think it's best if you stay away from my daughter, Lucy."

CHAPTER TWENTY-SIX

Isla

When I call West Park, I'm passed to a woman named Charlotte who, by the sounds of it, has been expecting my call. In fact, she already knows who I am and tells me she also knows Lucy. It turns out Lucy has been in to see her.

"I can see here we have an appointment booked for you. Can I ask what that might be in relation to?"

"My husband and I—we want to use the embryo."

"Ah, right, I see," says Charlotte. Her voice is kind, but it also unnerves me since she falls silent for a moment. "Have you been in touch with the surviving donor?" Even though she knows Lucy's name, she doesn't use it.

"Yes, I have been," I say.

I turn the coffee machine on and press the button for a double shot when Charlotte puts me on hold to find my file. If Lucy has taken the time to make inquiries about the embryo, it means this isn't a fleeting thought—it's more than that. She's obviously serious about this.

"Sorry for the wait," says Charlotte, now back on the line. "I have your file in front of me and I need to inform you that we've locked down the embryo."

"What does that even mean?" I ask, the milk spilling over my mug.

"As you know, one of the donors is deceased and the female surviving partner has expressed an intention to make a claim."

"Lucy," I say.

"Yes. Lucy," she repeats before pausing. "Isla, I would like you and Ben to come in for some counseling if that's something you're open to. And I'd like to suggest the same for Lucy. This situation is unique and complex, and if we can, we'd like to support both parties to work through things. Especially since both parties have expressed an interest in the embryo. At this stage, Lucy hasn't revoked access for you and Ben to use it, but at the same time, there is legislation that applies for any posthumous use of embryos and gametes. And I can tell you that we don't have an advance directive from the deceased donor that says he permitted this. Then, of course, there's the issue of the storage limit, which has almost been reached."

I pour the soupy coffee down the sink and push the button to make a fresh one, only I forget to slide the mug onto the drip tray.

"Ugh."

"I know this must be very hard to hear."

"I was referring to the coffee. Sorry. Never mind." I hesitate, but I need to get the question out. "What if Ben and I are opposed to Lucy using the embryo? Where does that leave us?"

Charlotte doesn't answer the question. Instead, she simply asks, "When can you and Ben come in, Isla?"

Charlotte makes the appointment and later confirms Lucy will be there, too.

"Things are already so complicated. If she goes ahead with this, how are we supposed to pile that onto Reese?"

"Isn't 'complicated' the definition of family?" says Ben, perfectly serious in tone.

"Oh, come on, surely this would be something pretty huge for Reese to handle."

Ben sits up straighter. "But would it be? Or would it be huge for you?"

I close the laptop.

"She's your best friend. And finally there's the opportunity to have her back in your life after everything that's happened. If Lucy ends up having a baby, couldn't that actually be something nice for Reese? Doesn't it all come down to how we decide to look at this?"

"Nice? It would be weird, Ben! This was not the plan. And this changes everything. How can we possibly have Reese enter into a relationship with her if she has a baby? It would be her biological sibling!"

Ben lifts his arms in defense. "Just putting it out there. I honestly don't think it would be an issue unless we decided to make it one."

I twist my body so I'm facing Ben. "I don't want her using it." I take a deep breath. "I know it makes me sound like a horrible person, but—"

"Actually, Isla, there are no buts…"

Ben turns the TV off and slumps into the couch, letting his neck lean against the top of the couch.

On Tuesday morning, I realize at the last minute that Reese has a dental appointment. She's been feeling better since Ben and I told her about Lucy, and has started asking questions about her, which I've tried to answer as honestly as possible.

"No cavities!" says Reese, tapping her teeth as she settles into the passenger seat of the car and admires the brand-new ice-cream-shaped eraser she earned herself as a reward from Dr. Cleverley.

"Good job, Button."

"Remember when I told you Bailey is adopted? Well, her mom said she can't meet her mom and dad because they're both in heaven," she says on the way home. "She wants to meet Lucy."

"Bailey wants to meet Lucy?"

"Yeah," she says, as if it's a perfectly normal request. "She wants to ask her some things for our investigation."

"Oh, okay, well...maybe one day she'll be able to meet her." One step at a time, I tell myself. Surely if any adult in my life is going to understand how delicate this situation is, it'll be Ellen, Bailey's mom. Who knows, maybe she'll be a good person for me to talk to about things.

"Can we see Lucy today?" presses Reese.

How can I let Reese spend time around Lucy when we're at odds about something so huge—something that, no matter the outcome, will affect Reese too? At the same time, if I say no, she'll cotton on to the fact things aren't right.

"I think she's busy today, Button," I reply, in the hope I can buy some time. This is something Ben and I are going to need to talk about as soon as possible.

"What about tomorrow?" she asks.

"She's busy all week, I think. I'll have to check with her."

"Tell her I need to ask her if she has curly hair underneath her straight hair. Does she use a machine to make her hair go straight?"

We get out of the car and Reese heads straight to the sofa. She flops onto it and opens up her notebook. "Lucy has blue eyes and I do too. That's because it's *genetical*."

"Genetic," I say, feeling a bout of nausea swirl through me as I start unpacking the groceries we picked up before the dentist. I check my phone. Another two missed calls from Mom. I keep ignoring them because I don't want to have to deal with her as well right now.

"Could we see if she has photos of Nate because I want to see his eyes. And his hair. And I have to ask Lucy if she can roll her tongue."

"She can't."

"How would you know?"

"Because I know everything about Lucy."

"Then why can't we see her?"

"Because she's busy."

"No, she's not. She's here for the whole summer. With Shirley. In Sorrento."

I turn around to face Reese and rest a hand on my hip. "How could you possibly know this?"

"Because Peaches and I were listening to you and Dad whispering for fifteen hours under the stairs."

"Is that how the box of crackers got there?"

She shrugs as if she has no idea what I'm talking about. "So can we see her?"

"Reese, stop pushing me, okay! No means no."

She snaps her notebook closed. "But you didn't say no! You just said she was busy!" She crosses her arms. "You lied!"

Somehow I forget I'm holding a bag of oranges and they tumble out of the netting one by one, thudding to the ground.

"You are the worst, Mom! I bet Lucy doesn't lie. I bet Lucy would be a good mom and not grumpy like you! You ruin *everything*."

The oranges. Peaches barking. Reese yelling. Mom's pressure. Lucy potentially having a baby. Ben and I potentially *not* having a baby. It's all too much.

Reese's voice booms through the room. "You always tell me not to lie and then you lie, lie, lie! You're a big liar and Mrs. Raynor says liars need to think very hard about their actions!"

That's the moment I burst into tears.

CHAPTER TWENTY-SEVEN

Lucy

I arrive at West Park before Isla and Ben. Charlotte welcomes me and breaks the ice by telling me about her holiday plans—she's booked a road trip with her daughter. They're planning on traveling the east coast of Australia in a camper van.

"Try not to be nervous," she says encouragingly. "Often these sessions are all that's needed to iron things out between donors and recipients." I know she means well, but Isla and I have a history.

Ben enters the room first, wearing a pair of navy shorts and a white shirt with his cuffs rolled up, exposing his tanned skin. He blinks a couple of times before a timid smile creeps onto his face when our eyes lock.

"Lucy...it's good to see you," he says softly.

"In the flesh," I say, standing up to greet him properly. We might be here under unusual circumstances but this is still Ben, the guy who was once one of Nate's closest friends.

He hesitates with his arms outstretched and then pulls them back, but it's too late because I've stepped into the hug. "It's good to see you again." He pulls away and takes a seat while Isla and I exchange nods.

"Lucy, hi," she says, before taking a seat.

"Thanks for coming."

Charlotte begins by giving an introduction as to what to expect from the session. Then she reiterates to us as a group why we're here: to see if we can navigate this situation so everyone is at peace with the way forward, whatever the outcome.

"I'd like some clarification if possible, Charlotte," says Isla.

"Sure."

"Obviously you've invited us all here today to talk about things but I'd really like to get an idea of exactly what rights each of us has. If each of us wants to use the embryo—who actually gets the last say?"

I keep my eyes pinned on Charlotte even though I already know the answer. I don't want Isla to hear it from her. I clear my throat.

"Charlotte, before you go into things, I'd like to say something, please."

"Go ahead," she says, nodding.

"You both should know that I've withdrawn my consent for you to use the embryo. I—"

"Wait, she can do that?" says Isla.

"Isla..." says Ben, reaching for her arm. He rests his hand there and doesn't move it.

"Lucy is within her rights to do that," confirms Charlotte. She goes on to explain the laws here in Victoria but it seems Isla is only half listening.

"Wait, so what does that mean? If we want to use it, do we need to make some kind of appeal or something?"

Ben gives me a sympathetic look, but I can tell that underneath he's hurt. "Isla, please. Let's just take it easy, okay."

She fires him a look and then turns her attention back to Charlotte, who leaps in:

"Ben, I think it's very normal for there to be a reaction like this from Isla. Obviously emotions are running high on both sides, so let's all take a deep breath."

"I don't want to hurt either of you, and at the same time I don't know how to make it easier for you," I say.

"Ben, Isla, there's another issue at play here that you may not be aware of and this ties in with the legalities about the donation and the posthumous use of the embryo. You see, Nate and Lucy at the time of donation didn't put anything in writing that allowed for the use of the embryo if either party was to pass away."

"What are you saying exactly?" asks Ben. "That we wouldn't be able to use it anyway?" he says, answering his own question.

"So how can Lucy use it, then?" Isla asks.

"There's a process involved, with no guarantee of the outcome," explains Charlotte. "That aside, my understanding after talking to you both separately is that Reese has recently been made aware of the fact that she's donor-conceived and that Lucy is her donor parent. So let me ask the three of you—do you want Reese to have an ongoing relationship with the donor parent?"

I'm the first to say yes, followed by Ben and Isla.

"Well, that's a start. What I'd like to do now is talk a little bit about another point that's just as important."

The three of us look at each other.

"Your friendship," says Charlotte. "While it might take some time for Ben and Isla to accept the loss of their right to use the embryo, I imagine it's also going to be difficult to accept the fact that Lucy wants to use it. Of course, we don't know the outcome of that or whether it will result in the birth of a child that's biologically related to Reese. But regardless of how things turn out, I imagine this whole process, given your history as friends, is going to be something quite difficult for Lucy as well since she mentioned before that her intention here isn't to hurt anyone. How about we talk about it?"

Charlotte is effectively asking us to lay it all out on the table in front of her. When neither Ben nor Isla says anything, Charlotte prompts me. "Lucy, if this was to be amicably resolved, what would that look like for you?"

"I'd like to make it work. I know we can do that but at the same time I know you're both upset and it *does* feel like I'm taking something away from you. But this embryo is a part of Nate and me. I'm not a mother yet."

"And we have Reese," says Ben quietly.

Isla stares at her lap.

"Isla, please, say something," I say. Suddenly, I'm crying. "I don't want to do this without you. I don't want to do this without you in my life. I can only do this if you give me your blessing."

She scrunches her eyes closed and presses a hand over her face. "I can't support it—I can't support it because it's not just about me. It's about Reese, too."

Of course. It always comes down to her fears about Reese.

Half an hour later, when Charlotte calls the meeting to a close and Ben offers an apologetic smile on his way out, we are no closer to resolving anything. And having a baby feels further away than it ever has before.

When I get home, Mom is waiting in the living room, the table set and my favorite dinner on the table—seafood risotto.

"Thanks, Mom," I say, pulling out a chair.

"You look as bad as you did on the day of the funeral," she says as she puts my plate in front of me. "Stop slouching; it's not good for your posture."

"I can't see this working, Mom. It's either a baby or Isla and her family in my life. I don't think there's any way I can have both. You know what the worst part is? I could go through all of this and still not end up with a baby, losing her and Reese and Ben in the process."

Mom sits down on the chair beside me and puts her arm around my shoulder. "I know how much it hurt when you lost her the first time, Lucy, especially since you lost me, too. But this is the chance for you to build a life for yourself with the creation of your own family."

"But I consider *Isla* family, Mom. This will hurt her. I don't want to do it without her finding peace with it but I might not have a choice."

"Do you want me to talk to her?"

I shake my head. "No. I think we need to leave her be for now."

Mom goes to speak and stops herself, then tries again. "I can be here for you, Lucy. If you want to have this baby, and decide to go through with things, I can help you. You could move here—with me...I promise you that if that's what you want, I will do better this time."

"Move in here?"

What she's proposing...it would mean bringing my entire life back here to Sorrento. To start afresh. Alongside *her*. For years I've taken conscious steps to avoid my mother—to keep her at an arm's length despite Nate's constant gentle nudges toward finding a way to repair what had long ago fractured. Of course, it isn't like Mom and I detest each other, but my resentment about her behavior and the choices she made drove a wedge between us that until now has remained firmly in place. But now, looking at Mom, the sincerity in her eyes, the deep longing to hold me, to feel useful and wanted, but mostly to have the love she holds in her heart accepted, is something I couldn't deny her.

Despite her mistakes, there's something wonderfully human about Mom offering to *be* there for me. She's a woman who acknowledged her mistakes and actively worked toward becoming the best version of herself she could be.

"Just something to think about," she says, patting my thigh. A flash of embarrassment crosses her face when I don't immediately answer her.

"Mom, wait...I...thank you. I think it could be something to consider. *If* it eventuates."

CHAPTER TWENTY-EIGHT

Isla

The following afternoon I get home from taking Reese to Bailey's for a play date when Ben tells me my mom has called. More than once.

"I told her you were tied up but she said it was urgent. Actually, her words were, 'This is of utmost importance,'" he says from the bench seat in the front garden, where he's trying to get his lawn aerator shoes on. According to the saleswoman at Bunnings, they were this year's hottest Christmas gift for men. I'd been skeptical but bought them anyway, and Ben has diligently been wearing them in the hope of transforming our summer lawn into the envy of our neighbors.

He stands up and starts walking across the grass. "Ha! These shoes are fabulous," he says with a chuckle. I don't know how he can be in such a good mood after the appointment at West Park, especially since he was so quiet on the drive home, and I know he didn't sleep much last night, but this is Ben, and I shouldn't be surprised. He has a way of bouncing back that gives Reese a run for her money.

"We'll talk more later. I've been thinking about things and I think we should talk to Lucy again. Maybe if we can help her see how complicated this will be—especially for Reese—then she'll change her mind."

"Isla, are you actually serious? They told us we can't use the embryo. We can't make this into a situation where we can't have it, so neither can she." He shakes his head.

"I didn't mean it like that."

"No? Then how did you mean it because that's exactly what it sounds like. She was your best friend. You used to care about the things that made her happy."

Is that how it looks to Ben? Is it possible he's right? Did I ever stop caring about Lucy's happiness? Or do I simply have a track record of putting my life ahead of hers?

Ben's expression softens and he looks up at the sky. "It's hard for me too," he admits. "I think that we need to focus on Reese now—she's the gift we never thought we'd have and up until now we were doing okay as a family."

"Then why does it feel like we just lost a baby?" I say, trying not to cry.

His reply comes after a beat. "Because we did."

"Firstly, I still can't believe you went and disclosed things to Reese without regard for the consequences. Then I learn there've been further developments in this saga." Mom's arms flail about in a way that is out of character for her. She's normally so poised, able to choose her words carefully, but she is clearly flustered. After avoiding all her calls, she picked up her car keys and drove right over.

"Coffee?" I ask, unimpressed by this impromptu visit.

"None for me. Do you have any dandelion tea?"

"Don't even know where I'd buy some. How about a regular black tea?"

"I'll have a water, then. Sparkling. Slice of lemon."

"I only have tap water."

"Well, I suppose that will have to do, then." Mom opens her bag and takes out a small spray bottle. She closes her eyes and spritzes her face and neck. "I've been pondering this incessantly since I saw you. The question I have is why, Isla? Why was this necessary?"

Mom accepts the glass of water from me and takes a sip. "Whenever you're ready you can answer the question," she prompts.

"We decided that Reese deserves the chance to have a relationship with Lucy."

"Hmm. What is that relationship going to look like, exactly?"

"We're still figuring that part out."

"What if Lucy decides she wants input on how you raise your daughter? What, then?"

My patience with Mom is wearing thin. "Lucy has her own life."

"That now includes Reese."

"It always included Reese, Mom! The only thing that's changed is that now she can spend time getting to know her. This is a positive thing for Reese. I know it might not seem like that to you—but so many donor-conceived or adopted children spend their lives *looking*, Mom. Looking for the people who helped them come into the world. Imagine that for a second. Walking down the street, seeing someone who shares a physical trait with you that leaves you wondering whether that person could be the one who helped give you a life?" I realize in this moment that deep down, despite Lucy wanting a baby, this *is* how I actually feel. I just wish things weren't so complicated because Lucy having a baby *does* change things again. If Reese continues a relationship with Lucy, it will also mean cultivating a relationship with her child, and that means we will need to work out how this can all work together for the sake of everyone involved.

Mom sits there, lips pressed together. "And what about Lucy's baby? Where does that leave you and Reese?"

"How do you know about Lucy wanting to have a baby?"

Mom gives a small shake of her head. "I paid her a visit."

"Mom! You did not!"

"It was the only thing to do."

"You're impossible! We might not see eye to eye on this, but that's going too far, even for you."

"You are talking about a potential biological sibling here!"

"Stop yelling at me, Mom!"

"How much do you need?" Mom reaches for her purse.

"Mom, what are you doing?"

"You'll need a lawyer. Your father knows a good one in Melbourne. Edwin... Edwin Sperling... or Sterling..."

"I'm not going to call a lawyer, Mom. It's not my embryo. It's hers. And she might not even be able to use it."

"You need to protect Reese so you don't lose her."

"No," I say firmly. "You need to stop interfering in my life."

It's then I realize that Mom's hands are shaking. "Mom, listen to me. There might be challenges but I am not going to lose Reese." I hope I sound more convinced than I feel.

"Oh, please. If it was you in Reese's shoes, you'd be out of my life in a heartbeat."

I blink and focus my attention on her as she sorts through her handbag to find a tissue. "Why would you say that?"

Mom blows her nose.

"How does this have anything to do with you and me, even as a hypothetical?"

Silence envelops us.

"Mom! Answer the question."

Mom's arm reaches for the counter as she tries to steady herself. Her knees buckle and I lunge forward to catch her as she starts to fall.

After checking her out in emergency, the doctors send Mom home for a rest. We don't speak about the last part of our conversation until two days later when I drop in to check on her, mostly on Ben's insistence.

"Hey, Dad, where's Mom?" I ask as I step into the kitchen and deposit a casserole dish on the stone countertop.

"Where she's been for the past two days. Upstairs in her bedroom watching the soaps," he says as he sorts out the contents of his tackle box.

I do a double take. "I thought the doctors said she was fine."

"She *is* fine, Isla. She's being dramatic. It's what your mother does when things don't go her way. Let me go upstairs and let her know you're here."

"I already know she's here, Lewis," says Mom from atop the staircase. "I'm not feeling up to having visitors, Isla. I'll see you next week for brunch."

"Mom. Seriously? We need to talk."

"Elinor, really, come on down here and act like an adult."

Very rarely have I heard Dad speak like this to Mom. It's obvious there's a certain level of tension between them. Growing up, I rarely ever heard Mom and Dad argue, though I know they had the odd disagreement from time to time. It was normally behind closed doors, and possibly even by appointment, knowing Mom.

Mom gives a theatrical shake of her head and glides down the staircase. She doesn't look the part of someone who's spent the better part of the morning in bed watching soaps and feeling under the weather. She's wearing lipstick, her hair is styled, and she's even gone to the trouble of wearing earrings.

"Casserole," she says, eyeing the dish.

"Nobody cares about the casserole, Elinor. Talk to your daughter or I bloody well will."

"Lewis," spits Mom, in a way that indicates she wants him to stop there.

"Isla, your mother told me what transpired the other day. I think you did the right thing in being open with Reese. Lucy is a fine woman—always has been, despite what your mother thinks of Shirley—and I am sure Reese will be better off for knowing the truth of her existence. Denying her a relationship or the chance to know the identity of her donor parents was..." Dad bows his head.

Mom's expression is stony. "Lewis, please. Enough."

"I'm sorry, Elinor, but she needs to know."

"Know what?" I say, feeling the hairs on my arm prick up. Neither of them answers me.

"Elinor," he says.

"I'm not feeling well. I need to head back to bed."

"Will somebody tell me what's going on! Dad, please say what you need to say."

"The reason your mother's been so determined for you to keep the truth from your daughter is because she's afraid of losing you. Because of the lies we've told you."

"Lies? What lies?" I slam my palm against the countertop. "What lies, Mom?!"

"Please, Isla, calm down."

"I will not calm down!"

Mom turns her body away and goes into the living room, where she sits down on her wingback armchair and crosses her legs. Dad and I follow her.

"Before your father proposed, we had a brief..." She shakes her hand dismissively. "Separation."

"We broke up, Elinor."

"Yes, we did. Because my mother didn't approve of me marrying him. She thought... well, it doesn't matter what she thought, but I was expected to listen to what she thought was best for me. Obviously when it came to marrying Lewis, I didn't listen."

"Your mother traveled overseas, Isla. She spent a year in France, and when she returned, we reunited and I asked her to marry me."

"But I was... already pregnant."

I blink. Blink again. And then suddenly, it feels like the world has slowed down and everything is in slow motion.

"Did you go to France too?" I ask, already knowing the answer.

"No. He did not." Mom stares into her lap, then closes her eyes.

I look up at Dad. "You're...not my father."

Dad holds my gaze with his, his dark eyes sincere. "I am your father, Isla. Always have been...your father."

It can't be true. My dad, the man who taught me to read, to drive, to play chess, and to make snowmen. The man who took me out on fishing trips and sailing adventures as rewards for my good grades is not the man I thought he was. He camped out in the backyard with me when I was seven and let me and Lucy turn his study into an art studio when I was twelve. Mom got pregnant by a man she barely even knew. She never kept in touch with him, nor does he know of my existence.

"You know what the worst part of this is?" I say, shaking a finger at Mom. "You made a decision to keep this from me my whole life, and then you made that decision based on *your* fears and you imposed it on *me* without me even knowing!"

"Isla, please. When you say it like that it makes it sound so awful. My doctor—he told us, 'Never tell. Whatever you do, do not tell.'"

"And you listened to him!"

"We thought we were doing the right thing. We didn't know what else to do." Mom chokes on her last words. "I have lived my whole life afraid of losing you."

"You kept this from me too," I say to Dad, wiping the tears from my chin with the back of my hand.

Mom stands up to get some tissues.

"I did," he says, his voice small.

"There's no point in lying for me, Lewis. I insisted he keep it from you. Your father is a good man, and if you're going to be angry with anyone, that person should be me," says Mom.

I stand up. "I am angry. And not just because you lied. Because you made me lie to my own daughter! You projected your fears onto me for your own selfish reasons, and honestly I don't know if I can ever forgive you!"

Mom presses a hand to her chest and starts sobbing.

I grab my handbag and keys and make my way to the front door.

"Call me when you get home," says Dad. "To let me know you're okay."

"You and me—we have so much in common. I *look* like you," I say, my voice shaky.

His hair, wavy if he lets it grow too long. Dad's skin, that like mine, burns in the sun. Mom's tans. Dad and I both love fresh tomatoes, hate beetroot, and detest coriander. We have the same taste in music, cheer for the same football team. We only need to look at each other to know what the other is thinking. I'm close to my dad. Only we aren't linked by genetics. We are linked by something entirely different.

Love.

It has to count for something.

Correction.

It has to count for everything.

I look over to Mom. I no longer see a controlling mother; I see a woman who's lived her life in fear of losing the things she loves the most. I do not want to become my mother. I do not want to make the same mistakes as her.

CHAPTER TWENTY-NINE

Lucy

When Isla and I were younger, we used to play a game. If ever one of us knew the other was sad or having a bad day, we'd reach out to one another. We'd usually do this by turning up on each other's doorsteps with a gift. These so-called gifts usually weren't special store-bought gifts, but our special possessions. I once turned up on Isla's doorstep with my treasured copy of *Charlotte's Web*, and she turned up on mine with a silver trinket box she ended up telling her mom she lost. We didn't have many disagreements, but if we ever did, we'd resolve them our way. One of the conditions was we were never, *ever* allowed to say no to a doorstep gift.

After all this time, I'm thankful that Mom kept the keepsake box from my teen years for me. I rub the dust off the lid and open it, almost gasping when I see the shoes.

A memory floods my mind. I'm twelve years old again, and Mom is nowhere to be found. There's a loud rap on the bedroom door and then a creaking sound.

"It's just me," Isla calls out, and instantly my mood lightens. "What are you doing?" she says, flopping onto my bed.

I shrug. "Nothing."

"I know things with your mom are hard and you wish they were different but I have a present for you," she tells me, unzipping her backpack. She takes out a shoebox and places it beside her. She's decorated the box with her precious scratch 'n' sniff stickers and glitter paint.

"This is for you," she says.

"Today's not my birthday."

"I know." She points to the box. "Go on, open it!"

I lift the lid and peer into the box, moving the scrunched-up tissues she squashed in there to make the gift look a bit more exciting. It looks like the way my gran shoved old tissues into the creases in the couch.

"Jelly sandals?" I say in disbelief.

Isla nods, her smile lighting up her eyes. "Yes!"

"I love them and I'm never going to stop wearing them. Thank you." I hug her.

"You're my best friend. I'd do anything for you. Anything at all. I'm always and forever here for you. No matter what."

"That's what best friends do."

No matter what life lobbed our way, I knew Isla had my back, and I had hers.

She was grounded for two weeks when her mother found out she gave away her brand-new shoes, but later, she told me it was worth it—even when she had to polish the leaves of every indoor house plant they owned.

I take the shoes out of the box and place them in the gift box I've purposely stuffed with tissues instead of cellophane. And then I write my note:

Dear Isla,

You came into my life during a time I needed you most and for that I'll always be grateful.

These shoes belong to you, but I'd like to pass them on to Reese with a reminder of what they represent—some of the most important things in life: love, friendship, and forgiveness. All I ever wanted for Reese was a good life. She got one thanks to you.

I forgive you and I also forgive Elinor. Nothing about our situation was or is easy. We all come to the situations we are faced with in life from different angles, with different fears and opinions. You are a good person, Isla. Please never forget that.

I would love nothing more than your blessing but understand if this can't be so. And if that's the case, I hope one day you can find it in you to forgive me. I will be here waiting for you if you want to come home.

Your best friend,
Lucy x

I drive to Isla's and ring the doorbell. At first I think nobody's home but then the door creaks open and Ben appears.

"Lucy, hi."

"I just came to drop this off for Isla," I say, handing him the wrapped parcel. He eyes it with a confused look on his face—I've covered the brown paper in stickers like we did when we were younger.

"Isla's not home. But why don't you come in anyway?"

"Oh, no, I wouldn't want to cause any—"

"It's fine, really. I'd like you to come in. It'll be good to chat, actually."

I stand there quietly contemplating whether I should when he calls out, "Reese! Come downstairs, we have a visitor!"

He must sense my discomfort then because he nods his head in reassurance. "Come on. Let's crack open a beer. For old time's sake. For Nate."

I step inside and can't help noticing that Isla's home is a home in every sense of the word. From the moment I step through the front door, it becomes obvious how hard she and Ben have worked to make this a loving home for Reese. The hallway wall is covered in photographs of Reese throughout the different stages of her life—newborn, toddler, what I imagine was her first day of kindergarten, and beside that photograph is one that is obviously her first school picture. There are photos of the three of them eating ice cream together, on a boat together, in the snow together. At the end of the hallway, just before we reach the kitchen, is an eye-catching triptych of three frames—black and white, each holding the definition of the words beneath them: family, love, home.

I briefly admire the frames when a honey-colored cavoodle comes up to sniff me.

"Say hello to Lucy, Peaches!" says Reese, crouching down to cuddle her. "Hi, Lucy," she says, her voice suddenly taking on a tone of shyness.

"Hi, Reese, how are you?"

She smiles back at me. "I'm good." She gets on her tiptoes and stretches her neck, all the while staring at my face.

"Button, why don't you give Lucy some space to breathe."

"Underneath your straight hair do you have curly hair?" she asks, ignoring him.

"No," I say, "but Nate—he had wavy hair and when he was little it was curly. His mom, Janet—she has curly hair."

Reese lets out an excited "Oooh!" as if she's just opened a Christmas present.

"We can talk some more about this later, Reese, but for now, why don't we let Lucy have a seat."

"I'm going to go upstairs to work on my report, and then when I come back I have seventy-two questions to ask Lucy."

Ben laughs as Reese skips away and back upstairs. "I hope she's not too intense for you."

"Not at all—it's lovely, actually. Nate would have loved her."

"I'm really sorry, Lucy. How are you doing?"

"As well as expected. I guess?"

He gives an understanding nod and motions for me to follow him into the living area of the house—a large kitchen with white shaker cupboards and an island with a black stone top.

Ben opens the fridge. "Can I get you something to drink?" He's already pulling out a jug of what looks like red cordial, but I know it's herbal tea because that's what Elinor used to keep in her fridge in summer. Raspberry tea, two slices of lemon, and a sprig of mint. "Isla always keeps this red stuff in the fridge. Otherwise a beer?"

"The red stuff will be fine," I reply.

Ben helps himself to a beer from the fridge while we dive into small talk, bringing each other up to speed about our lives.

"Ben, I want to apologize. I really don't mean to hurt you both," I say, once we've exhausted the talk about my renovation, his business, and the weather. "I—"

"Hey, it's okay," he says softly. "Really, it's okay. I'm not going to sit here and fly off the handle."

"You're not angry?"

"I can't say I'm not a little disappointed but we have Reese—she's everything to us. And you've lost so much. I can only imagine what that feels like, so I think if I can push aside my own feelings about it and look to what we already have, it makes it easier to let go."

"And Isla? How does she feel?"

"I think what Isla's finding hard right now is the fact that a lot is happening at the moment—coming to terms with the fact that she won't have another child, being transparent with Reese, having her meet and get to know you ... it's a lot to become comfortable with all at once," says Ben, choosing his words carefully.

I tear my gaze away and fix it on the tree in the backyard, pregnant with lemons, some of which have pooled in the grass beneath it.

"I think we need to talk about it some more," continues Ben. "It might take a while for everyone to get used to the idea," he suggests. "She just needs some time. Let me talk to her. I'll bring her around."

Reese appears in the kitchen then, carrying a photo album and a notebook.

"Lucy, I want to show you photos of me as a baby and then you can show me your photos," she declares. She drags a kitchen chair next to mine, sits down, and opens the album.

She flicks through page after page while I try to keep my emotions at bay. And when Ben discreetly pulls out his phone to take a photo, I pinch my nose. He gives me a nod of understanding. "I hope you don't mind," he says. "She's missed out on these moments—I figured she'd like to look back on this one, one day."

I can't help worrying about where Isla fits into this—what she'd think if she were here.

But I needn't wonder because a moment later, the front door opens, followed by the sound of footsteps down the hallway and into the kitchen.

She stops in her tracks when she sees the three of us sitting together.

"What's going on here?"

Reese is the first one to talk and, of course, explains everything, including some of her seventy-two questions, of which I've only managed to answer five so far.

"That's great, Button," she says through a pained smile.

Reese turns back to me and fires another question my way, which Isla interrupts. "Reese, I think Dad needs some help watering the garden. You can finish asking Lucy her questions later."

She exchanges a look with Ben, who gets up and says, "Come on, Button. Then we can have some ice cream!" which seems to do the trick.

"What are you doing here, Lucy?"

"I just came to drop something off for you. I really didn't mean to stay or even see Reese... I know this is hard for you. I should go."

"Lucy, this is huge for me. It's not what I anticipated when I decided this would be the way I'd start a family. We had an agreement whereby you donated to Ben and me. You said you never wanted children and that was the arrangement. That was what I felt comfortable with and now you're changing those terms. I'm sorry, but I think it's just too much at once. I don't even know how to talk about it with you." She flips the switch on the coffee machine, which grinds into motion.

"I understand."

She puts a mug on the drip tray and flips around to face me. "Do you? Do you have any idea what you're asking of me? Of Reese? It would be her biological sibling. I just gave up on having another child, Lucy, only this time, this is it—no third chances."

I stand up. "I know how this makes you feel. You're worried about Reese but I actually don't think that's what the problem is because I know we could make it work if we wanted to. I think the main issue is that I'm taking something that belongs to you." My throat closes up. I clear it and the words come out squeaky, like they don't belong to me. "And for what it's worth, I'm sorry about that."

Isla closes her eyes. "Fine," she concedes. "If this is what you need to do, then this is what you need to do."

"I'm sorry," I whisper.

I really am sorry.

CHAPTER THIRTY

Isla

Reese and Bailey are swimming while Ellen and I sit in the backyard, poolside.

"Before we know it they'll be back at school and we'll be packing school lunches again," she says.

"Let's just hope there's no more schoolyard dramas," I say, playing with my straw.

"About that. I think I owe your daughter a thank-you."

"For what?" I ask curiously.

"For standing up for Bailey," she says as if I should already know this. "She's a fierce protector of her friends, Isla. You and Ben must definitely be doing something right."

"I'm sorry, are we talking about the same thing here? Reese got into trouble multiple times after Mitchell called her a fake baby."

"Yes, but she only stepped in when he started teasing Bailey. Called her a bird face at the book parade."

I give her a blank stare.

"The book parade? You're saying she was defending *Bailey*?"

"Yes. I thought you knew. She told Bailey she would never ever let anyone hurt her because they were best friends."

I put my drink down. "Reese never mentioned she wasn't bothered by the teasing. I didn't know Bailey was having a hard time. I thought she was upset about Mitchell teasing *her*."

"Oh, Bailey said that Reese was upset the first day but after you explained things to her she was fine. Actually, Bailey also mentioned that Reese just met her donor parent. How's that going? It must be such a special time for you all. Bailey wishes she could have met her biological parents. She met her biological grandmother, so she's happy with that."

I can't help but stare at Ellen in admiration—the way she's talking about this like it's nothing to be feared, like it's simply part of life, leaves me speechless.

"I'm sorry—am I speaking out of turn? Bailey told me. I hope you don't mind."

"No, it's fine. This is all a bit fresh. We only just told her."

Ellen smiles encouragingly and then stops herself. "Is everything okay?"

"You seem so comfortable talking about Bailey being adopted. How do you manage that?"

"You're finding things hard to navigate?"

"Yeah. I am."

"Well, we can talk about it," she says, almost chirpily. "If we want our girls to feel comfortable about their identities, we should feel comfortable about them too, right?" Sensing my hesitation, she reaches out a hand. "Reese told Bailey she's excited about getting to know her donor parent. She wants Bailey to meet her. I think that sounds healthy."

Ellen's reassurance fills me with hope I haven't felt in a long time. Maybe Reese is a lot more resilient than I gave her credit for.

"What's her name?" she asks.

"Lucy. And she is—*was*—my best friend. We were inseparable... until one day... we weren't."

"Mmm. Okay, this sounds like a long story. So, first up. How'd you meet?" she asks.

I smile to myself, remembering the day like it was yesterday.

The day I met Lucy was the last time she ever ate burnt pancakes. Looking back on it now, it all came back to my jelly sandals. Later, she told me that those shoes, the color of her raspberry-stained fingers, were precisely the kind of footwear she dreamed about owning when she lay in bed at night, imagining what it would be like to get dressed and step right out of her cornflower-blue-fronted house. She'd walk past the front gate that needed a good spray of WD-40, down the street, and onto wherever life beyond Blossom Park Drive would take her and her jelly-sandaled feet.

I was walking my bike down the street, blood streaming down my leg from the graze on my knee when I'd turned the corner too fast and lost my balance. There she was, sitting on the front porch steps, plate on her lap, feeding her leftovers to Evie, her golden retriever, reading a book, while her mom was . . . well, who knows where her mom was. She had luscious, shoulder-length hair and was wearing a blue seersucker jumpsuit that looked like it was a size too small. She shoved the piece of pancake she was holding into her mouth, swiftly licked her fingers clean of raspberry, and clasped her fingers around the dog's collar.

"Stay, Evie," she whispered, her eyes glued on my shoes. Evie broke away and bounded up to me for a pat. She got up and came to the gate.

"Sorry about that," she said, grabbing Evie by the collar. "I like your sandals," she said.

"Oh, thanks."

"You're bleeding," she said, noticing my leg.

"Yeah. Do you have a tissue?"

"Do you have far to go?"

"Three blocks. Or maybe four. I'm kind of lost. We only moved in a couple of weeks ago."

"I'll get you cleaned up and then I'll help you get home."

I released the bike from my grip, letting it fall onto the strip of grass.

"Where's your mom?" I said, once we got inside.

"She's not here."

"Where'd she go?"

She stretched her arms up and tried to coax the first aid kit from the shelf with the pads of her fingers. "Where she always goes." The box tipped toward the girl's direction. She caught it just in time.

"And where's that?"

"The hotel."

"And when's she coming back?"

She shrugged.

"Oh. So where's your dad?"

"He died."

She rummaged through the kit and found two boxes of bandages. "Glow-in-the-dark or regular?"

"Glow-in-the-dark, of course! What's your name anyway?"

"Lucy."

"I'm Isla."

Lucy poured some antiseptic onto a cotton ball and gently wiped my knee, while I cast my eye around the kitchen. There were dirty dishes in the sink and an untouched stack of burnt pancakes plated on the kitchen counter. "Did your mom make those?" I asked, wide-eyed. It was the messiest kitchen I'd ever seen.

"Gross, huh?" she said quietly.

"Well, the good news is you'll never have to eat burnt pancakes again," I declared.

"What makes you say that?"

"Because my mom makes the best pancakes and they're never, ever burnt. I'll come by tomorrow and you can come over and we can have pancakes."

"Okay," said Lucy, her eyes lighting up. "That sounds fun."

"What were you reading when you were sitting out there?" I asked.

"*Charlotte's Web*."

"Any good?"

She nodded. "Really good. You could borrow it if you like."

"Really? I'll bring it back tomorrow," I told her. I'd always wanted to read *Charlotte's Web*.

She walked me back to my bike, tucked the book into the basket, and rode her bike beside me until we reached my home. Soon I would learn Lucy was not only the kind of person who poured love into you; more than that, she had the uncanny ability to leave you far better than she found you. What a thing it was to have a best friend like Lucy.

"So, what happened between the two of you?" asks Ellen. "Please tell me this has a happy ending. You obviously love her to pieces. She sounds gorgeous."

"I do. She is."

None of those feelings have changed. None of those feelings I have for Lucy will ever change.

"And look at what she gave you," says Ellen, pointing to Reese, who's now out of the pool and pretending to sell lemonade to Bailey through the play house house window.

Lucy gave me a gift. A daughter. She is everything I ever wanted.

Correction.

She is everything. She is enough.

CHAPTER THIRTY-ONE

Lucy

Mom drags me along to her evening yoga class on the beach. We roll up our mats and are about to start heading back home, making our way across the sand, when I notice Isla's figure. She's standing there, waiting for me.

"Go on," says Mom. "I'll see you at home."

Isla waves to Mom. "Hey," she says to me. "Can you spare a few minutes?"

"Course."

She slips her shoes off and we start walking along the stretch of beach. It's almost dusk and the sky is like a palette of pastel watercolors—peachy-pink morphing into powdery-blue.

"The doorstep gift," she says. "Your letter. It was . . . beautiful. Thank you."

"I don't know how to make this easier for you," I say. "But I also don't know how I can actually do this knowing it's going to hurt you."

"When my mom found out we were looking for a donor couple, she wasn't happy about it. What I mean is—she was really unhappy. Especially when I told her you and Nate had offered to donate your embryos."

I stand there, tight-lipped.

"You know what she's like. She has an opinion about everything and I didn't necessarily listen. I wanted a baby and we'd discussed the arrangement and I figured she'd have to get used to the idea whether she approved of it or not. The thing is, right around the time I found out I was pregnant, I also found out Ben's business was in trouble. We were in deep financial trouble after the fire."

"You never said anything."

Isla shakes her head. "I couldn't. You'd left for overseas when I went to put the house on the market, but my mom found out."

"Right... but I don't see where this is going. You were already pregnant. This doesn't explain why you cut us out of your lives."

"Ben lost everything, Lucy. We were in so much debt after the fire that he was about to file for bankruptcy."

"What? That's... crazy."

"He was using our personal finances to keep the business afloat. There were issues with the insurance and... well, the fact is, we came close to losing the house. We had no savings left and I was pregnant."

"I still don't understand what that has to do with Nate and me."

"My mom stepped in to save us, Lucy. She brought her checkbook and saved our house and the business and... it was..." Isla takes a deep breath. "It was conditional. I lied about changing my mind. I lied to you and Nate, and I lied to Ben too. I was apprehensive about the arrangement, but I think, with time, I could have become comfortable with it."

"Wait. Are you telling me your mother *bribed* you? To pretend Nate and I never existed?"

"Like I said, she wasn't happy about the idea of donation in the first place. She thought that Reese would be better off not knowing the truth."

"Like ever?"

"I think so. She knew that one day she'd be old enough to ask questions. I guess my mother thought I'd be able to keep hiding the truth from her."

"You let her manipulate you like that? Really? *This* is why you did what you did?"

"We needed the money. I felt like I had no other choice. It was wrong. I know it was wrong but I couldn't see any other way. If I didn't accept her help... our life would look very different from what it is now. We spent years saving enough money to pay back the money she loaned us. We put off having another baby because we wanted to gain financial stability. I figured that maybe one day we'd be in a position to buy our own house and at that point I could find the courage to reach out to you again and explain the truth to Reese, but then it all became harder and harder. The distance between us grew and I suppose I started to convince myself that my mother was right. My emotions and fears got in the way."

"I knew your mother had some pretty firm views about the way she wanted you to live your life, but this? This is terrible."

"My mother isn't the only one to blame. It was easier for me to acquiesce to what she wanted because of my own insecurities about the donation."

"Because of our relationship?"

"Yes," Isla admits, finally looking up at me.

I stand there, blinking, trying to take it all in.

Isla veers off to the right and plonks herself onto the sand. "Your note. Seeing you again. Hearing Reese talk about you. This is hard. And I'm disappointed about not being able to have another baby, but the thing is, I have a child. You don't. I owe you a blessing, Lucy. I cannot give you what you gave me, but I can give you my blessing. I owe you so much more than that." She looks out to the water and blinks. "Because you and Nate gave *me* so much more than that. You gave me Reese."

"You don't owe me anything—it was never conditional. Ever. I wanted this for you. I wanted to see you happy."

"I don't think I deserve you," she says.

"Oh, come on," I say.

She pushes her fingers into the sand and watches it trickle from one hand to the other. "I want you to know what it's like to hold a baby in your arms. Your baby. I want to support you with this. Ben and I—we put something in writing for the clinic."

"You did?"

"Yes, and I'm seeing a counselor and I've joined a support group for donor parents."

"Is it helping?"

"Yeah, I think so. I'm here, aren't I?"

"We can take this slow. We can work out what feels right as we go."

She shifts closer to me so our arms are touching and rests her head on my shoulder. "Lucy?"

"Mmm."

"I just found out my dad isn't my biological father."

My body stiffens. "What?" I whisper.

Isla's eyes are watery. "Can you believe it?"

I cannot comprehend what she's telling me. Lewis isn't her father? "What? How? I don't understand."

She gives me the rundown, and by the end of it, tears are streaming from her cheeks. "I just wish it hadn't taken *this* news to put things into perspective for me."

"I'm so sorry. What now?"

She shrugs. "I don't know. Got an instruction manual?"

I shake my head and let out a half-hearted laugh. "Don't look at me."

"Things with you and your mom—they're good now?"

"We're working on things, but yes, I think we're going to be fine."

She smiles. "That's good. Hey, I brought something for you," she says, reaching into her oversized tote.

She hands me a drawstring bag. I open it and peer inside and that's when I tip my head back and truly laugh.

Adult-sized razzle-dazzle-pink jelly sandals.

She pulls another drawstring bag from her tote. "Matchy-matchy," she says in a singsong voice.

"I love you," I tell her.

She gives my shoulder a nudge so hard I almost tip over into the sand.

"I love you too."

A couple of days later, Isla drops Reese off at the marina and hands me a cooler filled with snacks and drinks. Soon I'll be heading home to Melbourne to sort a few things out—one being my search for Nate's letter that Helen, my fertility lawyer, keeps reminding me about. Isla thought that it would be good for me and Reese to spend some time alone getting to know each other, and by the looks of it, Reese is excited. She's got a camera slung over her neck and she's holding the notebook that never seems to leave her side.

"Have a fun adventure, Button. I'll see you in a few hours," says Isla before she pecks her on the cheek.

We wave goodbye and then Reese takes me by the hand. It feels strange but lovely.

"How many fish do you think we'll catch?" she asks me as we make our way to the boat.

"Maybe a hundred if we're lucky."

Reese laughs.

"Okay, here we are."

"This is your mom's boat?"

"Sure is. Like it?"

"I love it."

I help her onto the boat and then hold the life jacket up for her to slip her arms into. Then I go up front and turn the engine on. I pat the seat next to me. "You coming, Captain Reese?"

"Did my mom really love fishing?"

"She definitely did. We used to go fishing off the pier every summer. She was good at it. She was good at lots of things, actually."

"Like what? School?"

I cast off and then check my line and Reese does the same with hers. "Not just school. She was good at everything. One year, your mom got really interested in saving injured wildlife. So you know what she did?"

Reese shrugs.

"She organized for our whole class to walk from Sorrento to Portsea and we raised lots of money for them. She got an award."

"She did?"

"Yep. And you know what else? The school still to this day takes students on that walk to raise money for wildlife."

"They do?"

"Every April."

"What else?"

"She was a great friend to me."

"And you were best friends."

"We sure were. The best kind of friends. Your mom found me when I was feeling sad and alone and she and your Grandma Elinor—they helped me."

"Where was your mom? Why didn't she help you?"

"She was kind of tied up. I don't know if your mom told you, but when we were younger we made a promise to each other."

"What was that?"

"Well, I was going to see the world and she was going to change it."

Reese laughs. "How do you change the world?"

"I think she wanted to do lots of things—like make things better for people."

"Like a nurse?" Reese wrinkles her nose in confusion. "I can't imagine Mom as a nurse. Anytime she has to put a bandage on me, she gets all shaky."

I smile. Isla always was a bit squeamish about blood. "Ah, maybe not a nurse, then. More like a politician."

"Oh, my dad doesn't really like them."

"Well, some of them aren't very likable, but some of them are. Lots of them work hard to make things better for people—jobs, health, things like that."

"But my mom sells houses."

"Yeah. I think she changed her mind along the way. That's okay, though. Sometimes people do that. People are allowed to change their minds."

Suddenly, Reese's rod almost slips out of her hands. "A fish!" she gasps.

"Fish! You got a fish!"

By the time we're ready to turn back, we've caught four fish: three whitings and a trevally. The trevally was too small to bring home, so we gave it a name—Murphy—air-kissed it goodbye, and released it back into the water, right before we took a selfie together.

"Before you were born, your mom used to dream about you, you know?" I say to Reese when I cut the engine and wait for Isla to arrive.

Reese adorably scrunches up her nose, trying to decide whether I'm serious or not.

"It's true. She used to say things to me like, 'Lucy, I had this dream where I had a baby and she was perfect. Her name was Reese.'"

"What if I was a boy?"

"She was going to name you Xavier."

"Noooo."

I laugh. "Anyway, what I want you to know is that your mom and dad love you so much it never stops. And me? Well, I love you too—in a different kind of way. If I'm honest, I'm still working out this kind of love because it's very new to me."

"I was like a present," she says.

"Yes," I say softly. "You were the most precious present your mom and dad could ever get. And you were also the most precious present I was able to give anyone. That makes you special. Very special."

"I think you're special too," she whispers.

"Thank you." I put my arm around her shoulder and give her a gentle squeeze. "So tell me... tell me everything you want to know about Nate and then I'll tell you anything you want to know about me. First things first. Are you left-handed?"

"Yes!" she says. "Are you?"

"Sure am!"

"Can you roll your tongue?"

"I can't, but Nate could. He was right-handed. But there was this weird thing he used to do. Whenever he'd see bright lights he'd sneeze."

"Nooo way! I do that too!" She claps her hands over her face.

"You do?!"

"Yes! Everybody thinks it's funny but I can't help it. Mom and Dad call me Sneezy whenever I do it."

"That's what I used to call Nate," I say.

"I know you're sad about him but I don't think you'll be sad forever."

"No?"

"No, I think you'll be happy again soon. When my cat, Snowball, died I was sad for two weeks. I hope Peaches will live forever because that would make me sad for more than two weeks for sure. Grandma Elinor says that happiness always has a way of finding us if we let it."

"Yeah?"

"Yeah, and she also says that sometimes it's our job to help happiness and love find other people. She tells me lots of stories about how she does this. One time, lots of years ago, she found a little girl who was sad. She was a friend of my mom's. The little girl was sad because her mom was sad and my grandma swooped in and took her under her wing. She did everything possible to make the little girl and her mom happy again. She looked after them and loved them. And it worked because she had love in her heart and she put it in the little girl and her mom."

"I know that little girl and her mom," I say, wiping my eyes. "Your very special grandma gave them a wonderful gift."

I help Reese unbuckle her life jacket and then crouch down so I'm at eye level with her. "Reese, there's something I would like you to know." I take her hand in mine. "I want you to know that you can ask me anything about me or Nate and I will always answer you truthfully. You can think of me as a very close friend who loves you very much."

She goes over to her backpack and opens it, pulling out her notebook. "I'm already undertaking my investigation." She opens the notebook and points to one of the pages.

"Your *investigation?*"

"Yeah. Me and my friend Bailey. We need to finish our investigation on who we are and what makes us special. Mrs. Raynor—she got us to do a project for school but I didn't get to finish my answers because I couldn't find the answers. But me and Bailey, we decided we do want the answers because otherwise it's like a mystery."

I manage to make out the words, *Who did I inherit my blue eyes from?* in bold writing, scrawled in purple marker.

"You can't know who you truly are unless you know where you come from. That's what Dad said."

"He told you this?"

"He told Mom that." She peers into my eyes. "Does your dad have blue eyes like you?"

I swallow. "No, his eyes were green."

"Where's your dad now?"

"My dad died when I was a little girl."

"Like my age?"

"I was a little older than you. But not by much."

"That's too bad."

"I met your mom not long afterward. She helped me through that time."

"And she's helping you now because Nate died?"

"Yeah, I suppose she is."

"She's good at hugging."

"She really is. Your mom—she told me you were into science."

Reese nods. "I'm going to be a scientist for sure."

"Nate loved science. Mostly he was interested in environmental science."

"Like trees and stuff?"

"Yeah, like anything to do with the earth. Do you know what his job was?"

Reese shakes her head.

"He was a photojournalist and used to travel the world so that other people could discover hidden parts of it. And before he did that, he did some dangerous missions so that people like us could see what was going on in the world. Like where there were wars—he would go out and take photos for newspapers."

"Whoa! He must have been so brave. Do you have photos?"

"I do have some photos. Would you like to see some?"

Reese nods again and slides closer to me—so close, I can smell her shampoo and the sunscreen on her skin.

I take my phone out and hold my hat up to shield the sun so she can see better. "This is Nate in the Galapagos Islands last year. He was getting ready to scuba dive."

"He has a big smile."

I smile and scroll ahead. "This is us visiting a volcano in Hawaii."

"Ooh, that's cool. I haven't seen a real volcano, but I made one once."

"Hello! Mind if we join you?" comes Isla's voice. By "we" she means her and Peaches, who has just been picked up from the groomer's. She's carrying a straw tote bag and is wearing a white-and-yellow sundress which shows off her perfectly fake-tanned legs. "Who's hungry? I brought burgers!"

"Starving!" says Reese. "Hey, Peaches!" she says, cuddling her.

"Mom, did you know that Lucy and Nate visited a real volcano?" She holds up the phone so close to Isla's face that she has to take a step backward.

"Hawaii," I offer. "She wanted to see some photos of Nate."

"He was brave and adventurous, Mom."

Isla crouches down and pecks Reese on the lips. Reese puts her palms against her mother's cheeks and smiles, which makes my heart expand. The two of them share a closeness I might never know.

"Yes, he really was brave and adventurous," says Isla. She pulls a paper bag from her tote and hands me a bottle of juice.

"What else was he?" asks Reese, directing her question to me.

Isla, who is unwrapping one of the burgers, tilts her head, intrigued by her question.

"I think you should ask your mom to tell you more about him," I say finally, my eyes meeting Isla's.

"He was Lucy's biggest fan, Button." She hands Reese the burger and then peers into the bucket beside her. "So, how many fish did you catch today?"

CHAPTER THIRTY-TWO

Isla

Mom and Dad finally agreed to give me the space I need after I avoided their calls for a week. Eventually, I called Mom back and asked her for whatever details she could give me about my biological father. All she could tell me was his age, the town he was born and lived in—Colmar, a town in north-eastern France—and his name. Gabriel Lecuyer.

I've spent the past week searching for some kind of online presence for him to no avail.

"Do you really want to find him?" asks Ben. "Maybe you're having a knee-jerk reaction to this," he suggests.

"Of course I want to find him," I say without looking up from my laptop. We're both in bed and I've broken our rule about no devices in the bedroom for the third night in a row. It's glaringly obvious to me now that being able to piece together my identity is important to me. In the space of days I've been forced to reassess everything I thought I knew about my life and who I am. There's no doubt about it: I love my dad, but I hate how Mom and Dad went about keeping this from me. I need time and space to cool down—to process everything—but I'm also overwhelmed by a fierce desire to find out who exactly Gabriel is. So when Reese comes to me every morning with a question about Lucy and Nate, I no longer feel a sense of fear about whether she'll reject me or

Ben. I understand, finally, that on a deeper level she's simply trying to obtain the information she needs to process who she is.

"You could do one of those DNA tests," suggests Ben.

"Mmm, maybe," I say, scouring Facebook again.

"Or you could do something else."

"Like what?"

"You could go to France." He eases the laptop closed, rolls his body closer to me, and kisses me. "Go find him, Isla."

Over the days that pass, it feels like the life I knew has started to crumble. I look in the mirror and ask myself what made me *me*. Of course I know who I am—I'm Isla Sutherland. Reese's mom. Ben's wife. A successful real estate agent. Collector of shoes and lipstick and activewear. But I start to notice things about myself—the shape of my face, the bridge of my nose, my Cupid's bow, and the way my left eye droops a little more than the right. Do I share any of these physical traits with my biological father? Unlike Mom and Dad, I'm allergic to bees and suffer from motion sickness. Are these traits ones that can be handed down from family? Then there's the question of family history. Knowing I have a biological father out there somewhere makes me wonder about the kind of family he comes from. Is there a possibility I share more things in common with my grandmother on my biological father's side than Grandma Connie on my mother's side? And what if I have siblings?

I'm in the bathroom applying my make-up when Mom shows up. Reese is at Bailey's and Ben is at work, which means I'm the only one available to open the door, and she knows I'm home since my car is in the driveway.

She hands me a bunch of flowers from her garden—dahlias and a spray of roses.

"I've come to apologize," she says from the doorstep. She then opens her handbag and takes out a worn photograph of her and a man that was clearly taken some time ago. "That's the only photo I have of him."

The image is grainy, but I can make out a mop of dark hair, a strong nose, dark eyes, and tanned skin. He looks so *different* from Dad.

"Where will this leave us, Isla?" Mom asks quietly.

"Too soon to say," I reply, unable to let go of the part of me that's angry.

She bows her head and nods. "Understandable," she whispers. She goes to turn away but hesitates. "With regard to Lucy. I think perhaps you did the right thing to go against my advice." She takes a moment before continuing. "I think that perhaps my advice was not the best advice after all. I think it's time for me to take a step backward."

When I look up and into Mom's eyes, she offers a smile. "You don't need to say anything. Take your time. I will support whatever decisions you make about your life from this day forward."

When I head over to Shirley's, she informs me that Lucy is on her way home from being out on the boat.

"She's heading back to Melbourne tomorrow."

"When do you think she'll be back?" I ask.

"I don't know that she will be coming back," she replies, and I can hear the tinge of sadness in her voice. Just when the two of them have managed to find a way back to each other, Lucy is leaving again. Shirley switches the kettle on and pulls two mugs from the overhead cupboards. "Who knew things would get so complicated, eh?"

"Oh, you have me to blame for that," I say.

Shirley shakes her head. "We become mothers and suddenly the world expects us to be perfect, Isla. The truth is, no mother is perfect. Sometimes we get it wrong, sometimes we get it right."

"And sometimes we fail trying."

She squeezes a bottle of Morning Fresh into the sink, sending a stream of bright green liquid soap into it, and plunges her hands into the water. "Most unforgiving job in the world."

"I could have been a better friend. I've spent so long trying to protect Reese from feeling different, and if Lucy has a baby our family *will* be different. I just hope I don't let her down this time."

"What is it you're worried about, love?"

"Reese will have a biological brother or sister outside of our immediate family."

"Lucy's not like family?"

"Of course she is..."

Shirley lifts an eyebrow. "Would Lucy having a baby make your daughter unhappy?"

"Actually, I think Reese would be excited about it."

"You're worried about what other people will think, then?" continues Shirley.

"People judge," I say. "And I just want her to feel like she fits in."

Shirley smiles sympathetically. "That's the thing. We are all different, Isla. All of us, at one point or another, feel different in some way, don't we? It's how we deal with it that matters. We can embrace our differences, or we can spend our lives trying to pretend they don't exist. I know which I'd rather."

She rinses the last plate from the sink and dries her hands on a tea towel. "Enough about that now. We have some work to do, you and I."

I question her with my eyes.

"We can't very well let her stay in Melbourne alone, moping. One of us will have to head down there to check on her."

By this, I know she means me.

"How do you feel about Reese spending some time here? With me?" She winks at me.

My answer comes surprisingly quickly. "Actually, I'm sure Reese would love that."

CHAPTER THIRTY-THREE

Lucy

After being away for several weeks, returning to the house Nate and I wanted to call home sends an avalanche of emotions through me. I close my eyes and all I can see is Nate, wearing a tool belt around his waist trying to figure out how to install wood paneling or a new light fitting. We ate fish and chips in the middle of the living room for three nights straight before our dining table arrived. I love the home and everything about it but there's no mistaking it—it doesn't feel like mine without Nate here to enjoy it with me. Suddenly, it feels like the ceilings are too high, the views too pretty. The pale-blue–colored walls painted in Elation only serve to remind me of the life I'm supposed to be living, and not the one I've suddenly inherited. I want the house to remind me of Nate; instead it reminds me of the future we were supposed to have.

The first place I look for the letter is my suitcase. My clothes from the trip to France are still in there—I didn't bother unpacking before the funeral. When my suitcase reveals nothing, I unzip Nate's. The sight of his clothes—haphazardly rolled up and squished in—takes my breath away. Reaching for a T-shirt, I bring it to my face and inhale.

Would you be okay with this, Nate?

As expected, there's no answer. Just the sound of summer rain thwacking against the steel roof.

*

After a week of searching, the letter still hasn't turned up. I spent most of the week doing everything Mom had predicted I would if left alone and to my own devices. Which in actual fact equated to a lot of moping and little else. Mom has been calling me twice a day, sometimes more often, and has even insisted on visiting, but I managed to persuade her not to after I forced myself to get a cut and color. After that, I came home and put on some lipstick and a pretty blouse over my pajama bottoms for a FaceTime call.

Isla and I, on the other hand, have been text messaging. Reese asked if I'd be coming back to visit soon because she has lots of questions for me.

I nestle into the hanging egg chair on the patio and pick up the book I'd started reading before my trip to France with Nate. I turn the first page and that's when I remember.

Nate's letter.

I tucked it into the book I was reading and didn't bring the book home with me. No, the book is still in France. In Chamonix where I left it.

Later that evening, Isla turns up on my doorstep with an overnight bag and a bottle of wine.

"Your mom sent me," she declares.

I hold the door open and she steps inside, taking in the surroundings. "Lucy, this place is…my gosh, it's beautiful."

"I need to talk to you about that, actually."

"Oh?"

"Got any colleagues in Melbourne?"

"You want to sell it?" she says, sounding surprised.

"It's too big for me. We renovated it and decorated it but we never got the chance to make it our home. Being here reminds me of what I lost, not what we had. We were travelers, Isla. So really the only place that truly feels like home to me is Sorrento. Once I settle back into work, I'll be able to work from anywhere."

"I'll find you somewhere perfect. Whenever you're ready." She pulls her phone out and shares a contact with me. "Ruby. She'll be able to help you put this place on the market. It'll get snapped up in a heartbeat."

"Let me show you around," I say, motioning for her to follow me. I give her a tour of the house, and when we reach the spare room, I hesitate. As in, I can't find the words to speak.

"Lucy? You okay?" asks Isla.

I haven't been inside this room since returning home. This room—spare room or nursery, baby or no baby.

"We were in the process of deciding. It could have been a nursery."

Isla rests a hand on my shoulder. "Could still be a nursery," she says gently. "Assuming that's still what you want and you don't sell the house." She walks over to the window and peers outside.

"*If* I get to use the embryo."

"Not so straightforward, huh?"

I explain how I'm in the process of making arrangements for the embryo to be transferred interstate and even then it might not be so simple to obtain the approval to use it.

"Nate wrote me a note before he died, saying he wanted to become a father, and I need to find it." I couldn't explain it, but even if the letter won't be enough proof for me to be able to gain permission to use the embryo, I still want it.

Isla appears a little stiff, like she's holding her breath.

"What is it?" I ask eventually.

"How do you think Nate would feel about you having a baby now? On your own?"

"He'd want me to be happy."

"And would you be? Is having a baby going to make you happy?"

I nod. "Yes. It would. I've realized I put off having a baby for all the wrong reasons, and just because my mom made some choices in her life that hurt me, doesn't mean I'd make those same mistakes. I want this. I think Nate knew what was holding me back, too. He was always hinting that I should work on my relationship with Mom. I think he'd be happy about this."

Isla steps forward and hugs me. "I think he would be too."

We make our way downstairs, where Isla spots my passport and frequent flyer card.

"You planning on going somewhere?" she asks, sounding surprised.

"Overseas."

She picks up the passport and flicks through it. "Overseas where?"

"France."

"You mean, as in *Europe*? France? French people?"

"Uh, yeah? I leave in two days. I need to see if I can find the letter. Plus, Nate loved skiing and it makes sense for me to properly say goodbye to him in the place we were last together."

Before I can say another word, Isla blurts, "I'll come with you."

We stay up until 2 a.m. talking on the recliners on the patio, my king-sized comforter laid over the both of us as we stare at the stars and sip on wine.

"Do you think I'll ever reach a point of forgiveness when it comes to my parents?" she asks, leaning her head against mine.

"If I can forgive Shirley, then I think the answer is yes."

"They lied to me."

"They didn't know better. Or at least if they did, they were afraid of what the consequences would be."

"I can relate to that," she says, slightly slurring her words. "And these are the consequences," she says, pouring more wine into her glass. "I'm so glad I saved Reese from feeling this way. How could I have been so...?"

I take her wine glass from her. "Stop being so hard on yourself."

"I feel like a weight's been taken off my shoulders. I carried the fear and worry around like a heavy coat all these years. I should never have worried." She reaches for my hand. "What if I find him? My biological father? In France? What if he wants nothing to do with me?"

I thread my fingers through hers.

"We work that out when we get there. Together."

CHAPTER THIRTY-FOUR

Isla

"Guess what, Button?" I say after dinner the following night.

"What?" replies Reese.

"Lucy and I have decided to take a trip. To France. Do you know where that is?"

She pretends to think. "Mmm, an island somewhere?"

Ben laughs. He's taken two weeks off work so I can take this trip, which is really saying something since this is one of his busiest work months.

"It's in Europe," Ben says. "Which means it's a very long boring flight away."

"I don't want you to go on a long boring flight away. Can I come too?"

"I knew you'd ask that. So I came prepared." I hand over a gift bag filled with things I know will keep her occupied.

"Baking kit!"

"Yep, Dad can help you with that. And Dad and I were wondering if you might like to spend some time with Shirley while I'm away?"

"Shirley makes me laugh. I like her," she says, nodding. "And I have twenty-two questions to ask her. Does this mean you and Lucy are best friends again?"

Ben and I look at each other and smile. "Yes," we say at the same time.

"Could we watch the video? Nate's video. I want to see what he recorded for me," says Reese.

"Yes. Of course. Let's watch it now."

She moves toward the two of us for an embrace. I know I speak for Ben when I say it feels like we are the luckiest parents in the world.

Reese snuggles in between us when Nate appears on our TV screen. Ben clears his throat and I know this is as emotional for him as it is for me.

"You sure you're ready, Button?" says Ben, pausing the video.

"I'm sure," she says, eyes glued to the screen.

Ben's hand folds over mine, and together, we press play.

"Hi, Reese, it's me . . . I'm Nate and I thought you might like to know a bit about me. So, uh, I'm thirty-four years old and I'm a photojournalist. I'm married to Lucy—happily married . . . very happily married, actually. In case you're wondering, we don't have any kids, but someday I'd like to have a dog.

"What else can I tell you? I love sports. Especially surfing and snow skiing. Lucy and I usually head to the snow every winter. Up until recently she was working as a TV presenter for a TV network, which means she's all-around amazing—I mean, she's literally an amazing woman because she's smart and kind and generous. She's really creative, too.

"So what else? I'm a regular guy. I don't do Facebook or Instagram and I'm pretty disorganized but I'm good with my hands. If I had a motto for life, it would simply be to be happy. And eat ice cream. I hate tomatoes and never touch onions and my favorite food is spaghetti Bolognese followed closely by chocolate-mint ice cream. Fun fact! There is not one day in my life that passes that I don't eat ice cream.

"I kind of wish you were here to ask me about all the things you want to know, but I guess at the end of the day I want to let you know that I think I'm a pretty decent, honest guy who's lived a great life, and I'm happy. I hope you are too.

"Reese, there's one more thing I think you should know. Lucy and I, we think about you a lot. I don't know when you'll get to see this video, or if you ever will, but I imagine you might at some point wonder whether we ever thought about you or if we even cared.

"We did. We do. You're actually one of the things in life we are most proud of, because you are the biggest gift we were ever able to give the world..."

Ben wipes his face and then squeezes my hand.

"There's another video after this one, sweetheart, but maybe we could watch the rest together with Lucy? How does that sound?"

"I like that idea."

"We love you, Button. You are the best gift we ever were given."

CHAPTER THIRTY-FIVE

Lucy

I return to Sorrento to pick Isla up on our day of departure, then we head to Mom's to drop off Reese, who will be spending the day with her. When we enter the house, Mom's in the kitchen.

Mom's face lights up when Reese steps into the room. Today Reese is wearing a striped cotton dress the color of sunshine.

"Reese! Have we got our work cut out for us today." She presents her with a hanger from which a chef's outfit hangs. Mom has organized a bake-off for her local charity group and clearly wants Reese to look the part.

"I'm wearing a *uniform*?!"

"Of course! I take my baking role very seriously and so should you." This from Mom, who's wearing a frilly apron and is covered from head to toe in flour dust.

Reese gets changed and skips back into the kitchen donning the costume that fits perfectly aside from the chef's hat, which partly covers her eyes.

"Okay, time to go!" says Mom, clapping her hands. "Bon voyage!"

After Isla gives Reese a hug that lasts almost a minute and a half, we wave goodbye.

In the rearview mirror, I watch Mom and Reese waving.

"Is this what it's going to be like? Our new and unique family?" asks Isla.

I don't have the answer, but I think it has a nice ring to it.

If I'm thankful for anything on my trip back to France, it's having Isla by my side. She's been to France only once in her life, only visiting Paris, and she hasn't stopped snapping photos since our arrival. This is our first stop, where we settle into an Airbnb we've rented. With only ten days at our disposal, we have a few days together here, and then I'll head to Chamonix, almost a four-hour car ride away. Isla will join me next week after she's had a chance to do some searching. We both know this might not be enough time, but I understand her reasons for coming all the same. If she's unsuccessful in finding Gabriel, she'll at least return home with the memory of the town she was conceived in and the knowledge that she tried to find him. Before leaving home, I employed the services of a local guide I met in the region years earlier, Cyndi, who can help point Isla in the right direction since Isla's French has long ago been forgotten.

"Do you remember when we were fifteen and made a vow to travel the world before we turned thirty?" she asks as she stops in front of yet another boulangerie. She takes me by the hand and drags me into the shop, the scent of fresh pastries making my mouth water.

I wink at her. "I did travel the world before I turned thirty."

"I wonder if it's too late for me," she says, with a dreamy look in her eyes. "Reese would love it here. So would Ben . . ."

"Earth to Isla. You have a life back home."

"Eh, but we have ten days here and I'm going to make the most of it. Éclair?" She flashes me a cheeky grin.

*

A few days later, after Cyndi arrives at the apartment, I say goodbye to her and Isla and head for Chamonix, arriving just after midday. Being back is strange. It feels like I could wander down the main street and bump into Nate at any moment. The Christmas decorations that adorned the streets when I was last here are gone but I can still hear the music playing in my ears— the youth choir singing as they walked down the street in their Christmas costumes. Snowflakes falling. Nate's lips on mine. Me and him, leaning against a lamppost dreaming of a future that would soon be taken from us.

I finally pluck up the courage to ask about the book I'd been reading when I realize I haven't had a thing to eat all day except for one of Isla's leftover pastries for breakfast this morning. I push open the door to the café bar and take a deep breath. That's when I freeze. My feet won't move. The couple who've entered behind me step to the side and past me when it becomes clear I'm not going to move for them.

"Is everything all right? Can I help you?" asks a barman who's approached me.

I tear my eyes away from the corner lounge Nate and I sat at the last time we were here, and the conversation replays itself in my mind.

"But I didn't make a decision. I can't make a decision unless you have a thought that matches mine."

"A thought," I repeat.

"A thought that is open to discussion about making a decision."

"Right." I pause. "What are we talking about again?"

Nate laughs and tips his head back to drain his glass.

"Having a baby."

"Do you need to take a seat?" he asks, his eyes, filled with concern, searching mine.

"Um, no, I'm fine," I say, shaking my head.

Eye contact, Lucy. Eye contact.

"Um, I know this sounds a little crazy but I left a book here before Christmas. It was a copy of *The Nightingale*. It has a green cover—and it's pretty worn." That book, its dog-eared pages, cracked spine, frozen in time with Nate's note in it.

"I'm sorry, I haven't seen it. If you're looking for something to read, there's a bookstore downtown so maybe you could try there."

He goes to walk away. I grab his arm. "Sorry. I'm sorry. It's just...you don't understand. That book is special to me." I feel a sting of tears threaten. "I don't want another book. I left something inside *that* book. A piece of paper. A note. A very... important note."

He casts his gaze to an older guy who's working behind the bar.

"What does she need, Jeremy?" he calls out in French.

"I'm looking for a book," I say, approaching the bar. "My husband. He died. And I can't have our baby unless I find that book."

His brow lifts. "Okay. So, tell me about the book."

I describe it to him. It's one of my favorite books. Since it came out, I've read it every summer.

"Let me ask around," he says. "We usually get seasonal staff in over Christmas. Here today, gone tomorrow. One of them might have picked it up and taken it with them."

My eyes widen. "How will we know?"

The guy smiles. "I'll send a group text. Come back and see me this time tomorrow. Hopefully I'll have an answer and then you can..." He hesitates, an endearing smile forming on his lips. "Have a baby."

It doesn't sound promising. But it's a start.

"Excuse me!" comes a voice from behind me as I exit the bar and start walking down the main street. "Is this the book you're looking for?"

I spin around. The man standing in front of me, who looks vaguely familiar, is holding up a tattered copy of the book. *My* book.

Our hands brush as he hands it to me. I stare at it in disbelief before looking up at him. "How did you find this? Where did you find this?" My heart starts hammering in my chest.

He doesn't answer me right away but tilts his head, his eyes narrowing.

"Hey, aren't you the...?" He blinks. "Your husband—the skiing accident."

The scene enters my mind like a flash. Me, after Nate's accident, at the bottom of the slope, unable to form a coherent sentence. A gentle voice.

"Tell me what's wrong, sweetheart."

"You're the guy who... You helped me. You were with me." He held my hand in the hospital. Brought me coffee.

He nods.

It's him.

Blue-Eyes.

"I think I need to sit down," I say, suddenly feeling like it's hard to breathe.

Blue-Eyes springs into action. "Here," he says, guiding me back to the bar, one hand gently resting on my back. "Let me get you some water," he says, once I've taken a seat on one of the lounge chairs.

A few minutes later, he emerges from behind the bar with a tray of sparkling water and two orange juices. "Just in case you needed a sugar hit," he says.

He extends his arms for me to take a glass. "I hope you don't mind but I read the book. Twice, actually."

"You liked it?"

"It was moving," he says, breaking into a smile. "I found it on the table over there, but I left early because I was coming down with a cold so I took it home, went to bed, and started reading it…"

The letter. He's said nothing about the letter.

"There was, uh…a note in it…I…" He rubs his face. "Obviously I didn't know who it belonged to. We get so many tourists coming and going…Well, yeah, I'm ashamed to admit that I read it. I kept it in the glovebox of my car because I wondered if maybe one day…" He shakes his head. "Wow, what were the chances of you coming back for it?"

What *were* the chances?

"I'm Lucy, by the way."

"I know."

I question him with my eyes.

"The note," he whispers.

"Oh. Yeah."

"I'm Connor."

Now he has a name, I figure it's probably time to thank him. "Thank you for taking care of me that day. I never got a chance to let you know how grateful I was."

"It was nothing. You had a lot going on. I'm really sorry to hear about…"

"Nate."

"Nate," he repeats. "That was tragic." He presses his lips together and his voice softens. "So how are you?"

"Okay. Not okay. Sort of okay. Definitely not okay. Somewhat okay. Definitely okay. And then repeat. Sometimes all of that in one day."

"The ups and downs of grief, huh?"

I nod. It's easy to talk to Connor—maybe because he's a stranger, or maybe because he witnessed part of my suffering on the day I lost Nate.

"It's like this place has his stamp on it. He loved it here," I say, gazing out the window.

"How long are you staying?"

I shrug. "Not really sure. Now that I've found the book, I can go home."

"You traveled how far exactly?"

"I really love this book," I deadpan.

"Me too," he counters, and then he smiles again.

"I needed to find the letter Nate wrote to me."

"It was ... a ... beautiful letter," he says, shyness creeping into his voice. "That's pretty cool, Lucy. I'm glad you found what you were looking for."

I take a sip of the orange juice. "Does this have vodka in it?" I say, pointing to the glass.

He laughs. "Yeah, it does."

I smile and take another sip. "So tell me, what did you love about the book?"

It turns out that Connor is originally from Canada, tells great jokes, and loves to ski and travel. He's a graphic designer and runs his own business from wherever he likes, and usually he only works in Chamonix in November and December. This year he stayed on, mostly because he wasn't entirely sure where his next travel stop would take him.

"Have you ever been to Australia?" I ask.

"Never, but it's in the cards, and no, I'm not going to ask you if you have a pet kangaroo. Will you come back here next winter?" he asks.

I know this place will be one I return to—I'm just not sure if I'll return alone.

I grip the book tighter. Only time will tell.

CHAPTER THIRTY-SIX

Isla

My time in Colmar passed quickly, too quickly, and it soon became evident, even with Cyndi's help, that finding my biological father was going to take a lot more time—time I didn't have. As I spent my last evening wandering the fairy-lit cobblestone streets, admiring the medieval and Renaissance timbered houses that sit alongside the river, I questioned whether the timing was right. There were other things I needed to focus my attention on: Reese, Lucy, my parents. As I stumbled upon a night market buzzing with locals and tourists bundled up in thick coats, I decided that I would come back here to find my father, but I'd do it alongside my parents.

I pulled my phone out of my pocket and texted both of them:

> *I didn't find him and I don't think I need to. At least, not just yet. I love you. x*

We are going to go on an early-morning ski run in Nate's memory. The final goodbye. It has been a while since I last skied. New Zealand, two years ago, but I am up for the challenge, not because I'm adventurous but because this will be for Nate.

She found his letter—a guy, Connor, with blue eyes and a smile that would turn a block of chocolate into a gooey mess, produced it with her book. He casually popped past the chateau last night with another book to loan her. She passed one back to him, and then she tucked her one away in her suitcase and didn't say another word about him or the book.

While Lucy is still sleeping, I take an early-morning stroll through the village, and by that I mean a 7 a.m. walk in the dark. I come home and make pancakes. I fix a coffee with a double shot of espresso for Lucy and take it to her room.

She's lying in bed, staring at the ceiling, her face moist from the silent tears that are rolling down her cheeks and onto her pillow. The letter Nate wrote her is resting against her chest.

I close my eyes momentarily and there we are again, throwing pillows at each other, writing letters in secret code, eyeing off the world's best jelly sandals, stuffing our T-shirt bras with rolled-up socks, and spraying Sun-In in our hair. Riding our bikes with neon spoke beads adorning our wheels, and streamers hanging off our handlebars when we stop, pull out our jump ropes, do ten jumps, and then race each other to the convenience store.

"Knock, knock. Want me to come back tomorrow?"

Lucy nods and scrunches her eyes closed.

"Is it okay if I come in?"

She nods again, sniffling this time. "I don't think I'll ever get used to the empty spot beside me." She opens her eyes and holds my gaze. "Even if the application is successful, there's no guarantee the embryo will take, and if it doesn't, he won't be there to hold me."

But I will be, I think to myself.

I want to tell her it's okay. That it will be okay. That it'll work out for the best. But I can't. I can't lie to her. We don't know what the outcome will be. Nobody does. There's only one thing to do. I crawl into my best friend's bed and wrap my arms around her. Like old times.

*

We take the gondola to Plan Praz and disembark. It's an unusually sunny morning, with spectacular views of Mont Blanc, its glaciers, and paragliders who've taken off in the snow and are flying above Chamonix.

We pull our goggles over our eyes and fasten our helmets.

"He loved it here," she says, taking a deep breath. "I'm going to miss this place."

It's easy to see why. Lucy and Nate spent their life together—the life they built for themselves—traveling and discovering adventure. It's who they were. And now, it's time for her to step forward. It won't be easy, and I don't know how things will turn out once she makes the application to request permission to use the embryo she created with Nate, but I do know she won't be alone. She has me, and Reese, and Ben, and Shirley. She has *family*.

"Ready?" I say as we click our boots into our ski bindings.

She nods. "I'm ready."

"This is for you, Nate," I say.

"I love you," she whispers. And then she pushes off down the slope, with me right by her side.

If she falls, I'll be there to catch her.

EPILOGUE

Lucy

Three Years Later

It takes us three years to coordinate our trip back to France. Firstly, Isla needed to organize time off work that coincided not only with Ben's schedule but that of her parents, who will meet her and Ben in Colmar in two weeks. Reese, about to start secondary school in February, will stay on in Chamonix with me. I promised her I'd take her to Italy, starting our road trip at Lake Como and making our way down south, dropping Mom off in Tuscany for a wellness retreat she's organized for twenty women. At the end of the trip, we'll all meet in Paris before flying back home. Nate would have loved it.

We are at Les Planards, a ski area for beginners, and the morning is crisp and sunny, and filled with children's laughter and half-constructed snowmen.

"Where do we hire the sleds from?" asks Reese.

I give her the directions and keep an eye on her as she approaches the nearby kiosk. I'm busy building a snowman, something I haven't done in years; it's one of the things I most looked forward to on this trip. That and my visit to Brévent, where I'll ski again—for Nate.

As Reese makes her way back toward me dragging a red sled, out of the corner of my eye I notice a man approaching.

"Nice work. Don't forget to give him a name," he says.

I look up and smile when I register who it is.

"Connor?"

"Lucy." A smile breaks across his face and it reaches his eyes. I don't remember his smile having this effect on me. I'm smiling back, happy to see him. Actually, I'm *excited* to see him. He loaned me a copy of *The Book Thief*, and I never got the chance to tell him what I thought of it.

I stand up and hug him. "Nice to see you. I wondered if you might be up here."

"I've been coming back every winter."

"Really?"

He nods and then registers that I'm not alone.

"Hello," he says to Reese, who's been patiently waiting with the sled in hand.

"Hi," says Reese with a wave, exposing a mouth full of braces. "I'm Reese. Nice to meet you."

Connor introduces himself and looks at Reese, then me, then back to Reese, almost certainly registering the resemblance between the two of us.

"Could I try it out?" she asks, referring to the sled.

"Sure, just don't go too far," I say.

"And who's this?" asks Connor, crouching down.

"This is Leo, my son."

"Your son?" he says. "That's wonderful. So you...met someone?" he asks, but I'm almost certain he already knows the answer to that question.

"Not exactly," I say, and I realize I haven't stopped smiling.

"It's complicated," chimes in Reese as she starts tugging the sled away. One thing we all love is how Reese has embraced the uniqueness of our family.

"Yeah?" he says.

"Not really. Only for some people. But we don't worry about them," she says.

Leo points to Reese. "Come! Weese!"

"Can I take him with me?" she asks.

I nod. "Stay in this area where I can see you both, and be back soon. He has a lesson at two."

Connor grins. "He's learning to ski?"

"He sure is. His dad would not have had it any other way."

"You seem happy, Lucy."

"I am." I lift my glasses away from my face. "I read your book. I loved it, actually."

"Well, I'm glad to hear that."

"I read it a few times, actually. Do you have any other book recommendations?"

He grins again. "Mmm, maybe I do. There's this one book, I don't remember the name of it exactly, but the story starts with two characters—a guy and a girl—and they meet in the snow in the strangest of circumstances..."

I laugh. "And how does this book end?"

We watch Reese and Leo slide down the slope on the sled, their laughter reverberating in our ears. Leo jumps up and demands, "Again! Again!" and it's exactly the kind of thing that would have made Nate proud. Reese picks him up and makes her way back up the slope, tugging the sled behind them. She adores him. We all adore how much they adore each other. I take a few photos with my phone, keeping my promise to Nate's parents, and turn to face Connor.

"So, the book?" I say. "The ending?"

Connor's eyes meet mine. "Well, I haven't figured that out yet. It all depends on whether she agrees to meet the guy for drinks after a day on the slopes."

"She'll say yes for sure."

"Yes?" He smiles again.

"She wants her book back. So, yes. Definitely yes."

A LETTER FROM VANESSA

Dear Reader,

I hope you enjoyed reading *A Child of My Own* and spending time with Isla and Lucy! If you are interested in learning about my upcoming releases, you can sign up for my newsletter. Your email address will never be shared and you can unsubscribe at any time.

I wanted to write about the power of female friendship in this novel. To me, it's a love story between friends that highlights the unique and special bond some of us are lucky enough to experience in our lifetime. The selfless act of helping someone else become a parent is a fascinating one to me. *A Child of My Own* is a story about altruism, but it's also a story about forgiveness and enduring love.

I love hearing from readers, and if you've enjoyed this book, please consider leaving a review or saying hello! You can reach me via Facebook, Instagram, or my website, where you can also sign up for my newsletter updates.

With love and best wishes,
Vanessa

www.vanessacarnevale.com

vanessacarnevalewriter

@vanessacarnevale

vanessacarnevale

ACKNOWLEDGMENTS

My deepest gratitude to my editor, Lucy Dauman, for your wonderful guidance and support in helping shape this book. I honestly couldn't have done it without you! To the entire Bookouture team, it truly is a pleasure to work with you all. You're such a hardworking, dedicated, and friendly team, and I am so lucky to have you championing my books.

Alli Sinclair, you've been a treasured support to me over the years in my writing and personal life, and I'm blessed to have you around.

To the Golden Girls, who know who they are, I am so grateful for your love and friendship. Thank you! Thanks also to Claudine Tinellis, Michelle Parsons, and Chrissie Mios for your friendship and support.

Thanks to Mum and Fulvio for all the ongoing encouragement that means so much to me.

I'd also like to thank the wonderful people and organizations that assisted with my research: Kate Bourne, Claire Byrne, Monash IVF, VARTA, Jessica Marcy, and Julie Dinoto. In particular I'd like to thank Sarah Jefford for being so readily available to answer my tricky questions via email. Without your help I would not have been able to write this book. Any mistakes surrounding donor conception laws and processes are entirely my own.

To my wonderful readers, being able to write books for you is one of my life's greatest pleasures. Thank you for all your support and interest in my novels. I hope to be able to write many more for you.

Last but not least, infinite love and thanks to the precious people in my life: Fabio, Christian, and Alessia. Love you to bits and beyond.

READING GROUP GUIDE

DISCUSSION QUESTIONS

1. What did you think about Isla's attempts to prevent Reese from learning more about her identity? Could you empathize with Isla's reasoning for keeping it a secret and was it justified?

2. What thoughts do you have regarding Lucy's decision to fulfill Nate's wishes to become a parent? Do you think her decision was made too soon after his death?

3. Isla struggles with her worth as a mother. Why do you think this is, and is it relatable? What qualities make a good mother?

4. Lucy and Isla have complicated relationships with their respective mothers. How have the actions of Shirley and Elinor impacted their daughters?

5. Isla has been lied to by Ben and by her mother. Lucy has been betrayed by Isla, and feels her mother let her down when she was younger. What does it take to make relationships survive despite the mistakes we and others around us might make?

6. One of the major themes of the novel is forgiveness. What does it take to truly forgive another person once they've hurt you? Why do you think Lucy was able to forgive Isla for what she did?

7. Do you think Elinor experienced healing after finally disclosing the truth to Isla about her biological father's identity? How do you imagine the relationship between Isla and her mother might be changed after this?

8. Have you ever experienced an enduring friendship like Lucy and Isla's? What makes friendship between two females special?

9. Elinor and Shirley have their respective flaws. Despite these, could you relate to these women, and did you sympathize with them?

10. What did you think of the ending? Could the book have ended in a different way?

Q & A WITH VANESSA CARNEVALE

Q: Where do you get the inspiration for your books?

A: This is one of the most common questions readers ask me about my writing. Readers are fascinated about how an idea can turn into a book. As an author, I, too, am fascinated by this process and these are questions I sometimes struggle to answer definitively. Sometimes all it takes is one idea in the form of a thought or a question to spark another series of questions, and so on, until I know I have an idea for a story. Other times, I might read a news article, or have in mind a certain theme. More often than not, it's a culmination of all these things!

A Child of My Own is my fourth novel, and I knew at some point I wanted to write about friendship and motherhood. Some of my favorite books are those that deal with complex female friendships, and I especially love stories that deal with childhood friendships. I didn't want to write about any kind of friendship, but female friendship that was enduring and able to stand the test of time despite betrayal, lies, physical distance, and challenges. I wanted to explore the things that make friendship—like love—worth fighting for. This is what I had in mind as I wrote *A Child of My Own*. Sometimes in life friends will come and go, but what if you simply couldn't entirely let go of a friend despite how much they'd hurt you?

I'm lucky enough to still have friends from my early primary school years and early secondary schooling years. Despite the fact that we don't see each other all that often, we know we will *always* remain friends we've grown up together, been through ups and downs together, and know each other inside out. To have this kind of friendship stand the test of time makes us very fortunate.

While friendship is a key theme of the novel, I was also keen to explore the flawed relationships we all experience, sometimes in our own families, and sometimes between mother and daughter. As a mother, I understand there comes a time for parents to realize they must let go of their children and allow them to make their own decisions in life—something Elinor struggles with despite Isla's age, and not for the right reasons. I also think there comes a point in life when children realize that their parents aren't perfect—they're not simply parents—they're humans. And like all humans they can and will make mistakes. Isla and Lucy, of course, learn this the hard way.

My most recent books deal with situations that might make readers question what they might do in a particular situation and one of my favorite parts of the process is sitting down with a group of friends and talking about it with them. Over wine and a meal, we toss around ideas and potential scenarios in what sometimes feels like a Book Club discussion before the actual book is written! I always feel inspired and refreshed by these collective brainstorming sessions, and it's a nice experience for my friends who feel like they're part of the process too!

Q: Forgiveness is a key theme in the novel. How easy or hard was it for Lucy and Isla to forgive their loved ones?

A: It's this concept of forgiveness that I wanted to examine in this book, as I really do believe forgiveness allows relationships to find a pathway to healing and resolution even though it isn't always easy. I intentionally wanted some of the key characters in this novel to be flawed, and in some ways even unlikable. I know there will be readers who will find Elinor, and possibly even Isla, intolerable! However, I wanted these women in their brokenness to have the chance to heal and start over after experiencing love and forgiveness. Isn't that what we all would like after we make mistakes in life? A second chance?

At times while writing the book I gave a lot of consideration to how easy or hard it should have been for Lucy to forgive Isla. At times I wondered if readers might think she forgives her too easily because she doesn't harbor a huge amount of anger and resentment toward her. In the end, this is exactly how I wanted her to be. I didn't want Lucy to be consumed with bitterness as a result of how she had been treated—I wanted her to be a model for how we can look beyond a person's flawed behavior and actions and remember the goodness in them while understanding their motives and helping them heal a part of themselves.

Q: Family secrets are a cause of conflict and drama in this novel. Ben kept a huge secret from Isla, as did Elinor. Isla heads down the same path with her daughter. Can you talk about this aspect of the novel?

A: Writing about family secrets and their destructiveness was something I was keen to explore because so many families seem to have them, and they are so often the cause of conflict and destruction within relationships when the truth inevitably comes out. I find it fascinating when history seems to repeat itself within a family, but more so, as an author, I was intrigued to look at how fear might cause people to keep secrets in the first place. Ben lied to Isla about the financial loss of his business and was afraid to disclose the truth to her, while Elinor projects her fears onto Isla due to her own insecurities surrounding her own secret. At the same time, Isla allows her own insecurities to lead her down a similar path with her own daughter. Each of these characters fears losing the ones they love by being honest with them. Yet, when the truth eventually surfaces—that's when things can really fall apart!

Q: Can you tell us a little bit about your research process?

A: I very much enjoy researching and spend quite a bit of time on it before I start writing and there are a couple of reasons for this. I often need to make sure that what I have in mind for the plot is actually plausible, and often, this information will affect the plot itself. I often marvel at how authors of long ago wrote books without the help of Google to answer their questions! I am forever researching everything from paint colors to furniture trends and mouth-watering cuisine to feed my characters.

As part of my process, I also usually reach out to experts in their respective fields, because I can't get all the information I want online. For *A Child of My Own* I spoke to legal professionals, real estate agents, a school teacher, a skiing enthusiast, a friend who'd experienced an ACL injury, and even a former funeral director who was able to advise how Nate might be repatriated from France to Australia. I think readers might be surprised to know that sometimes I will research something for hours for it to only appear in the book as a single line, or worse, to be cut all together from a manuscript during edits!

Q: Lastly, what is your writing process like? How many drafts do you write?

A: I think a lot of people are surprised to learn that I don't always write in linear order. Sometimes I will start writing a book with a key scene or a moment of major conflict. This helps me get to know the characters in their most fiery and emotional moments! From memory, with *A Child of My Own*, I started with the scene where Isla and Lucy met, which now appears in Chapter Thirty. Writing this scene early on helped me discover some of the dynamics regarding their friendship, as well as their respective backstories.

I write using a program called Scrivener, which I love because I can re-order scenes and chapters as I go, and I tend to do a lot of this. I'm often asked about how I fit the writing in, and one of my answers is that I try to squeeze my writing into the spare moments of my life. Scrivener is great because it syncs between my phone and laptop and I can write snippets of scenes on my phone while I'm waiting for my son at soccer training!

As part of my usual process I semi-edit as I go, so once I have a completed draft it's probably more like a second draft. The upside of this is that I have a slightly cleaner draft to work with but the downside is that it takes me a little longer than I would sometimes like to have a completed draft. Usually at this point I try to let the manuscript rest for a week or so while a trusted writer friend reads it and provides me with feedback. Following this, I revise the draft, edit it, and then send it along to my editor!

ABOUT THE AUTHOR

Vanessa Carnevale is an Australian author of women's fiction. She is also the host of Your Beautiful Writing Life retreats held in Tuscany and Australia.

Vanessa loves to travel, and spent several years living in Florence, Italy, a place she considers her second home. She lives in Australia with her husband and two children.

You can learn more at:

Website: VanessaCarnevale.com

Twitter @V_Carnevale

Facebook.com/VanessaCarnevaleWriter

Instagram @VanessaCarnevale